Robert Michael

infinite word press

523 W. Roanoke Street

Broken Arrow, OK 74011

Dark Mountain

Robert Michael
Copyright 2012

ISBN: 1475179286
ISBN-13: 978-1475179286

For Tracey. Your love and faith sustain me.

Forever.One.

CHAPTER ONE

T he blood was what bothered Brian the most. His emotions were torn between desire and repulsion. He lay in his bed flat on his back staring at the ceiling. The darkness was a comfort. It calmed him. He could feel his body pressing into the lumpy mattress beneath him. He could make out his posters eating up dark holes on the dingy white walls of his bedroom.

He regretted going to see Molly at the cabin. It didn't help matters at all. In fact, he felt more confused now than ever. If he hadn't held his sister in his arms this afternoon things would have been different. If he hadn't tried to console her and listen as she spun her tale maybe he wouldn't be here wondering whether he should cry, scream, or kill someone. He was ashamed to even think about it.

He lay there biting his lip and wondered why he was so screwed up. *Why is my family so screwed up?* He knew that many of his friends felt the same way about their families. They had no idea.

He couldn't stop thinking about the blood. He didn't know what to do with it. As Molly recounted what she had seen that night almost a week ago, he couldn't help but think about the blood. He had seen the room. He had just stood there, transfixed. It was the color of red clay mud. It was smeared everywhere and flies careened drunkenly around the room. The room smelled awful. But it didn't matter. He couldn't take his eyes off of all the blood.

The ceiling in his room had turned a sickly yellow over the last few years. His father, Victor, rarely did anything around the house and so painting was a low priority. But, as Brian stared, the ceiling turned a dark brown. As he watched, mesmerized by his mind's own creation, the ceiling developed large cracks. Out of these cracks blood oozed forth, running in large, corpulent droplets across the ceiling. They rained around his bedroom pattering over his sheets, hitting the grimy bare wood floor.

He blinked hard to get the image out of his mind. The pattering continued. He glanced to his side and looked out of his window. A large moth softly smacked against the window, its wings beating hopelessly against the clear barrier. Brian stared for a moment, the moth beautiful and awful against the backdrop of the moon shining through the brisk early autumn Arkansas air.

The moth disappeared and Brian lost interest in the moon. The blood was gone, at least. He could feel his body sweating through the sheets. He could feel the effort it took not to shake. He turned on his side, curled in a ball, and determined not to think about the blood. He would never be able to sleep until he thought of something else.

Molly. She was there by herself. He chastised himself for leaving her. Riddled with guilt and anger, Brian had felt numb and weak as he closed the door of the cabin and practically sprinted home through the woods back to the house. He barely remembered the journey. As he lay there in bed trying not to shake, he ran his finger along the welts along his arms where the briars and thickets had left their mark as he ran. It was a small punishment for the deeds he had committed.

It seemed odd to him how small decisions affected life's outcome so dramatically sometimes. Even the refusal to do anything at all worked against him. He wanted to cry again, but wouldn't let himself do it. Despite everything that had happened, he could only think about himself. And the blood.

As he slipped into sleep, the moth returned. Its blue-gray wings fluttered desperately. Brian imagined himself as the moth, free to fly. He imagined himself wrapped in night, illumined by the moon.

CHAPTER TWO

I rritated that he had let Janice invite herself over to see him off, Jacob Barclay stuffed his socks into the back zippered pocket of his luggage. They had been divorced now for four years and annually participated in the sport of sleeping together again for a week or two until one or both of them realized the foolishness of it all. Janice had come to her senses early this year. Perhaps, he thought, she did not approve of his plans to travel to the Ozarks to "live like Emerson."

"You know, I thought you said you were over the whole mid-life thing? Didn't you just say that last year?"

"I only said it because I knew that was what you wanted to hear. It worked, didn't it?"

He didn't mind making her mad any more. In fact, he had become quite good at being a jerk. He wasn't sure it suited him, but it sure seemed to fit the situation. He had become tired of the condescending and hurtful remarks almost a decade ago. He had stuck through it all, hoping it would get better.

"There you go again. You know, since we were married for twenty-two years, you would think the conquest of getting into my pants would wear off sooner or later."

Jacob looked up from his packing and tried to contain a grin.

"I will refrain from commenting. You are making it too easy."

Janice breathed hard through her nose, almost a snort. That was one of the things that galled him. It seemed after so many years, all the little nuances had added up to one big itchy boil. Still stunningly beautiful, still whip-smart and fit, Janice was everything his buddies at the precinct dreamed about. But, under the soccer mom exterior, behind the gorgeous wedding planner, caterer, and business owner, was a manipulative, sanctimonious witch.

"Humor is not your strong point. Don't try." She laughed as she tossed her head and elevated her nose and chin. One hand was pressed with fingers up against her chin and thumb at her strained, tanned throat, the other hand on her narrow hip. "In fact, the funniest thing you have done since we have been apart is this juvenile *excursion*."

Trying to ignore her, he grabbed his camp pants that zipped off at the knee and his Under Armor sport pants and placed them neatly on top of the pile. He glanced around the well-lit bedroom of his apartment and asked, "Have you seen my pocket flashlight?"

"Gee, I don't know, Jacob. Since I don't live here, I guess it would be hard for me to know where your flashlight is."

She paused and stared at him hard as he tried desperately to appear as if he were genuinely trying to remember the last

8

known whereabouts of his trusty flashlight. He really just wanted her to leave. He could sense what was coming, like a June storm rolling in, the humidity amping up, and the leaves turning over their green undersides in the breeze.

"Jacob. Look at me. Please."

Reluctantly, petulant, and really feeling like a child now, he stared at her; his eyebrows raised in protest, questioning. He could feel his mouth downturned so much the creases at the corners of his lips cracked.

Undaunted by his 12-year old imitation, Janice continued in clipped, New England tones, her hands held out in front of her, palms up. It was her idea of "come unto me."

"Don't do this. Stay. We can work this situation out. Besides, Phillip needs us to watch Alice and Narissa for a week while he and Vivian go on a short mission trip to Greece."

He almost turned back to his packing, but still managed to say, "I'm not babysitting those two."

"Jacob, they are still your grandchildren. And I've just gotten news that Clarice and Charles are expecting. So that's three. Come on. Am I so bad that we can't just put on grandparent faces for one week together?"

"Is that all?"

She looked confused.

"What do you mean?"

"Well, I'm not cancelling. Is that all you wanted my attention for?"

She looked hurt for a moment. "So we aren't going to discuss this, even?"

"We did. I am not doing it. That's it, babe."

He shrugged, turned and found his flashlight on his dresser and placed it in a side pocket. He flipped the luggage over and tried not to look at her.

She sighed. He knew without looking that she had her head down and was beginning to pace. This was how she resolved great world problems. He knew her moods and idiosyncrasies, knew her passions and her peeves. At one time—and from time to time, he had to admit—these special things that made her unique appealed to him. Now, they seemed to curdle in his brain, to fester among thoughts of hurting her. Not physically, that was more than just taboo in Jacob's mind. He merely wanted to put the emotional barbs in just far enough to see her squirm.

Leaving now would do just that. He really didn't mind taking care of Alice and Narissa. He thought that he would even be a better parent now than he was for Phillip and Clarice. He was less self-absorbed, more mature and better equipped than he was at twenty-two--unless you asked Janice. She would argue that he had regressed to his frat days at Syracuse. Now, almost fifty and retired from the Buffalo police, the thought of playing house with Janice almost turned his stomach. He had only let her talk him into coming over because he thought it would be a good idea to have sort of a send-off for his trip. Grease the skids, like his dad would say.

"Ok. So you don't want to cancel your trip. I can certainly respect that. You need some space, some time away. A retirement trip, right?" She tittered.

He glanced up and noticed that she wasn't looking at him and had indeed taken to pacing and staring at her stilettos.

"You can go away until November then come back in time for Phillip's trip. It means so much to them and you know on a missionary's salary, he can't afford to take them along or leave them at a nanny's."

He had to concede her logic. But he didn't want to give ground too readily.

"Alright. But I am staying right up to Halloween and won't be back here until the third."

Janice looked up, her eyes bright from the sun shining through the bedroom window. He could smell her skin from across the room, a light scent of some kind of flower blossom. He could see that if he took the wrong direction, he could really upset her. Her eyes were glassed over, tears forming as pools in the corners, moistening her mascara.

"Alright," she said; her voice was small and measured. He knew that she was expecting the other shoe to drop. He knew that she was thinking this, had even said it aloud in therapy. *Jacob always measures out arguments in waves of ultimatums and conditions.* The therapist had seemed sympathetic and claimed that true compromise came with few strings attached. *What did he know, anyway?*

"And, we aren't watching them at my place. It's too cramped here and it isn't close to the park like at your place."

He made this part up on the run, knowing that she would rather have it that way, anyway. It would give her the option of pushing him out in the event that the experiment bombed, rather than the messy moving out.

Jacob saw that he had surprised her. He could sense she was thinking he was making this too easy. He allowed her this small victory because he just wanted to get out for now, unscathed, unfettered, unburdened by the obligatory guilt. Only Jacob knew that he secretly felt the winner.

He checked the zippers on the luggage and came around the bed to grab her by both shoulders in the best supporting role he could conjure. He liked the feel of the satin A-line dress against her firm shoulders. He shook off that thought and looked her straight in the eyes and decided to tell the truth. Or, at least as much of the truth as he could and still get away without a bigger drama.

"Jan, hon. It will be alright. It's just a survival trip for an old guy wanting to test his mettle without hurting someone. I'll have all the technological methods of communication to keep in touch in case something happens. The manual for my radio says it will carry out a signal across the world, even on a cloudy day. I'm even lugging around extra batteries for that sucker."

She scoffed and blinked away the tears, but he could tell she was relaxing. She had been tensed, waiting for some other thing, some other dart he would fling at her to pin her down. He guessed she expected an accusation that he wanted to get away from her—which was the truth, on some level. But, part of planting the emotional hurt was to not do the obvious, not say the whole truth, but to hide it away like a little seed of nettle to plant later in the season when the crops all looked healthy.

"Alright, you big *jerk*."

This was her big joke for years. Calling him names she didn't really think fit. Cute, when they were in love. Now, it was just unnecessary.

"You gonna help me to the car with this?" He indicated the three bags on the bed and the fly rod at the door packed in a neat cylinder case.

"Sure, Nancy. You sure pack like a girl in your old age. " *Again with the school-girl insults,* he thought.

Another one on his list of her off-the-wall faults: she joked around like her dad. He remembered Christmases spent in Connecticut, her dad spitting drunken vitriol all week. He made fun of Phillip's curly hair, calling it a perm. He popped off about the public schools in Buffalo, Jacob's job being "too dangerous for the pay" and topped it with off-hand comments about mini-vans. Todd even spent the entire week calling his kids names like Rudolph and Oscar the Grouch. Jacob had been sickened by his wife's blind acceptance and worship of this mean, bitter man. Just when Jacob was having about enough of his behavior, Todd Herbert Beckworth the Third would inevitably perform some extravagant immoral stunt to the delight of Jacob and Curt—the other son-in-law—and the horror of the rest of the family.

One year, Todd had run naked (except for his LL Bean half-boots and knee-length black dress socks) down the front steps in his drunken state--the snow the only thing whiter than his backside--hugged the seventeen-year old neighbor girl in her parka and confessed his love. Jacob wished he had gotten that one on tape. It was all he could do, with his wife's diligent insistence, of course, to get poor Todd out of that jam. But, even though it didn't put him in jail, at least he was sober for the next two Christmases. And then the old Todd was back again.

Jacob had waited for years to watch to see if Janice would ever behave like her father. She stayed away from strong drink and since he had had enough during his first two years at college to last him a lifetime, it didn't bother Jacob any at all. The most she would do, though, was this superior name-calling that elevated her status and chastised him. She never aimed this blunt-sided humor against the kids, but he had seen her do it at work, belittling her workers, chiding them into obedience or some semblance of hero worship. It was odd that she never got some of her own medicine. She never experienced any fallout until he had the lawyer deliver the divorce papers. He had imagined for weeks the look on her face when she received the documents. And that maybe explained why she kept coming back for more.

Now, she moved effortlessly, an uncommon grace for her age, picking up the heaviest case and slinging it over her shoulder like Hemingway on expedition. She reminded him of so many famous actresses that aged well. Her features belied the fact that she was two years older than him and her movements were tuned by years of tennis, golf and a personal trainer named Sven. He envied her. She didn't even stagger going down the steps and never removed her high heels. The muscles in her slim, firm calves worked furiously to accommodate the extra weight of the bags. She never grimaced, grunted or complained, just lugged the two seventy pound bags as if she were a teenage bell boy.

Janice had sold her catering business after they divorced for a hefty sum, had invested it in a Canadian coffee shop that she sold back to the corporation for more than three years' revenue and now lived in a condominium in an affluent suburb of Buffalo. That made him even more envious but he managed to stay confident knowing that she needed very little from him. It made things simpler that way.

As they put his bags in his late-model Ford extended cab, he took the time to give Janice some consoling hugs, some heart-felt thanks for the help and made the same empty promises for which he had become famous. The morning October sun was especially bright, the air crisp and thin. His home was on the southern edge of the city and the fog from the Lakes had been blown north across the border for once.

"You know, this is my last ditch effort. Are you sure that this isn't going to turn out like British Colombia or Idaho?" He hated when she brought up his failed trips.

"I am better equipped, better prepared and I chose Arkansas for a reason. It has excellent trout fishing, plenty of open public lands and an inexpensive out-of-state hunting license. Besides, you aren't going to talk me out of it now." He smiled to assure her. "But, I will be back and we'll play grandma and grandpa if it means we can sleep in the same bed for awhile."

She grinned wistfully back. "Don't push it, grandpa. The couch has a pullout and the plan has been from the beginning to have the girls sleep with Grandma."

He shrugged.

"Guess a guy can't have it all, right?" He kissed her on the cheek, the smell of her skin causing him to keep his eyes closed for a second longer than he wanted. He was sure she noticed because she had that smug look on her face, her smile crooked, her perfect teeth exposed. He honestly hadn't seen that smile from her since their first "hook up" after their divorce. It was her way of telling him that he should know what he had been missing.

Soon, he had pulled away, watching her get into her new red Audi, waving and smiling a plastic smile he was sure she could see. And that was how he left Buffalo behind.

CHAPTER THREE

D riving was a sedative for Jacob, which was problematic. But from his disasters in traveling, he was aware of his shortcoming and made amends. He stopped frequently at gift shops, roadside parks, small quaint towns just off the highway, restaurants and sports stadiums. He drove down Highway 79, relishing in the new sparkling PNC Ballpark and Heinz Field, both nestled near the Monongahela River. He wasn't a fan of either team, but it sure was fun to see a city like Pittsburgh grow around a winner. He had even heard the Penguins were set for a new stadium after picking up Sid the Kid. It gave him hope that Buffalo would rebound. The Sabers were still competitive, but the Bills were miserable and the fans knew it.

He thought on these things, man-things. Surface concerns about hair loss, gut, sports, hunting, good boots and gear. And women. Of course, Janice had been his first and only love. But, since the divorce, he had struggled with the idea that he needed to branch out and try again. It just wasn't like him and instead, he always relished the few weeks each year he and Janice found time to rekindle their dying flame. They both knew the fire was dead, but neither of them could bring themselves to pour the water on the embers and stir it until it died. It had no more fuel, but contained just enough heat to keep them warm for a few weeks.

He listened to the radio, talk shows and weather reports. He hadn't caught on to all the technological gadgets, even though he had access to many of them through his work. They distracted him and he felt strongly that if he relied on them too heavily, he would lose his edge. They could be time-wasters and that was a formula for inefficiency. In his younger days he had maintained a strict regimen of diet and exercise, but like most men his age, had grown more and more sedentary and his muscle tone had faded. This was especially true in the last four years. He had really let himself go, eating more red meat and riding the stair climber less.

And the road churned by. As he drove through the mountains of West Virginia, he was amazed at the change of color as he drove south. It was still green in the central plateaus, but as Highway 79 snaked its way through gorges, through entire mountains and into deep, curving valleys, the trees turned blazing shades of red, orange and yellow. Maples and oaks and birches lined the hills on either side of the highway, thick trunks and healthy tree tops melding into vegetative soup as he sped merrily by at seventy five miles an hour. After about an hour south of Jackson's Mill where he had stopped to take in a Civil War history lesson and a potty break before continuing on, Jacob realized he needed to plan some trips closer to home.

Thumbing through some of the brochures at a rest stop west of Huntington, Jacob found information on the Appalachian Trail and began to imagine a trip like that in his mind. A rented vehicle for the drive down and hike back or hike down and fly back? His budget would accommodate just about anything right now, but it would dry up soon and he would be back to figuring out his future.

For now, he just wanted to hunt and fish and relax. Get away from people. Not worry about Phillip and his no-pay job and Clarice and her abusive husband. He didn't want to think about Janice or the women that called him once a month or left messages on his dating service forum.

He had opened the forum page online one day at the insistence of Harold from Forensics. Harold said it had made a difference for him. The red-head he married the year before was gorgeous, for sure, but she barely spoke and Jacob wondered if maybe she wasn't an immigrant. But, not only did Jacob not find a match, but found many of the women who responded to his simple dating profile to be too brazen, too sullen, too jaded or too homely. They were young gold-diggers, tired, divorced, emotionally wrought, sexually aggressive or physically inferior. It only served to make him feel lonelier. And inevitably he began to think about Janice. And that wasn't good.

He spent his second overnight stay in Lexington, Kentucky. Thinking this was his last real sign of civilization, he holed up in a suite at a new hotel and went into downtown to soak up some night life. The thing that struck Jacob the most about Lexington was it was green. Several downtown buildings were lit with a leprechaun glee, bathing the surrounding buildings and the river in streaks of Irish green.

Dark Mountain

If Dubliners ruled Vegas, maybe it would look like this, Jacob thought.

A bar along Maxwell, near the University of Kentucky and within view of the veritable shrine to basketball, Rupp Arena, pumped out upbeat country rock-a-billy. Smiling with youthful anticipation, Jacob entered; he was glad he had stopped to purchase a pair of new boots and some jeans that would fit. His worn t-shirt and open short sleeve button up he left un-tucked. He felt loose and free and he looked it. Wanting desperately not to look like an out-of-towner and even more desperately not to appear divorced, he tipped his new hat to the bouncer just inside.

The music assaulted him, the drum throbbing and the whining guitars shrieking. A female with considerable talent blithely twanged about leaving her no-good man. A fiddler, his blonde hair cascading around his shoulders, took up a haunting counter to the lead guitar. It was classic. Jacob remembered his college days studying Criminology at Syracuse. He had picked up dozens of dates in places just like this: live band, lots of noise and plenty of scantily clad, happy ladies. The only difference was that, unlike at Syracuse, no cigarette smoke suffused the air. Instead, he could smell cheap perfume and sweat, the yeasty smell of beer on tap and drinks spilled as young and old alike danced with abandon.

"Whatcher poison?" The bartender cleaned a glass and leaned forward to yell over the raucous. She was lean, about 45 and still wore her hair feathered to the sides. He imagined he could smell the hair spray she used to keep it in place.

"Just a Coke," Jacob replied. He could feel his head beating, the blood at his temples pulsed heavily. He expected a negative reaction to his order, but received none. She set down the glass she was cleaning, and quickly filled his glass from a spritzer. He noted she didn't add ice and when he reached for the glass with his left hand, he saw her glance at fingers. He figured her for divorced twice, three children and no alimony checks coming in. *Stop stereotyping, Jake*, he chided himself.

As he looked around the bar, he spent the better part of an hour, two more Cokes and two requests for his number, people-watching. It was interesting to him to watch the subtle and overt hunting of the opposite sex. And twice, he noticed, of the same sex. He increasingly found this to disturb him less than it would have twenty years ago, but he still hadn't grown accustomed enough to it to not be surprised.

Around eleven-thirty, he had decided he had enough. Feeling bloated from cola and pretzels, he paid his tab and stepped down from the stool by the bar. He tipped his hat to the bartender and left her a five-spot on the heavily scratched bar top. As he did, he noticed a poster behind the bar with a picture of a missing boy. He thought that was odd. In Buffalo, he'd see posters like that in bus stations, grocery stores, convenience stores and city buildings. Rarely would one be up at a bar. He noted that the picture was probably taken a few years ago when the boy was ten. The poster indicated that he was fifteen. The boy had piercing eyes that despite the grainy copy, were distinctive under the slight forehead and razor-thin nose. The eyes were evidence of a shrewd intelligence and wit. Jacob recognized those eyes. They weren't too different than the ones he looked at in the mirror.

Jacob recalled his own teen years; disappointed in his father, he had dreamed of running away to flee from the shame of his father being in jail. His fractured family finally spread out more to start over than to get away from each other. By the time Jacob entered college, his father, Matt, had served his time for embezzlement but failed to seek out his family again. Jacob's mother had moved on, lived in North Carolina and married a loan officer named Paul. His sister was travelling Europe as a literary agent sub for American imprints. He got one card at Christmas his senior year and never heard from his father again. His sister occasionally sent him an e-mail or some invitation to a social networking site. He responded infrequently, mostly with updates about the kids.

After over twenty years serving as a detective, Jacob had seen what could happen to runaways. It was rarely a happy ending. In fact, most young people were served better by staying in whatever situation afflicted them than braving the world at large.

Jacob made his way back to his suite with these things on his mind. He checked the truck from his third-story window and looked out over the small city at the winking lights. He wondered about all those people. As great as city life had been to him—a job, the convenience of modern technology, and the illusion of security—he realized that violence and danger were at the core and the cusp of all civilization. As his professor had stated all those years ago, we as humans are animals. Reasoning, calculating, cunning and selfish, the human race is destined to turn upon itself even (or especially) in times of affluence or cultural attunement. The doom of great civilizations had a common theme: the false sense of invulnerability and the denial of forces outside our control—nature, the world around us and our own fallibility. Jacob had never truly been an eco-friendly sort—he hunted, fished, ate steaks, pork, and fish, drove a gas-guzzling truck, and occasionally left the lights on at night—but he was acutely aware that he needed to be prepared for a future that may require a dependence on survival. He knew he needed to hone skill sets that others ignored. As his friends grew fat and lazy, soothed by the comforts of technological innovations, he had prepared himself for the worst. It wasn't that he felt he was cynical, just a realist.

Growing up in Boy Scouts had taught him to be prepared. Without a father to guide him, his mother had found solace in the male role models that were available in Scouting. It really was invigorating for Jacob to experience nature, the outdoors and the camaraderie of fellow Scouts. Even after he entered college, he spent summers and breaks taking trips to various "adventure" outings—white water rafting, canoeing in the Canadian wilderness, forty-mile hikes, rappelling, rock climbing and spelunking.

Now, as he looked out and wondered about the people behind all those lights, he wondered how they would react if all those lights were extinguished forever. He sighed and ran his fingers thoughtfully around the felt brim of his new cowboy hat as he set it on the dresser. He pulled off his over shirt, un-tucked his t-shirt, slid off his jeans and left them in a pile on the floor by the air conditioner. The cool early October air wafted through his open patio door, gently moving the gauze drapes. He knew he should be tired after so much driving, but for some reason he was strung like a piano wire waiting for the hammer to strike.

He paced around the little room, picking up the remote and then discarding it without a thought. He opened the drawers he had no intention of using and sought out the obligatory Gideon Bible and finally plopped down on the springy mattress.

He hadn't read the Bible in a year or two. He had occasionally visited the congregation where Phillip attended, a three-hundred member affluent Baptist Church. He couldn't remember what denomination. It always made him wonder, because right across the street another Baptist church met, and at the corner a Free Will Baptist church had set up shop in a closed grocery store. Why couldn't they all get together and worship? Was it socio-economic? Surely, their doctrines weren't so different they had to maintain *three* buildings in a city block.

All the reasons that religion appealed to Phillip were lost on Jacob, but he didn't judge. It was good that Phillip had found a calling, something about which he could be passionate. He found his wife, a career—such as it was—and a purpose in life. Jacob knew that was a lot better than he had done at Phillip's age. Jacob had gone into detective work looking forward to an early retirement from the beginning. At least he had accomplished one thing.

He riffled the pages, the red edges a blur as he tried to pick a passage at random. He sometimes liked this exercise. Often, it would provide more wisdom than a stale fortune cookie. Tonight, he stopped at the book of Colossians. Having no idea about the title, he closed his eyes and traced his finger down the page and then he looked to see the verse his little game would produce. His neatly clipped nail hung just below verse two of chapter four. It read, "Devote yourselves to prayer, being watchful and thankful."

He considered these instructions for a moment. He was always watchful; that was trained into him. He didn't understand prayer. He knew it was a conversation with God. However, it always seemed somewhat cocky to him that if God was God, what right did Jacob Barclay have talking to him? Showing thankfulness was something he did maybe once or twice a month. And at Thanksgiving. Jacob felt that humans—Americans, especially—spent entirely too much time feeling sorry for themselves to be thankful. And he wasn't immune to that foible.

He decided he could wrap the three commands together and get it over with. He said a quick prayer, making sure to be thankful for the beauty of nature, his children and grandchildren, his own health and then asked God to watch over him and keep him safe. Much of the content of the prayer had been borrowed from the prayer leaders from Phillip's church and Phillip's own prayers at holidays. The prayer was simple, he knew. But he put as much of his heart into it as he could muster, really not expecting too much but comforted, nonetheless.

He lay there for some moments, staring at the dead television in the semi-dark. The bathroom light spilled across and left a rectangle glow across the screen. Glazed-eyed, he looked into it and thought maybe he was as at peace as much as he had been in months. He almost drifted off to sleep, the Gideon Bible still resting on his slowly rising chest.

Eventually, he slipped under the covers without setting the alarm. He wasn't concerned about the time; he was in no hurry. He fell asleep in minutes, dreaming of SLR film cameras and deer.

CHAPTER FOUR

O n the road again, Jacob felt content to set the truck on cruise and not stop until he got to Paragould, Arkansas. He knew there were faster routes into the mountains, but these winding, two-lane roads between Caruthersville, Kentucky and Paragould reminded him of his trips with his college buddies as they traversed the great Canadian wilderness. In fact, if he were to retrace his steps to becoming this hermit, the modern version of Emerson and Joseph Conrad, he would have to say it began his junior year at Syracuse.

He had just broken up with Amy Nixen. This was not as traumatic, now almost thirty years later, but at the time he was devastated. His dorm mates decided that to cheer him up they needed to go on a "primitive." To them that meant no walkman's, no FM radio, and lots of alcohol. It was convenient at the time to travel into Canada and so the four of them: Jacob, Danny, George and Chris drove across country. By the end of the first week, they were practically broke and the trip had begun to have the feel of a jaunt across

Europe. They stayed at the barns of generous farmers, did odd jobs for room and board and spent many nights huddled together under a tarp after a raccoon destroyed their only tent. They had started out aiming to trek to the Northern Territories, thinking that held the most adventure, but most of them weren't prepared for the colder temperatures. They headed west and ended up in Regina.

They had no plans about when to come back at first, but soon the booze ran dry, everyone got bored of sleeping in tents and in strange beds and he had forgotten all about Amy. It was the first time in his life he had done something constructive to combat a letdown. So, he was hooked. From then on, when he had any difficulties--relationships, work, the Bills went a long losing streak—Jacob would plan an extemporaneous "primitive."

Sometimes he would take the kids or Janice, but most often, he would head off by himself. Usually, he would travel in state, but after awhile the New York State Parks, and the streams and woods of upper New York began to lose their appeal to him. He wanted to branch out.

That is how six years ago he had ended up in British Columbia. He had planned a one-week outing. He ended up in a blizzard. He got lost and wandered off course by ten miles in the mountains just east of Vancouver. He broke his fishing rod falling through the ice on a lake he was not able to identify to this day on any topographical map. He broke two fingers on his left hand—thankfully, not the right—and had frostbite on his left big toe. The rescuers found him four days later. He was fine, except he had to have his toe amputated. Despite being told he was fortunate to survive--

and against Janice's will--he made a trip to Idaho the following year.

Again, he met near disaster. This time, it was foolishness and overconfidence that put him in danger. He was overlooking a bluff, glassing some bighorn on the next mountain when he noticed a draw that would lead him up to a spot where he could get some great pictures with his Nikon 35mm. He got out his Zeiss lens from his bag and was fitting it onto the camera when he heard what sounded like a large animal pouncing through the brush behind him. He swung around and dropped the $600 lens. Reflexively, more out of sentiment than fear of cost, Jacob dove to catch the falling lens. He managed to save it just as it was going to bounce off a rock and probably plummet forty feet to the bottom of a ravine.

However, in saving the lens, he paid a hefty price. He rolled ungainly, face first across the jagged rocks of the mountainside and caught his foot on the roots of a bush. He had badly scraped his knees, elbows and the palm of his left hand. The knuckles of his right hand ached where he had rapped them on the boulder saving the lens. Perched perilously over a drop of fifteen feet, the blood quickly began to rush to his head. He got dizzy and he struggled to push himself back up the steep slope. All the while he could hear the racket from the nearby brush. He figured it was a bear.

And he was right. He could smell it before he could see it. It lumbered closer, attracted to Jacob's scrambling. He had not brought a gun, only fishing and photography equipment. It was the first time he had ever left on an excursion without at least some defense. Fearful of his life, he regretted his decision.

He tried to stay still and watched in horror as the massive brown bear raised itself up on its hind legs about twenty-five yards away. It sniffed the air with its shiny black nose and then settled back onto all fours. The image of the beast's fangs as it tested its surroundings struck him to his heart. He knew from experience that the bear's claws and incredible strength could be the death of him.

Jacob lost the beast in the tall grass uphill. He could hear it huffing, growling low and deep. Then, several tense minutes later, he saw the bear cross below him on the ravine floor, lumbering its mass of matted fur laboriously. Relieved, sore and shaken, Jacob scrambled back up the steep slope and sat trembling on a large basalt boulder for an hour. He camped there that night on the bluff, but made sure to keep the fire going all night. In the morning, he re-traced his steps and headed home. He had had enough adventure.

It was shortly after the Idaho incident that Jacob, faced with his unhappy marriage, two adult children, and no way to cope with his displeasures, found a lawyer. He spent the money he had been intending to use for a trip to the desert of New Mexico on getting a divorce. Sometimes, you had to make sacrifices.

Now, five years later, this was Jacob's first excursion since the divorce. Despite Janice's insistence, there was no way he was going to cancel this trip. He wanted it for clarity. He needed it for his sanity.

He had been planning it since June. He met another ex-cop at the gym one day named Clark. Clark had grown up in Arkansas and had a very slow, deliberate accent. After discussing college football (*Hogs sooo—eee!*) for twenty minutes over elliptical trainers and watching the tight bottoms of the young mothers in the yoga class through the glass wall, Clark had mentioned the amazing trout fishing opportunities in Arkansas. Catching browns and rainbows really relaxed Jacob. Clark's mountain home seemed just the place he needed to relax. He mentioned some particular areas and they exchanged numbers. He researched it some more and planned out his trip.

And he was nearing his destination. Slightly irritated that the tank was almost empty, forcing him to stop, Jacob found a Shell station in a little town called Rector, just west of the state line. Jacob had been counting on getting all the way into Paragould without re-filling. He was in Arkansas now, at least. He pulled in and set the pump to working. He decided that it would be best to drive on through Paragould if he could find something to eat here and get some rest before heading out. He figured it was only three or four more hours of driving before he reached the town of Bexton.

He trudged his way into the station, his legs stiff from the long drive. It was unlike him to drive so long and so hard when he wasn't in a bit of a hurry. He pushed open the glass door, the obligatory bell chiming his entrance. The station smelled of oil and cheap cigarette smoke. He had noticed an open garage door on the north end of the station with a "CERTIFIED MECHANIC ON DUTY" sign.

Three other patrons wandered the store. One was an older woman, her cigarette in hand, blue smoke curling up from ashes just dying to fall to the dirty, scarred tile floor. It didn't appear that anyone had washed it in awhile. It needed a woman's touch, but evidently not the one standing chatting loudly to the attendant.

Her skin hung loosely beneath her elbows, wrinkled and limp, like an empty wineskin. Her hair was pulled back severely from her forehead, crow's feet extending back almost to her cauliflower ears. Her jaw was at an unnatural angle, her lips pursed as if she was dragging on an eternal cigarette. He guessed she was missing her molars. She gestured with her left hand, waving it and stabbing the air like non-verbal punctuation.

"And then she says to me, 'Margaret, I think you need to play it all down on red. You're goin' broke!' It's the last time I'm listening to her! And the last time I'm going to that casino! Crooked Injuns! Took all the tobacco sales from you, Walt, and now they're taking all my money at their casinos!"

"Yup," the barrel-chested man behind the counter put away a pack of Camel cigarettes and looked back over his shoulder. "You done any good down at bingo?"

She shook her head as if she were a trout trying to throw a hook.

"Themfisheaters cheat like Nixon! Only reason I go there is they gots plenty of coffee and donuts. They had the gall to pass around the collection plate asking for donations for the coffee supply. And every time I light up, they look at me cross-eyed and say things like 'Well, I never!' under their breath. Like I can't hear 'em!" Walt nodded his head and chuckled faintly.

"Humph. Sounds like 'em. Charlie Sutherby comes in here telling me stories. Ain't no one gonna shoot straight no more." He stroked his long mustache and glanced in Jacob's direction.

Jacob had decided to hang back for awhile and stay out of the way, scoping out possible snacks for his trip. What he found so far were packed with sugar and fat: Twinkies and cupcakes, candy bars and sticks of pepperoni. The closest thing he could find to nutrition was a packaged gray tuna sandwich that had expired two weeks ago. He picked up two bags of almonds, hoping the munching would occupy his hunger until he got into Paragould. With the time he was making, he could even swing into Jonesboro and get a decent meal.

"Hey, Mister. That pump ain't got no auto switch on't. Ya need to go back out there before you spill half my store of premium out onna concrete." He glared at Jacob, his hands flat on the counter. Jacob noticed three big gaudy turquoise rings on each hand with a matching turquoise belt buckle. The lady—Margaret, he presumed—turned then to consider him. The ashes fell silently to the floor. She didn't smile, but only squinted real hard, her crow's feet collapsing, the skin of her forehead coming together in folds. Her eyes were gray, her skin a tan so dark it appeared she had rubbed it on a freshly stained fence.

"Oh, sure," he said, turning to leave.

"Oh, and don'tcha leave outta here with those nuts, Sonny Jim."

Jacob, crazily reminded of Robin Williams, did his best not to smirk. Not wanting the circumstances of either a continued conversation or spilt gasoline, he decided to put the bags of almonds back and made for the exit without haste.

"Gotcha." As he turned, he caught the eye of a boy about fifteen standing by the magazine rack. He recognized the boy, but couldn't place him at first. His sandy blonde hair was long in the front, covering one eye. His Wrangler jeans looked worn, and Jacob noticed in his front pocket a bulge about the size of a candy bar. Its wrapper stuck up just above the hem of the pocket, confirming Jacob's suspicion. Then he noticed the eyes. A decided glint of mischief, but he had seen those eyes recently. And then it clicked: this was the boy from the poster he saw last night in the bar.

Surely, he was a couple of years older, maybe six inches taller and his hair was different. But he recognized the eyes and the set of the mouth. The stolen candy bar was his tip-off. As with most detectives, Jacob believed heartily in hunches. He looked up quickly, all this processing in his mind in a second. He decided he would come back in after he caught the pump and see if he could determine what the boy was about. He headed out the door, turning his back on the boy deliberately.

He went to the pump and caught it just as it topped thirty dollars; probably good enough until he got into Jonesboro or even Bexton. He checked his wallet. He wanted to pay cash for the transaction and watch the boy's face as he fumbled with several large bills. He wanted to see if the boy was a real criminal or just opportunistic and hungry. His hunch was the latter. He didn't get a vibe from the kid that he was in any way dangerous. In fact, just lingering at the scene of the crime, he was screaming "please catch me, I don't feel right about this."

Jacob rarely met individuals that crossed the law like that, but they were usually juveniles and he always recommended them to his close friend Alice Taft. Alice had retired a couple of years before him, having devoted almost fifty years of her life in social services. He loved her dearly because she had a genuine passion to help. Often, the caseworkers with whom he worked were jaded and cynical after just a few years of working with problem kids. Not Alice. She was tough on them, but they knew she cared and except for the toughest nuts, she always had a soft spot in her heart for them. Many of them even turned out alright.

He replaced the pump and entered back into the dingy Shell station.

He noticed the boy as soon as he came in, the bell dinging again. He was pretending to read a Field & Stream, but was scanning the attendant. Jacob glanced in the corners of the room. No cameras. The boy was lucky. Only one over the door and it was facing the cash register.

Jacob approached the counter, wallet in hand.

"You got the white Ford F-one-fitty?"

"Uh-yuh," Jacob returned, trying to sound natural. Walt squinted past him, looking at the pumps outside.

"You from outa state? Is that New York?"

"Yeah. You got change for a hundred?" Jacob pulled a wad of money from his pocket. All hundreds. "Or do you take credit cards?" He knew they didn't. He saw the signs when he entered the second time.

"Yeah, I'll take a hun'ert. You don't want them nuts no more, Mr. New York?" He tipped his head and smiled at Margaret. His teeth were yellow with tobacco. His breath smelled hot, like alcohol. To be able to detect it over the haze of smoke and the griminess of the oil, it meant he had either consumed quite a bit or something particularly strong.

"Uh, yeah." Jacob watched the boy out of the corner of his eye. He hadn't moved. Hadn't even turned a page. But his eyes stared somewhere between the top of the magazine and the cash register. His mind was humming and Jacob could sense temptation and regret wrestling within the young man. Jacob crossed back over to the rack and got the almond packets and grabbed a can of Hire's root beer from a barrel filled with ice by the counter.

"That'll be thirty-four, ninety five, total. " Walt licked his lips as Jacob pulled out a crisp hundred dollar bill. If Janice knew he carried around this much cash, her heart would stop. Even though she had plenty of her own, she hoarded it like someday she might need it.

"Oh. And, hey, I'll buy one of those Snicker's bars, too." He hooked his thumb over his shoulder in the direction of the boy still holding the magazine.

Walt looked confused.

"You know, the one over there in my nephew's pocket. Isn't that right?" He craned his neck around and looked the boy right in the eye. He could see what appeared to be fear or confusion at first, then it was almost like he just woke up from a long dream.

He answered in a strong voice, one that had just turned deeper, Jacob could tell. He remembered when Phillip talked like that.

"Yeah, unc. I was gonna pay for it though, you don't need to."

"Nah. Your ma would have your hide if you spent your birthday money on sweets. It's on me. Now, put the magazine down and go out and hop in the truck, I'll be out in a minute."

Walt and Margaret just stared, Walt's mouth hung open slightly.

"But, Mister, that boy yonder has been hanging out here since morning. You just showed up. Was he meetin' you here?" Margaret asked boldly. She had stubbed her cigarette out on the countertop leaving a black mark and a curling gray smoke rising. It wasn't the first time the counter had been mistreated in such a way. Its surface was pocked with black and yellow mars.

"Why, yes. Anyway, how much, Walt?" Jacob asked, smiling.

Walt looked confused again, his heavy brows furrowing together to make a white "V" across his forehead.

"Uh, the candy's on me, mister. You come on back and put fifty in the tank anytime, New York. But don't be leaving no juvenile delinquent 'round here scarin' all the patrons away."

"Sure enough. Thank you." Jacob smiled warmly. Walt handed him back his change and he heard the boy jangle the door as he left. Jacob followed close behind, watching the boy strut up to the truck and circle around the front.

As he went around the pump, the young man looked back to Jacob.

"You didn't need to do that. I was just biding time. I've got my own money and I planned on buying it. I got it out of the freezer and put it in my pocket to thaw." His cheek twitched. Jacob had embarrassed him more than anything else, it seemed. But it was a lie. The kid was smart coming up with a plausible alibi in less than one minute.

"Nah. That's not true. Besides, the guy didn't charge me for it. But you won't be able to hang out in there anymore."

He looked hurt, but straightened up and stuck out his chest. He shook his head in defiance.

"Don't matter. It stinks in there anyhow."

"You got that right. What're you going to do now?"

"Well, you said get in the truck, so I figured I would listen to you and see what you wanted. I am guessing you think you know me or something, doing what you did. I couldn't figure out your angle at first but I guessed it would be best to play along until I knew what game you were playing.

"Well, ain't you smart?"

He looked pleased.

"Smart enough to know you are a cop or something. What're you doing in Kentucky, anyway?"

Jacob tightened his lips.

"Son, you are in Arkansas. And you are wrong. I used to be a cop. My name is Jacob Barclay. What's yours?"

"Luke."

"You got a last name, Luke?"

"Yeah.Uh.Nettles. Luke Nettles."

Another lie. His cheek flinched again. He needed to teach this boy not to play poker. He would surely lose his inheritance.

"Get in the truck, we'll talk while I drive on into Paragould and get us a bite to eat. What do you say?"

"As long as you're paying." He raised his eyebrows with a knowing look. Smart boy. But something worried Jacob about how trusting he seemed. Sometimes cons conned the con. Jacob had experience with that maneuver and it left a lasting impression. Jacob climbed in and put his CD's in the back seat so that Luke could sit in the front.

"What you listening to?" Luke asked, sounding genuinely curious. Young folks are fervently hungry for the escape they get from music—have been for generations.

"Classic rock.Credence, Neil Young, Kansas, Moody Blues and Eagles.You know'em?"

"Uh.The Eagles? Saw them in concert. My dad made me go. Awful old, aren't they?"

"Well, if they were young, they wouldn't call it 'classic,' would they?" He fired up the truck and pulled out onto Highway 49 southbound.

"I will listen to about anything. Country, rock, alternative, it doesn't matter." He pulled the lever at his side and let the seat recline back, his hands behind his head. Jacob glanced over at him. The boy looked well-nourished with no visible bruises and he seemed to be in decent humor. Runaways were usually jumpy, fidgety, and had a glassy-eyed, deer-in-the-headlights look when confronted. They felt guilty for running away, but trapped or doomed.

Luke appeared to have options, attitude and intelligence. And just a little guile.

"What are you hungry for, Luke?"

Jacob saw him look over at him out of the corner of his eye, a smile playing on his lips.

"You really buying?"

"Sure. Why, you have deep pockets and want to buy me supper?"

"Hmmph. No. Not really. But, if you're asking what I want, I want a cheeseburger with bacon. Lettuce, no onion with a little mayo and a ton of ketchup to dip it in. Oh, and some fries. Don't matter where, just a good, juicy cheeseburger." Luke had a spaced out, dreamy look, a lazy, satisfied smile playing at his lips.

"Alright. I think we can fit that bill. But, you'll have to answer some questions for me first." As he glanced over, Jacob caught him rolling his eyes.

"You're the boss, mister."

Jacob raised his eyebrows in amusement. "You got that one right, hoss. My old lady couldn't get that straight and here I am."

Luke's countenance dropped. His frown took in his whole face. He shook his head and stared out the window in silence until they got to Jonesboro and pulled into a Carl's Jr. about twenty minutes later.

CHAPTER FIVE

J acob didn't figure Luke would be such a finicky eater. That was usually a trait reserved for children that were raised with a certain lack of restraint. It was rarely indicative of abusive parents, but may be a sign of neglect. He knew he was reaching—it was completely possible that Luke had developed the habit because his parents were affluent. His clothes and his attention to cleanliness were congruent to his status as a runaway. Jacob was curious, but suspicious. Something wasn't right.

Luke continued to strip the bacon off the cheeseburger and lay them all in a line.

"Man. What is up with these hilly-billies! Don't they know you need to cover the *entire* burger with the bacon?" He looked up as he finished and then picked up another French fry from the pile he had neatly arranged, the fries lying next to each other, in order of height from large to small. Jacob figured he'd never picked up a runaway OCD case before.

Luke looked over at him and gave him a shy smile. "Thanks again for the food. The fries here are great. They have some kinda batter on them. Sarah, a girl I hang out with at school, hates the batter, but I think it adds some other element that fries usually miss. You know? Like potatoes need breading, or something. I don't know." He shrugged and went back to stacking his fries, popping the short burned ones in his mouth.

"Where do you go to school?"

Luke hesitated. Pretended to chew and swallow with effort. *Gosh, this kid's good*, thought Jacob.

"Nelson High, a big high school in a suburb outside of Lexington. I've been going there for two years now. I'm a junior next year. Letterman in track. I run the four hundred meters and compete in the long jump. That's my fave. It's quality. I'm pro, 'cause I've got hops."

"Hops?Like in beer?" Luke didn't laugh at his lame joke.

"Nah, I can jump pretty far, see. I think I can get a scholarship. Not bad for a white boy from the South, if I do say so myself."

"Runaways rarely get scholarships, Luke. You'll have no address."

Now, Luke did laugh. He spit out the drink of Coke into a napkin.

"Hah. Yeah, there's that. Man, you're hilarious. You sound like my Dad." He looked at Jacob, a mischievous grin playing at the corners of his mouth. He looked sinister for a second. He continued in a condescending plea, "Gee, Jacob, would you be my pa? That would sure mean the world to me. What with me running away because my parents are such old farts!" He broke a fry and stuck both ends in his mouth, smiling, chewing and talking at the same time, "Give me a break, dude."

He laughed again and put the burger in both of his hands, his elbows on the table. He suddenly wished Alice were here. She'd straighten him up in a jiffy. But he was stuck with him. He had decided to play Good Samaritan and now he was handed a smart-aleck kid who seemingly was a well-adjusted, affluent, non-abused, run away. Go figure.

"Ok. So tell me your story."

"What? Just like that? No more warm up questions? I mean, I thought about lying to you earlier and decided, 'Shoot, tell him the truth, it'll make him nervous.' I didn't think you'd puke down your leg like this and pull up and shoot the ball, Jakie."

Jacob didn't like his tone, but decided to wait him out. Kids who had complexes this large had to be given some room. They had to feel like they were in charge before someone set them straight. The farther someone dragged them along, the more compliant they were when they jerked their leash.

The "Jakie" comment didn't faze him, either. It was Luke's attempt to rattle him. It was probably his first light stab, too. Later on would come comments about Jacob's mother and his sexual orientation.

"I'm just curious as to why a perfectly smart, well-fed, member of the varsity track team would off and leave home. Posters up all over Lexington prove someone out there cares about you."

"I guess you're right, mister. Someone does care about me." He continued to smile as he wolfed down his burger. Ketchup stained the corner of his lip and he extracted it with his tongue languidly, the bite of burger hanging precariously from his mouth. *Now, you're just being juvenile,* thought Jacob. *What are you going to do next, make me sit on a whoopee cushion?*

"If someone cares for you, why not stick around, get your scholarship, go off to college and get out into the real world on better terms? You're what, sixteen?"

"Fifteen. I moved up a year. I didn't mention that I made Dean's list last semester, did I?"

"Now I'm really confused, Luke."

"Yeah. I thought so when you told that backwoods clerk I was your nephew. I looked at you and thought, 'This dude's not right in the head, but I'll just go along. This ought to be good.'"

"I'm glad I can be entertainment for you."

"You really don't get it, do you?"

Jacob shrugged.

"Don't know why I'd be asking if I knew."

He took another bite his hamburger.

"Mmm. This is good. Good burger. They don't put too many spices on, but that flame broil, now that really does it."

"You know, I don't really have all day. I think I'll just leave now." He took his tray, his food untouched and began to head to the door.

"Hey!"

Jacob turned, thinking *the walk-away works almost every time.*

"Yeah?"

"You gonna eat those fries? I'm really into that batter."

Jacob looked confused. Luke laughed and took another huge bite of his burger. It was half gone already. Either the kid was hungry (like most young men), or he was used to eating without couth. Something in his cocky behavior seemed genuine. He wasn't just playing cool to cover up his fears. He really was a first-class jerk and he knew it—reveled in it, in fact.

Jacob turned and sat down fast, slamming his tray onto the counter. He could see Luke's smile widen. *So you think I'm cracking, huh? OK.*

"You know, I changed my mind. I am really curious how you came to be two hundred plus miles from home without transportation on your own at fifteen. Especially since I can tell you are used to getting your way and seem in no hurry to go anywhere or get away from anything."

"Who are you?"

"I told you. Something tells me you haven't told me everything straight about yourself, Luke."

"You'd be right, Jakie. I haven't been completely honest. And I'm sorry." He took another bite and licked ketchup off of his finger. "You'll just have to accept that apology, and that's it," he said, working the words out around the deposit of food in his mouth. He chewed loudly and picked up the next longest fry.

"What if I told you I know exactly the game you are playing?"

"I'd call you a liar, Jackie. 'Cause you don't." His eyes got big, his green irises sparkling with glee. *He thinks he's toying with me.*

"Ok. Game over, chuckie. While you were waiting in line for our food, I texted a friend of mine with the New York Department of Human Services, Juvenile division. She contacted the local sheriff. It seems someone's on their way to pick you up, right now." He glanced outside and watched as two cruisers pulled into the restaurant parking lot.

Luke didn't flinch.

"Did they bring the news crews? They're going to want to get this on film."

The hairs on the back of Jacob's neck stood up. It was his early warning detection system. Of course, he had realized for a while that not all was right with this situation. He thought back over the facts, quickly trying to figure what he was missing. Not knowing what was fact and what was fiction, he wasn't sure he could undo this riddle without help. He resigned to allow the situation to play out. A wise man once said, *"All things will reveal themselves with time."*

Luke sipped Coke through his straw and appeared unfazed by the approaching officers. Of course, Jacob had picked up on their arrival and on the spur of the moment he had made up the story about texting a friend to add pressure to the conversation to see how Luke would react. It wouldn't take long for him to call Jacob on this bluff. The officers went to the counter and chatted about kids and softball games. Not good for Jacob. Luke just stared at him and smiled. He never looked over his shoulder or seemed to notice.

"You planning on staging some sort of scene? I'm just trying to help, here, Luke. If that's your name."

"Hmmph.Trying to help. I see. You don't know me or why I would need help. You assumed since you saw a missing child poster that may or may not have looked like me that I needed saving. Did you ever stop to think that maybe I have something they want? Or maybe something they don't want me to expose?"

"I don't know. You tell me. I'm in the dark here, and I can't help you if we can't talk about it."

"What makes you think I want your help, Jakie? You already lied to me. I suppose it's only fair, I lied to you first. But, c'mon, I'm not asking you to trust me. You are asking me to trust you, but you lie to me in a way that is lame, number one. Second, it was unnecessary. You could have just asked me. I may or may not have answered, but at least I would still be considering whether or not to trust you. Now, it's not such a big concern: I don't trust you."

"Fine. So I screwed up."

"Yeah. You did. But I am going to let you off the hook. Just because you tried the whole 'walk away' bit, I have some respect for you. You have done this sort of thing before. So, outside of some poor judgment in the face of my attitude and some frustration, you screwed up. Everyone deserves a second chance. Right?"

"Sure."

Luke looked extremely confident. He probably felt in control. And right now, he was. Jacob was just as inclined to fold as he was to wait him out and allow him to reveal his hand voluntarily. He sat tight and decided to listen rather than talk.

The officers sat down next to them and Luke still didn't react. Maybe his hunch was right.

"Alright. Despite the unwanted company, I'll tell you my sordid story. Not because I want your help, understand. I just guess you are as worthy as anyone else to hear it out. Sarah was the last one I told and she's the one that told me I should bug out. Pretty good idea at the time. It may have saved my life." He said it so matter-of-fact that he may have been talking about the weather.

His detachment made it more real. Jacob had seen kids externalize incredible injustices and perversions of humanity. They had so many tools of coping, it was no wonder the human race persisted.

"I'm listening."

"I can see that. You are a good audience, Jakie. I mean that." He took another sip of the Coke and swallowed hard. He looked to his left at the officers and smiled boldly at the blonde one with the tattoo on his forearm. Ex-marine, Jacob guessed. He glared back at Luke and turned his attention back to his comrade.

"Anyway, I left about four weeks ago tomorrow. It's been liberating to just drift. I've seen a lot and done a lot. It seems like I've been gone longer. I've lived more in the last few weeks than I did growing up. Anyway, there's no way I'm going back to school again. Not even to run track. It's all a joke."

"No one's going to insist you do anything you don't want to, Luke. Just continue. You were saying you left four weeks ago. Did you plan out your escape?"

"Escape? I wouldn't call it that. It wasn't like I was in a prison. Our house is four thousand square feet, we have four vehicles, my dad makes upwards of a quarter million a year, cold. But, see, that's the problem. No. I'd say I didn't escape. I just chose to *step away*."

Jacob could sense a breakthrough. The kid was incredibly articulate and sane. Whatever was bothering him was way beyond Jacob's capabilities but he was at least a good listener. When he thought about it for one second, though, he felt strange that he never used this talent in his marriage or as a father.

"I see."

Luke smiled. He put the last two bites of burger in the wrapper and the last five fries and folded them together into a ball. Then he sucked the last of the Coke from his cup. It made a slurping noise.

"You know? I knew about what my dad did for a living since I was eight. I just never found it threatening or illegal. It's sort of like some sayings or jokes that you don't realize are wrong until you put it together. It took me years to realize that when my dad called someone a 'cotton picker' it was a racial statement. I had repeated that numerous times, too."

"Did your mom know?"

"Mom? Huh. Funny. She didn't care. Whatever got her the Escalade and the purses and the shoes and the credit card, it didn't matter to her if he was a drug dealer. No. She knew, I'm sure, but she didn't know. You know what I mean? She was aware, just not fully. There's no way he could keep that from her."

"Keep what?"

"Well, dad traffics in body parts: kidneys, lungs, hearts, brains. All the good, gory stuff."

"What do you mean, traffics?"

"My dad does autopsies for the county coroner, Jakie. But, that's just his day job. There are people out there that are plain evil. They buy body parts for rituals, sick experiments and feasts. Yeah, I know it's twisted, but people are just that way."

His face had turned sour. Jacob could tell he was struggling now. The officers next to them couldn't possibly have overheard over all the noise in the restaurant and Luke's reserved account, but they seemed to sense something. Intuition, observation, magnetism, whatever it was, the officers began to watch Jacob and Luke out of the corner of their eyes.

"How did you find out?"

"You ever read *The Tale of Two Cities?*"

"Yeah.Long time ago. Why?"

"Well, there's this guy, just a normal Joe, but at night, to feed his family, he would rob graves. Turns out to be a pivotal character in the novel—just like Dickens—but there's a scene early in the novel when his son follows him out one night and witnesses his father's nocturnal habits. That's sorta like what happened. It's just uncanny when you read it in a book at fifteen and realize that could be you. That's all."

"So, you actually witnessed your father harvesting organs?"

"Yeah. I did. It wasn't exactly 'Take Your Son to Work Day' or anything, but I saw the box, I saw the labels, the lists, the calls on his cell phone. All of it. He has a couple of regular clients that want nothing but livers. And they pay him *thousands* of dollars a year. Now do you understand? I want out. And they don't want me telling anyone what I know. Mom won't say anything because she doesn't want her life to change, and Dad because he wants to keep Mom happy. And honestly, Jakie, I don't think either one of them have a conscience about it. Me? I couldn't sleep."

That explained the circles under his eyes.

"Wow," Jacob said under his breath. He believed him. It was too crazy to make up.

"Yeah, wow. Now, if you will excuse me, I'll just thank you for the fine meal and head on down the road. I'm trying to make it to Saint Louis."

"You have family there?"

"Are you kidding? No. I've got tickets to see the Cardinals."

Jacob laughed.

"Besides, just getting this off of my chest has been great."

"That's fine, but what about all those people who he's stealing from? Don't you want to stop him?"

"Hey, I'm no body thief, but I'm no hero, either. Why else would I choose to run away instead of stick around and play snitch? I'm too enamored with my own skin, dude. Survival of the fittest, right? Besides, I understand it's sick, alright? But they're dead. Why worry about the dead, when I'm still living?"

"Well, at least you have your priorities straight."

Luke stood up and stuffed the sandwich and fries into his right front pocket. He glared down at Jacob, looking angry and hurt for the first time.

"Don't try to guilt-trip me." He threw down a wadded-up five dollar bill. "That's for the dinner. You didn't need to pay. Besides, maybe I was wrong to tell you, anyway." He turned, anger burning his ears scarlet and his fists clenched tightly at his sides. *Finally, a tantrum*, Jacob thought as he rushed forward and grabbed him by the wrist. He stuck the five in his hand when it opened up. Luke whirled, his other fist starting to rise in a haymaker. The officers tensed, expecting trouble. He heard the sound of a button being popped, a sound with which Jacob was familiar—one of the officers had just unfastened his holster.

Jacob froze, staring intently at Luke. He knew he should just let him go. Luke was only fifteen, but Jacob knew kids younger than that who were single mothers or gang members living on the streets. Many of them did not have the tools, the skills, the education or the opportunities that Luke had. Jacob figured he would be alright on his own. He would have it better than most, at least, but never be quite normal. Nothing wrong with that. Over half the people in the world weren't normal.

Even though he knew he should just let go, Jacob wanted to end things on better terms. Something was eating at him and he wasn't sure what it was. Maybe it was Luke's scumbag dad. Maybe something about Luke's story resonated with Jacob because he remembered growing up resenting his father and lost respect for his mother somewhere along the way and felt alone in the world before he was fully grown.

"Take it back. You need it more than me. It'll buy at least one hot dog at Busch Stadium."

He could see Luke relax for a second. He fussed with his bangs and glanced off to his right. He seemed embarrassed. Jacob could see that he was about to cry. The glance to the right had cleared that, but his eyes were still glassy.

"Yeah. Thanks," he said quietly, tucking the bill back into his other pocket. He released his wrist and let him go. Luke deflated, his arms loose and his posture calm.

"Who're they playing?" Luke turned. His attitude brightened slightly.

"The Phillies. Tickets are hard to come by, but Sarah hooked me up."

"She going with you?"

"No, she wanted to, but she has it good. Better than me, at least."

"Well, enjoy. Pujols is incredible. First ballot Hall of Famer."

Luke smiled brightly.

"Yeah. Hope to catch him hitting the long ball. There's a double-header Sunday. I got tickets to both games."

Jacob nodded. An awkward pause ensued as neither knew exactly what to say. They stood by the condiment bar, Jacob with his hands at his sides, Luke scratching his unruly hair.

"Look, I appreciate you wanting to help. That was kind of you. I don't want to be part of it. But if you are truly concerned, then look up Dr. Brackens who works for Billings County Coroner's office. All the evidence you need is on his I-Phone. "

"Thanks. I will. How did you know I was a cop?"

"I don't know." He shrugged. "You just walked in there all smooth and acted like you knew me. You flashed all that money like you thought that you were tempting me to steal it. The only thing that threw me off was the wad of cash. Dad always told me cops didn't make much money. He said that public servants were paid like indentured servants. Except for that detail, it was pretty obvious, I guess, but I had a strong hunch."

Jacob was amused, despite himself.

"Gee, thanks."

"Don't take it wrong. I've just got a knack for these things. It's why I'm so good with the ladies."

"I see. Well, it was nice meeting you, Luke."

"Mr. Barclay?"

"Yeah?"

"Promise me you won't have me followed or brought in until after the Card's game."

"I won't have you brought in at all, if that's what you want. You seem to have this gig figured out." Luke looked grateful, his mouth turned up in a quick smile.

"That would be great. Thanks. I will text you sometime and let you know where I am."

"Text me? How...?"

"Oh, you'll need your phone though." Luke reached into his pocket and handed Jacob his cell phone.

"That's how you knew I was lying?"

"Yeah. And you really should talk nicer to that Janice chick. She's hot. Your texts to her are rude." Jacob decided the kid lifted his phone while in the truck.

"Thanks for the advice. You just try to stay out of trouble. Don't let me hear you've been picked up for shoplifting or pick pocketing." He held up his cell phone.

"No problem. Have a nice trip." He turned then and left. The door swung open and he watched Luke strut across the street. He looked confident again. He had purpose and direction despite his past. Jacob was jealous.

"Have a nice trip." Jacob said to no one in particular. He looked over and noticed the deputies had returned to their conversation, evidently satisfied that all was well. For some reason, Jacob felt it wasn't. And yet he was sure that Luke would be fine.

CHAPTER SIX

S heriff Billy Joe Shoemaker sat in his cruiser, spitting sunflower seeds out of his open window. He was on a stretch of State Highway 62 between Lansdown and Bexton. The sun was going down, and his shift was about over. He clung to boredom with zeal.

He knew four cars went by in the last hour. Troy Thorton, the newspaper man from up at Ashton in his '72 Green Cadillac. Then Jesse and his wife Dolores Jean came, speeding as usual. He didn't pull them over. It would do no good. Besides, they paid their taxes and were all-around good citizens if they'd just leave the bowling alley alone. He was tired of losing by over eight pins to Jesse every Monday night.

Two other cars had passed, but half asleep, his nose buried in a pulp western, he wasn't sure who they were. The sounds of their vehicles registered in his mind, but he couldn't recall even the make of the car—whether it was a truck, a semi or a sedan.

So, Billy Joe was in a sour mood. He felt underpaid and over recognized. He couldn't get away from the constant questions, bickering and hollering. Not a whole lot of crime up in these parts, unless you counted domestic abuse of which there was plenty. Or vandalism.

Billy Joe didn't concern himself with either of these. He couldn't really classify them as crimes in his book. Women got beat, most times they deserved it, he thought. Plus, every once and a great while, some wimp would come home sloshed or with lipstick on his collar and his old woman would knock him up side the head with a frying pan, rolling pin or broom handle.

Billy Joe felt if they got it, they deserved it. He didn't take sides. It was in itself its own sort of justice, dispensed quite handily by the victim. They didn't need to include him, necessarily. And, if a kid wanted to paint his initials on an overpass or bridge abutment, what of it? He'd done as much or more when he was a kid.

Now, speeding? That was a different story. It served as an opportunity for Billy Joe to do his favorite thing: chase people. There was something intoxicating to him about flipping on the lights, hitting the sirens, and revving up the engine of his Dodge Charger.

It wouldn't hold a candle to the Diplomat he drove eight or so years ago, but its turbocharged engine was more than a match for all but the fastest cars. On the winding roads around Bexton, there were no long stretches for most folk to get up to speed. So, it came down to skill.

He had watched every episode of CHiPs and Dukes of Hazzard when he was young, and the chase scenes were his favorite. Smokey and the Bandit was probably his favorite movie of all time, but he didn't advertise any of these things because he didn't want to get made fun of.

Besides, he caught the irony that the cops often looked bad in those shows. It didn't matter to him, though. It was all about the chase. And there wasn't one driver that had outrun or out-driven him in his twenty years as township · police, county deputy or county sheriff.

But, tonight, Billy Joe had nothing going on and he fully realized he was in for another night of TV dinners, network sitcoms and then smoking a cigarette on the back porch while listening to the Dodgers or the Mariners play on the radio.

His social life had ended two years ago when Becky Chastain had moved away. They had been bowling partners, sometimes lovers, and confidants. She worked as a dispatcher and sometimes they would take vacations together, riding their Harley's to Sturgis.

Their matching leather jackets and red bandanas were punished by the wind and the weather, but they were happy. She got pregnant and when he said he'd gladly marry her, she said "No," and left town. Last he heard, she was living in North Dakota with a fellow biker who ran an eBay store for Sturgis memorabilia and accessories.

She had a boy last November and she named him Kit. Billy Joe was more than heartbroken; he had been blazing angry. He sold his Harley and all his leather and swore off riding motorcycles forever. And he promised himself he would never buy another item from eBay, ever.

"Whatcha doing out there, falling asleep?" came the rude voice of Estella Courtwright over his radio. She was the new dispatch. Sixty-two, red-haired, and mad at the world, she liked to tease Billy Joe something fierce.

"No. Just listening to your skin dry out, you old bag," He responded. He knew he was encouraging her. There was nothing she liked more than banter. It tested her limited intelligence, and that made her happy.

"You're not getting any younger, B.J."

He hated it when people called him that. Estella knew it, too.

"Why don't you catch some speeders coming down off of Blue Tick Mountain? We sure need some revenue. The mayor was in here at the office the other day fretting over the books. He said he'd have to cut some staff soon if we didn't get some more money in. No bake sales are saving Concord County, it looks like."

"Estella, can't you just shut up? Everyone with a scanner can hear your tripe. And use proper radio jargon, you underwear smudge. Out."

"Well, you got another hour, it looks like, so sit tight up there. Did you bring sumpin' to read?"

"Yeah, another issue of Sports Illustrated."

"You still placing bets with Vic?"

"You've been listening to too much office gossip, Stell."

"I'm not blind. I see you boys all hunkered over those papers, arguing over spreads. Why, there were about a dozen of your buddies over at the library t'other day moping about injury reports."

"What are you doing at the book store, Stella? You still pursuing Old Man Spencer? That man's got more dust on him than his books."

"You hush up about my main squeeze there mister. I'll haul off and get you fired if you don't watch out."

Billy Joe smiled. He loved giving her a hard time about
Old Man Spencer. He was an eccentric old coot, but had the
rugged good looks of a Sean Connery or a Clint Eastwood.
Lanky, with a crown of white hair and a full white beard,
Wesley Mark Spencer owned the used book store and the
department store across the street. His kin ran the
department store—profitably, too. But, his book store was
his love even though it never made a lick of money.

Many of the unattached ladies of the town, including a
few younger ones, had pursued Old Man Spencer for the last
decade since his wife died of a heart attack. He was still hale
and hearty himself. He was often found reading a book, or
walking the streets downtown talking easily to anyone he
met.

"I've got to go, Estella. You take it easy."

"I'll take it any way I can get it, you tub of lard. Out,"
she said mockingly.

Billy Joe sat in the cruiser another ten minutes, the only
sound the hiss of his radio, the quiet rustle of the trees in the
early autumn wind, and the racket of the birds, bugs and
animals of the woods around him. The field he sat in
overlooking the highway was surrounded by hardwood forest
all around. The hill carried up ahead and around the bend.
Usually, the sounds of the forest were a background noise.

Billy Joe thought it was much like in a city where the
rush of vehicles and the noise of industry and people would
eventually become a part of the backdrop of the city life.
You didn't notice it until you listened for it. It was never
truly quiet anywhere, it seemed.

Just as he was nodding off again, his book forgotten in
the seat beside him, he heard the sound of a truck engine far

off. He pushed himself up in the seat and tried to determine from which way the sound was coming. It was coming north and so it would soon pass by him and head up toward Bexton.

He reached for his console and began to turn on the radar when a white Ford truck passed him. He noticed the out-of-state tag and without hesitation, flipped on his lights and sirens, instead. He turned the Charger over and stomped down on the gas before he even put it in gear.

He peeled out. Dark, moist earth spit up around his fender wells, thumping harmlessly. The back end swung wildly, but he corrected expertly, and his tires dug in. Soon, he was racing across the field. He hit the asphalt and the tires barked.

The driver of the truck pumped his brakes and pulled over to the berm without hesitation. Slightly disappointed that the driver didn't make a break for it, Billy Joe pulled in behind him, angling his car slightly. He took down the license plate on his pad. Then he called into Estella.

"Estella? I pulled one over. From out of state. Speeding over by Joshua's Washout. I'll need you to pull up his info when I get back. Over."

Only the hiss of the radio greeted him. He checked his Timex and silently cursed as the seconds ticked off. Irritated, but knowing Estella had left early and Liz and her son Tommy wouldn't be in for another ten minutes, Billy Joe decided to stall for time.

He watched the fellow in the truck, his dark, short hair and long-sleeved shirt moving from time to time. He checked his rear view mirror every few seconds and Billy Joe could see his brown eyes and thick dark eyebrows. They were furrowed in frustration. Billy Joe smiled broadly. He loved getting up the skirts of out-of-staters. It would teach them not to come through his county speeding.

The fact that he hadn't actually caught the New Yorker speeding was irrelevant. It was a lesson in principle, anyway. Billy waited a little longer and then radioed in again.

"Unit one to base. Come in." Nothing but static greeted him. He looked up ahead and watched the man in the truck. The guy cleared his throat real loud, his fist to his mouth. Billy Joe could hear the crickets and cicadas screeching, the low rumble of the Charger's engine and the deep chug of the truck's exhaust.

Billy Joe decided he shouldn't make the fellow wait too much longer despite the fact that it was tempting. He stepped out, his jack boots scraping on the gravel alongside the road. He lifted his prodigious weight and his entire six-foot-five frame from the cruiser and placed his cap snugly on his melon-sized head.

He loved the way the gold hat band glinted in the sun. He preferred his deputy's black cowboy hat, but the county wouldn't pay for them when he sweated them through. They only would allow him the standard State Trooper caps.

He adjusted his hat, put his hand reassuringly on his revolver and strutted up alongside the truck. He enjoyed listening to the creak of his highly polished boots as he walked. He peered over the bed, curious and hopeful for drugs, contraband or black market rifles. He was disappointed again: there was only camping gear and a properly stored hunting rifle and what looked like might be a compound bow in a fancy case.

He caught the guy, probably in his fifties, staring at him again in the rear view mirror. Billy Joe put on his serious face. It was a look that had intimidated more than one man. With his stature, a gun, a badge and that face, most folks just didn't stand a chance.

He approached the window which was already rolled down, feeling pretty confident. He noticed that the woods had gotten quieter and the wind had picked up a bit. He looked the guy right in the eye.

"You know how much you were doing back there, mister?"

"Yes. Exactly. I was doing forty-five in a fifty-mile an hour zone. Officer." He looked him up and down and Billy Joe didn't see one bit of respect in that look. Bewildered and getting a bit angry, Billy Joe went on the offensive.

"I'll need your license and registration."

"Why? So you can go back to your cruiser and make me wait until dispatch gets in? I can hear you from up here, officer."

Now, Billy Joe was more than a little angry. He shot the guy a hard look, his face getting red and his ears burning. He saw spots for a second and knew he'd need to go see Doc Grant for some more heart medicine if he didn't get back into shape soon.

"You will hand over your license and registration, sir or I will extricate you from the vehicle and we will go into town to discuss this matter." He flexed his forearm over his piece and put his hand firmly on the door.

The guy didn't seem intimidated, but begrudgingly reached into his glove box and handed him his insurance card and pulled his license from his wallet. Watching him closely, he noticed a card in his wallet.

It was a card issued by many municipal police offices as identification outside of their precinct or jurisdiction. Billy Joe had a sinking feeling he had pulled over the wrong truck. For a second, he almost just let him go. But there was something in the lack of respect and the brazen attitude of this Yankee jerk that just plain upset him.

"There you go, officer. I hope all is in order." Billy Joe understood that the guy had decided it would be faster to just go along. He wasn't going to let him off that easily.

He took the license and turned it over and looked at it. He glanced at Jacob and back to the identification. Jacob was looking at him, incredulous. Billy Joe double checked the expiration date. Then he checked the back again.

"Says here you need prescription lenses, sir. I don't see your glasses."

"I'm wearing contacts for the trip. Easier to take care of."

"Don't they get dried out, driving all that way from New York?"

The guy hesitated. Billy Joe could tell he was gathering himself to speak normally.

"I manage. Anything else, officer?"

"Well, yeah. It says here you haven't marked to be an organ donor."

"Is there something wrong with that?" Something in the man's response really irked him. He spoke so quickly, so clipped. He had no regard whatsoever. Billy Joe hated uppity Yankees who thought they were better than anyone else. Only folks worse were Texans.

Billy Joe shrugged.

"Seems to me that a man would want to check that in case someone they knew would need a part or two. You know, in case of an accident."

"Did you pull me over to lecture me on my donor status or because you clocked me at an illegal speed, sheriff?"

Billy Joe didn't answer for a bit, just turned the license over again and then looked at the insurance card, thinking. He looked up and stared the guy in the face again, falling naturally into the intimidating stance that had worked so well for him over the last decade.

"You don't like us too much down here, do you Mr. Barclay?"

Jacob looked confused and then grabbed the steering wheel with both hands and stared out of the windshield ahead. Billy Joe could see his jaw working.

"I like you just fine, Sheriff. I don't take too kindly to being pulled over less than twenty miles from my destination on bogus charges."

"What are you insinuating, Mr. Barclay?"

"I am not insinuating anything, Sheriff Shoemaker. I am saying you pulled me over for no apparent violation. You probably pulled me over because my plates are out of state and you saw easy pickings." He turned and looked Billy Joe in the eye with a withering gaze.

Sheriff Shoemaker blinked twice.

"I'll be right back." He turned then and went back to his cruiser. He really just wanted to shoot the cocky mother in between the eyes. Just connect the dots, giving the guy a real uni-brow. He plopped back down into the seat, his feet on the ground outside and grabbed the mike.

Conscious of what Mr. Barclay had said earlier, he spoke quieter this time, "Unit one to base. Come in base."

"This is base, come back." It was Tommy. His mom was probably in the bathroom. It didn't matter. Tommy knew procedure well enough. He had been around the station for five years and Billy Joe had been busy showing the kid the ropes. He would make a fine deputy someday.

"Got me a hot-to-trot Yankee here speeding through Joshua's Washout. Need 4-1-1 on suspect. Copy?"

"Copy, Unit One. Just give me a second. The system's re-booting and it's slower than molasses in January, Sheriff."

"Take your time, Tommy. I want to make this sucker sweat for a minute anyway. How's your mom?"

"She's fine. She's out in the hall talking to Estella about the Lottery--Oklahoma's is up to seventeen million."

Billy Joe was amused. "Boy, what would you do with all that dough, eh Tommy?"

"Yeah, I know, right? Oh, wait, here it is. Give me a name, Sheriff, I'll look it up myself."

"Alright, it's Jacob Barclay. That's B as in boy-A-R-C as in car, L-A-Y. Address is on Frost Boulevard, Buffalo New York."

Tommy didn't repeat the information back or prompt him for the license number; he just waited.

Good boy, thought Billy Joe.

"Got 'im." Tommy hesitated. Billy Joe could tell he was digesting the information. The longer he waited, the more nervous he felt. It was as if several minutes had transpired instead of the seconds that passed until Tommy asked, "Uhhh... Sheriff? What do you want to know about this guy?"

"I'm guessing he's some cop or a big-wig. I guess I'll fix his wagon for speeding through Concord County Arkansas." He didn't feel as indignant as he was acting, but what was he to do?

"You're right about him being a cop, but he's retired, Sheriff. He doesn't have any criminal record or nuthin'. Whatchagonna do?" Tommy sounded concerned, and Billy Joe was touched.

He hadn't had someone look up to him since Becky left. And she just wanted to ride his bike more than anything else. Tommy really seemed to warm to Billy Joe, and that meant a lot to him. He wanted to impress the kid. He thought carefully. *What would Eric Estrada do?*

"Look, Tommy, this county is no place for folks to go speeding through the hills. This ain't some road in Germany, right?"

"If you say so, Sheriff. "

"But, this feller here, I just want to make an impression on him. That's all." He paused for a second, thinking of another detail. "Besides, Tommy, I just wanted to give you an opportunity to use the system. We need to make sure, just in case. I'll write him up a warning."

"Sounds fine, Sheriff. You wanna stop in and see us? Mom's ordering pizza from Mazzio's. I'll save you a slice." Billy Joe could count on one meaty hand the times someone actually extended a courtesy to him. The common misconception among most folk was that officers ate for free.

"Sure. I'll come on around after I wrap this up. I'll let you clean my gun and fill out my report if your ma will let you. Give you some real experience. What do ya say?"

"Really? That would be great! I don't think mom will care. Just come on by. You like pepperoni, right?"

"With extra cheese?"

"Of course."

"You got me dialed in, Tommy Boy. My mouth is waterin' just thinking about it. Beats the tar out of another TV dinner tonight."

"Glad to be of service, Sheriff. See you in a bit. Over and out."

"Unit One, out." Billy Joe's attitude brightened. He truly looked forward to spending time with Tommy. The kid was eager, loyal and wanted desperately to learn. Tommy was like Billy Joe when he was a kid: totally engrossed with being an officer.

Billy Joe's dad was a state trooper, and had died in a traffic accident on an icy road in January when Billy Joe was ten. His uncle Carl had taken him and his mom in and had instilled in him a strong passion for driving fast, listening to the police scanner, and chasing ambulances and fire trucks to see tragedies first hand.

Billy Joe took his ball point pen from his front pocket and touched it to his tongue. He pulled out the warning form from his console and slipped it into his clipboard and copied Mr. Barclay's license number and other information.

He signed it and then sighed. He looked ahead, the night falling around, the Ford's rear chrome bumper reflecting the red and blue strobes of his lights into the trees along the road. He rubbed his chin and decided it really was best to let the fella off easy.

He groaned as he exited the car and crunched and creaked his way back across the short expanse to stand beside the driver's side.

Mr. Barclay looked up at him, patient and silent.

"What you have here," he ripped the yellow copy of the warning off the pad and stuck it in the window, "is a warning, Mr. Barclay. And here are your license and insurance verification."

Mr. Barclay took the warning, insurance card, and identification wordlessly. He placed them in a neat pile in the seat next to him and placed both hands on the steering wheel. It had a two-toned leather grip, Billy Joe noticed.

"That all, officer?"

He nodded. "Thank you for visiting Concord County. Enjoy your stay and have a safe trip, sir."

"Yeah. Thanks." He turned the key and put the truck in gear. Billy Joe expected him to peel out. He just pulled calmly back onto the road and his tail lights disappeared around the bend ahead. Billy Joe stood there for a moment, his clip board in hand, a slight sheen of sweat on his forehead. He removed his cap again and wiped his brow with his forearm. His only thought was about pizza as he turned back to his vehicle.

CHAPTER SEVEN

J acob was tempted to speed now. He was infuriated. In his head, he swore. He gripped the steering wheel violently and desperately fought the urge to drive reckless. He knew the Sheriff had redeemed himself, but part of him wanted the Sheriff to give him a ticket. At least that way he had a reason to hate the man. As it was, Jacob only had the guilty feeling he was again assuming things about people irrationally.

His friend, Clark, had been from Arkansas and he seemed to be a very normal human being. He didn't seem to harbor resentment for "Yankees." Yet, at every stop he had made so far in Arkansas, assumptions had been made about him and in turn he had thought the worst about them.

He guessed it was human nature. He had seen the same situation as young black officers dealt with the realization that civilians—and sometimes even their co-workers--often didn't look past their color of their skin.

He tried to concentrate on his goals ahead. He had planned to stop in at an outfitter and get some basic equipment, maybe a fishing report and gossip. He wasn't sure he was up to visiting with any more people tonight. Maybe it was best that he find a hotel room and get some rest first. It had been a long day . Between the incident with Luke this afternoon and Sheriff Shoemaker this evening, his skills in patience and personality were being stretched to their limits.

As he pulled into Bexton, he noted his hotel on the right, a Denny's conveniently located alongside. The town was small. Highway 62 ran directly through town, intersecting Main Street. He noted that as the highway narrowed to accommodate angled parking for the Concord County Courthouse and the Bexton Public Library, it became a street named Broadway Avenue. This was the street on which his hotel was located.

Of course, if he had a GPS device, a voice would proclaim this fact to him. He remembered it from the map Clark had given him three months ago.

The white pillars of the courthouse were lit by a yellow lamp that accented the clock above the front port-cochère. The streets were clean, but the sidewalks were in disrepair. He pulled into a spot just north of the main street intersection and thought it best to walk around a bit and become familiar with the town.

Only a few couples were roaming the sidewalks, window shopping. A row of barbershops, antique dealers, insurance agents, real estate brokers and hair salons dominated the north side of Main Street. The two-story buildings looked old and ill-kept. Bricks were spalling, their faces falling off in chunks, the mortar dark with mold.

Main Street was well-lit and he could see a newly remodeled building up ahead. It looked like someone was trying to restore the historical aspects of the building. Its bright colors and updated signage made it stand out from its neighbors.

"VICK'S OUTFITTERS, SINCE 1917" the sign proclaimed. Its interior glowed and he could see several people rummaging about inside the large glass windows. Camping gear and mannequins in fishing vests and waders, fly rods, and creels donned the front display. A gas lamp provided ample light to the entrance that was quaint, filled with wrought iron, light brown stucco and European flair.

Debating over whether to make his way over to the store now, he determined he didn't want to haul all his new gear the two blocks back to his truck. Instead, he headed east on Main. It came to a veritable dead end two blocks later. Most of the buildings were abandoned, for lease, or contained clothing stores, a photography studio, and another real estate agent.

At the end of the street he saw the police station and next to it, a smaller, squat building that said "County Sheriff." Two cruisers sat in front and a gray sedan. As he walked by and headed back west on Main, Jacob saw another cruiser take the corner. He recognized the man driving right away. It was Sheriff Shoemaker.

At first, he was tempted to duck into a dark doorway of an abandoned building on the south side of the street. But, as his headlights swung wide, Jacob held up his hand and waved. Later, he would not be able to attribute why he did this, but it didn't matter. Billy Joe was oblivious to him. He cruised into a spot behind him and got out of the cruiser as if he were in a hurry.

He bounded up the steps into the Bexton Police department carrying his clipboard and the double doors closed behind him. Jacob shook his head. He made his way back to the truck and then drove over to Vick's.

He sat in the truck for a minute, filled with thoughts. He figured it was too early to go to bed; he wouldn't be able to sleep anyway. He kept thinking about Luke and asking himself if maybe he had made the wrong decision.

Alice would have insisted that he turn the boy over to Social Services. Of course, that was the legal thing to do. For the first time in his life he had gone against his better judgment and against the law that for years had dictated his every action and thought.

He ejected the Credence disk and rummaged around for the case. He saw there another CD case that didn't belong to him. It had interesting artwork and a dark motif. The cover read "Straylight Run." Luke must have left it, he figured. He opened the case and inside was a note written on the backside of the Carl's Jr. tray paper.

Mr. Barclay,

I just can't keep calling you Jakie. You are too cool for that. Thank you for all you did and promised to do. I think you will like this music. You really need to expand your taste. Remember what I said about Janice. If you are half as cool to her as you were to me, then, I guess maybe you two might have some nicer things to say to each other. Anyway, I'm just a kid. What do I know.

Sincerely,
Luke Prater

He stared at the note for several minutes wondering where God made kids like this. His kids were special, but this kid seemed to be just a little different.

Jacob put the CD in the player and listened to the first two songs. He wasn't sure what to think of the music, but he figured it would grow on him if he listened to it enough. Jacob thought about his actions more. At the time, he felt he was just acting on instinct. Maybe he hadn't made the best decision for him, but the best decision he could for Luke.

He ejected the disk at the end of the second song and gathered his keys and checked for his wallet. He had left it on the seat next to him. He picked it up, slammed the truck door and walked to the entrance of Vick's.

As he approached the front door, a young couple was coming out. The man held a fly rod, and the woman laughed at him and playfully punched his arm.

"You don't have to fish past lunch. I'll have a shore lunch fixed for you if we catch some trout."

Her eyes twinkled and her blonde hair fell across her beaming smile. If Jacob had been younger, this smile would have easily stolen his heart. The young man stopped, and Jacob thought maybe he had been caught staring. Instead, the young man reached back and held open the door for Jacob.

"She says she will be closing soon. You may want to hurry. She's nice, but I think she doesn't like working late."

The man spoke to Jacob as if he knew him. His spontaneous kindness, his woman's beautiful smile, and their laughter brightened his mood instantly.

"Thanks. Much obliged." He returned their smile.

"Not a problem." He continued on, and put his arm around her slim shoulders. He could hear them laugh as he escorted her around their red Jeep Cherokee.

"Shut the door! You born in a barn?"

A diminutive older lady with gray-white hair in a bun and a bright red cardigan shuffled up to him looking half serious.

"You closed?" He asked, just a little subconscious, but feeling better than he had all day.

"No. I just told them that because they'd still be in here jawing with me, giving each other love looks all night. Kinda creepy if you ask me. Don't they have a cabin or proper house to carry on like that in?"

Jacob smiled and shrugged. "I don't know them. They just held the door open for me. They seem like nice folks," he said and let the door close. She shuffled off towards one of the mannequins and flipped the "Open" over. She waved outside, evidently to the young couple and smiled. She turned to him, the smile disappearing.

"Well, what do you want?"

"I'm camping, fishing, and hunting over near the Ozark National Park for a few days and wanted to see if you have a supply of rations and some other gear. I'll also have some questions if you can answer them."

"Hmm. I see. You set up with Naomi? The outfitter?"

"Yeah. She told me to come see you."

"She told me you'd be here. You're from New York?"

"Yes. Buffalo."

"Never been there." She turned and indicated that he should follow.

"My husband, Louis Vick, owns this place but he busted his hip two weeks ago and now I'm holding down the fort. I suppose I know about as much as he does."

"This always been his place?"

"Well, it was his daddy's and his granddaddy's before that. But, yeah, we've been supplying camping, hunting and fishing gear all across northern Arkansas for three generations. Louis is eighty and I'm...well, never mind what I am, but you can say we know a thing or two about outfitting."

"Good. You came highly recommended." They made their way around to an aisle full of backpacks. There was a huge assortment.

Jacob took in the small store, then. It was cramped only because there was so much gear packed in to such a small place. Boxes lined the walls, and an old-fashioned cash register sat near the front. The store was light on decoration, but there was a sign on one column in the center of the room. It read, "SMOKE AT YOUR OWN RISK. THOSE GUNS YONDER WORK LIKE A CHARM."

Across the aisle from the backpacks he saw hundreds of rations and cooking supplies.

"Here's all you'll need. But let me tell you, if it says it has meat in it, don't trust it. It's just reconstituted. I can't vouch for the taste, but I can say with assurance it ain't your momma's pot roast."

He laughed.

"Thanks for the advice."

"I'll leave you alone for a sec. I gotta go spit my teeth out and make sure Louis hasn't rolled out of bed." She didn't smile, but he could tell she was happy. She turned and trudged up a set of stairs set against the west wall. He saw her disappear through a doorway and then her voice echoed back downstairs.

"Ain't got cameras, young man, but I got eyes in the back of my head. You even think about stealing, I'll pull that double-barreled shot gun off'n the wall and fill you full of buckshot. You hear?"

He hollered up the stairs after her, "Yes ma'am! I will pay for everything I pick out."

He heard her rummaging around and some muffled talking. He could hear her chiding Louis and doting on him.

He picked out about a box of dried vegetables, beans and herbs packed in individual pouches that were essential in camp cooking, some extra thick baggies with double zippers, a small "oven" which was heated by gel tabs, a few meal bars and some tubes of protein paste.

He knew from experience that the tubes tasted disgusting, but if he was caught in a jam, they would provide him enough nutrition to manage. He looked at several bags of prepared meals: beef stroganoff, sweet and sour chicken, beef tips and broccoli, spaghetti and meatballs.

He turned up his nose, realizing that unless the flavor profile was sweet (he sometimes enjoyed the blueberry cheesecake), he wasn't going to enjoy the packaged meals any more than the protein paste.

He had enough beef and chicken bullion, rice, ramen noodles and extra water tablets to make a ton of healthy meals. He fully expected to lose ten pounds in the next week and put on five pounds of lean muscle, especially in his legs. He knew how to push himself enough to get fit and it seemed like each year it took less and less.

Jacob browsed around, looking for other gadgets and tools that might be useful. He settled on a collapsible cup, a water boiling system that was the size of a thermos and would fit on a small propane bottle, and a package of hand warmers.

He piled his treasures on the little counter by the register and waited patiently for Mrs. Vick to return. He was pleasantly surprised at the reception he had received. He was charmed by her obviously forced gruff nature and her pretend cantankerousness.

He had always liked personalities that worked hard to be larger than life, when behind the scenes they were simple, caring folk that didn't care to be taken advantage of, trodden on or pitied. He imagined Mr. Vick to be tough as shoe leather with a heart of gold and as cuddly as a teddy bear.

He thought that he had been unkind to the Sheriff; although, he was sure the Sheriff had fit about every stereotype of a back woods cop. Jacob knew hundreds of police officers, detectives, security professionals, sheriffs and FBI agents. Most were just regular folk like him.

Despite his feelings of guilt, it was still hard to trust the Sheriff. His mind was set. Even if everyone in this spitball of a town were as wonderful as the Vicks, he could not forgive or overlook the distrust he had for an officer of the law that disregarded it or twisted it to fit his own agenda. The law was there to protect the rights of every citizen, not coddle to the whims of its servants.

Jacob heard movement at the top of the stairs. He looked up and watched as Mrs. Vick gingerly and deliberately made her way down the steps. He withheld comment, not wanting her to feel rushed. She had her head down, making sure she put a foot firmly on each step and concentrated on her balance. He noted her luxurious head of white hair and her slim frame. Mrs. Vick was a beauty for her age he realized. Mr. Vick had himself a rare prize.

"Oh, so you're still here. Good. And I see you are ready to check out?" She commented.

"Yes, ma'am. I found plenty here I can make use of."

"Well. I would say good, but I would want to have a talk with your grammar school instructor, mister." Jacob looked confused, but kept a firm smile since he knew a lesson was coming forthwith.

"Grammar school?"

"Who taught you to finish a sentence with a preposition, young man. It isn't proper. I taught grammar and literature for forty years at the local high school. None of my students would talk like that, at least not in front of me."

Jacob thought back to what he said and realized his error. It was an idiomatic expression he commonly used and never realized its grammatical taboo. He suspected he could still learn a thing or two from Mrs. Vick, the least of which was proper grammar.

"Why thank you for listening so intently, Mrs. Vick. I will pay more attention to my preposition use in the future and try to edit my words before I speak them."

"That is a fine thing to do. Most folk don't think before they speak and so they say all manner of silly, untrue things. They partake in hyperbole and synectode, run-on sentences and poor subject-verb agreement. And what I see on the internet would just put most grammar school teachers to an early grave I tell you."

"Internet, huh? I didn't figure you for an internet user."

She looked hurt. She gathered up some of his things and punched some buttons on the register.

"I was using the internet before Al Gore thought of it, young man." She grinned. "Just because I look older than the hills and I use a register made in the 1800's doesn't mean I am incapable of using modern technology. It hurts my eyes, but Gene--that's my son--he bought me a twenty-one inch screen and showed me how to increase the text size and now I even use it to read my books. It is so hard to see some of my favorite books without using some magnifying device unless I buy them from Amazon and download them to my computer."

"I see. Well, it's nice you can keep up that way. Have you thought of putting your merchandise on the web?"

"It crossed my mind, but mister, let me tell you, it isn't easy packaging some of this stuff," she gestured at the wall of backpacks and ski gear. "Besides, the shipping would eat us alive. If we lived in Little Rock, Bentonville or Fort Smith, I wouldn't think anything of it, but we are in a rinky-dink little hole here if you didn't notice.

"Besides, we do well here. Everyone knows us and everyone recommends us. I would say we have close to sixty percent of the market in North Central Arkansas of camping equipment. Wal-mart is our only competitor and they don't carry near as much as we do. You can't buy Orvis fly equipment, or Scott Rods or Weatherby or North Face or Swiss. Pretty much, you can buy Coleman or some knock-off of it there and that's it. I like Coleman, we carry almost everything they make, but we don't limit ourselves."

"I can see that. You have one of the best stocks I've seen."

"Well, thank you. Well. That will be three hundred and fifty six dollars." She grabbed a tube of lip balm and a package of chewing gum. "Any order over two hundred and we throw in two small items I notice you will need. That lip balm is something new we're trying out. It is a copy of that Burt's Bees stuff. We carry it, too. But try this out and let me know what you think.

"With the weather cooling down, you'll need to protect your lips. It'll keep them from drying out and also protect them from the cold by creating a layer. And the gum is great in case you don't brush much, which if you are like most men who trudge into the woods for days, I figure you won't brush at all. It will protect from gum disease and hunger."

"Wow. That's great. Thank you."

She practically beamed, her false teeth gleaming in the lamplight.

"It's what I do, son. Will that be cash or charge? We don't accept checks."

He flopped out four one hundred dollar bills, counting them twice, and bundled up the bags to go.

She opened the register and looked at him quizzically as he started for the door.

"Sir, don't you want your change?"

He looked back and smiled.

"Keep the change and start a new register fund. I appreciate your help and your grammar advice. You tell Mr. Vick to get well soon."

Mrs. Vick just stared back at him, the till open and the bills still in her hand.

"Well, I never in my whole life." She muttered. He pushed through the door out into the Arkansas night feeling better than he had since Janice had showed up at his door a

week ago in a plunge neckline sweater and high heels,
looking ten years younger and purring like a kitten.

CHAPTER EIGHT

T wo days later, Jacob sat on a ridge overlooking a farm deep in the woods of Arkansas. He was on the border of public land and the Ozark National Forest. He cradled a hot cup of cocoa in his hands, the warmth of the cocoa soaking into his bones chilled from a rough night spent nestled in the leaves. He had left his compact sleeping pad behind to make room for more gear.

He sat on a rotten log that had fallen on one side of a fence line that followed the ridge out to a small shelf where it dipped back down toward the small meadow and circled around to a dirt road that led up to a small white farmhouse and a modest barn.

His .22 caliber rifle lay propped against the end of the log. He managed to kill a squirrel last night before retiring to bed and had mixed most of its meager meat into his ramen noodles and chicken broth. It was salty and gamey, but it was the better than the burger he had eaten in Paragould.

Several head of cattle grazed on the side of the hill and he spotted some geese on a pond behind the barn. He watched as the farmer hauled some bales of hay around and stacked them neatly just outside of the barn.

What a peaceful, simple way to live, he thought. Jacob admired the man down there who he knew was up even before he was this morning. He saw the thick sides of the milk cows inside the darkness of the barn and heard the lowing. He could tell even from half a mile away that the farmer was well into his fifties and possibly retirement aged. Despite this, he moved with the determined pace of someone accustomed to a lifetime of hard labor.

After his adventure in town, he had followed a long, winding dirt road called--ominously enough--Crippled Turkey Road, to a top of a bluff. He had parked his truck in an oval turn-around and locked it. He left most of his possessions inside. After about three miles into the dense forest and underbrush, Jacob had realized he had left his cell phone on the front seat.

Janice had always hated how absent-minded he could be. It came in spurts, especially if he was particularly sidetracked. He didn't worry about the phone too much. It was probably best to get as far from civilization as possible for this leg of his trip. Jacob decided that he would call Janice as soon as he got back.

For the rest of the trip he would always be in walking distance from the truck and so he figured he could make it up to her. He planned on hiking and hunting a few days before he came back and traveled to some good trout fishing on Army Corps of Engineers land on the Buffalo River. Then he planned to travel over toward Bentonville and canoe down the White River hitting some spots with his fly rod and just relaxing before he headed back to New York. That was his general plan, but he didn't have any real prescription for days or time.

It was strange for him to feel consideration for Janice after all they had been through. Jacob had not always been callous and unforgiving of Janice. He knew that what Luke had said affected him in a positive way. It was harmful for him to harbor angry feelings. Besides, this trip was as much about healing and getting in touch with his survivor instincts as it was a mid-life crisis luxury. Long ago, taking trips as a coping mechanism had turned into a cathartic experience intended to cleanse him of his "demons." He was difficult to be around, sometimes. These lonely trips softened his harder edges.

Jacob tossed the remains of his cocoa in the brush at his feet and wiped the collapsible cup clean. He popped it closed and stored it in his bag. He liked how compact it was and wished that much of his other gear was as thoughtful as that simple gadget. He shrugged into the pack, wishing for the first time he had come with a friend.

He wasn't prone to loneliness, but watching the farmer had made him long for some companionship. Part of him was compelled to go on down into the valley and ask the old guy if he wanted a hand with the work in exchange for a good cup of coffee and a game or two of chess or dominoes.

But he knew that would defeat the purpose for trip. The first day, the separation could be bitter and hard. He determined to push through. No need to panic.

He picked up his rifle and checked the magazine. It was missing one cartridge. He popped one out from his dispenser on his belt, kneading the small bullet and looking curiously at its ruddy point.

They were varmit rounds, but they were accurate, the rifle light and the action simple. This early in the season, there wasn't much game he could legally hunt, but he was also only one man. A turkey, a deer or wild pigs would be too much meat for him to process.

He firmly believed in not killing more than he needed to survive. He slipped the shell into magazine and popped it back into place, satisfied with the metal snap that indicated that the magazine was locked. He made sure it was on safety and slung it over his shoulder, the leather sling biting into his collar bone.

He made his way down the mountain on the western slope away from the farm. As he descended, the sun disappeared. The woods were still damp from the light frost that had settled that night. Leaves crunched under his boots and he tried in vain to keep quiet as he shuffled along or to step lightly. The leaves either slid precariously or crunched loudly at his attempts to muffle his steps. He tried the heel-to-toe method he had learned in Scouts and it worked better.

He still felt he sounded like a herd of elephants tromping through the woods. He resigned himself to the noise and concentrated on his bearings. He searched for outcroppings of rock or game trails to improve his stealth and to give himself valid landmarks by which to ensure that he didn't backtrack or go in circles.

By mid-day he had traveled about three miles through fairly open ground. He had avoided the thickest undergrowth and chosen expanses of forest that evidently had been carefully tended by farmers or horticulturists because they were marked by very little downfalls and large, fairly spaced trees.

Since they didn't have to compete for the sun, they grew thick and full branches that often began just a few feet from the ground creating a lush canopy of gold and red leaves.

The layers of leaves upon the ground were from previous years and the decay from their detritus he could smell every second of every day. He was glad he was not allergic.

He stopped briefly for lunch, eating some turkey jerky and some slices of dried pineapple, raisins and figs. He admired this old-growth forest so resplendent with color. He took in the warming air and was glad again to see the sun peer out from behind where he had been walking.

It radiated through the canopy of leaves, dappling the ground around him and dissipating the whirling fog and melting the fine layer of frost. A faint breeze met his face, blowing gently from the west and he could feel moisture lick his unshaven face.

As he munched contentedly on his small meal, feeling his body regain energy and the listless exhaustion of his limbs decrease, he watched a family of beavers roll playfully over the brush and leaves north of him. They crested the rise and he listened as they scurried off down the slope and a faint splash as they entered a pond he had noticed earlier.

They had evidently dammed the small creek that wound around the lower end between the mountain he had just come down and the rise of the one he was preparing to scale.

Thankfully, the mountains here were less than eleven hundred feet but they fell sharply at times into valleys barely four hundred feet above sea level. The land was dotted with small ponds, many of which began as beaver dams. He had spotted three small ones along shelves on his trek down the last mountain.

Many of the mountains in this range remained un-named. The locals, nestled in cabins and run-down houses along practically impassable dirt roads that wound for miles in and out of this barely inhabited area, had names for every valley, mountain, pond, creek and hillock. Not all of them were marked on even the best topographic map, though.

On his way up the mountain, he had stopped briefly to talk to one of these locals. Jacob had traveled the same broken road for two hours and wanted to know how much further it would be until it ended. It seemed on his map to only be about twenty miles long.

"It's up yonder a pace." He had pointed up the road and then his finger drifted off to the east. "Then you follow the road around. There's a washout at Clem's Creek there and then you follow the left fork of the road. The right is Jeremiah Talbot's land. It's his private drive and he's likely to shoot you if'n he don't recognize ya."

Jacob had taken it all in, trying to get past the slurred, lazy, slow speech. The man had seemed honest and genuine, but Jacob could smell his body odor from inside the truck. Jacob could only guess the man's occupation to be a mechanic with all the grease that stained his torn t-shirt and the frayed jeans with one back pocket torn off and a belt cinched about it as if the pants were two sizes too large.

He had made a solemn promise not to take the wrong fork in the road and was disappointed when he arrived at his destination and realized he didn't remember taking a fork in the road. It must have been a well-disguised driveway because he didn't see a mailbox, a no trespassing sign or a "WELCOME TO THE TALBOT'S." He had an ominous feeling as he unpacked his gear and locked his door.

The morning was bright, but he felt naked and watched at the same time. He couldn't shake the feeling for several minutes, and then a large doe jumped out of the underbrush to his left and bounded down over the hill and across Crippled Turkey Road into the thick forest on the south side of the road.

His brief encounters with the locals, excepting Mrs. Vick, had all been varying degrees of disaster. The shop where he had procured his license to fish and hunt had given him additional advice. The old fellow had bellowed on for about an hour, giving sage information, recalling past hunts and several times, Jacob was sure he had mixed up memories of the war with recollections of key events.

Then Bill, the manager at the Bexton Inn, had provided very little to put him at ease about the locals. He had looked at Jacob's identification and glanced up at him, his eyes sad and shook his head.

"Tsk. I am from Florida originally. I thought we had some hicks there in the Everglades, but these folk out here take the cake, man." He was in his forties, his hair long and tied back in a braid. His hair was pulled back so severely, it made his forehead seem to shine in the bright lights of the hotel lobby.

Dr. Phil blared his nonsense psychology on a television with blurry reception. This noise and the rush of cars driving by on Highway 43 provided a backdrop of sound as the audience on the television applauded dumbly and semis rumbled by, shaking the glass of the hotel.

"Really? I think some of those hicks in Florida were originally from up north."

Bill's eyes grew wide and his lips twitched nervously.

"I'm sorry, I didn't mean..."

"No. I was joking." Jacob smiled. "But why do you think people here are so bad? The Vicks seem like salt of the earth." He tried to sound doubtful. He had learned that by playing the devil's advocate, people would produce concrete facts to back up their views. Sometimes an investigator had to read between the lines since most people naturally embellished in the face of questioning. But by taking the opposite position, he stood a good chance of at least knowing where the other person really stood.

Bill twirled the silver ring on his right hand and then plucked at his skull earring in his left ear lobe. The guy was pinned and pricked in a dozen places and that was just what Jacob could see across the counter.

"Well. I've only been here a couple of years, but everyone seems right nice to each other. But if you are from outta town, it takes them awhile to warm up to ya. At least, that's my experience."

"So, they're protective of their turf. What's new? You ever been to Harlem? Downtown Philly?Parts of Miami?"

"Well, yeah. But it's not the same, really. I know what you're saying, but there's something different about these people, you see? Those places are hard places to live and the people there are protective of their own.

I guess everyone can relate to that. But, here, it's hard in a different way. Everyone struggles to make a life, but these hill folk seem to think differently, act differently. They believe in things you and I wouldn't think twice about. I mean, they're something scary sometimes."

Jacob could tell there was something more he wanted to say. He kept plucking at things—his cuffs of his long sleeve shirt, his pearl buttons, and several times he tugged hard on his skull ear ring, stretching the lobe until it hurt to watch him.

Something about the way he was acting, the way he breathed as he talked, made Jacob want to dig deeper. A sense that something here needed investigated tugged at his conscience.

This guy didn't know he had been a cop. Jacob looked him in the eye; with a jerking movement, Bill slid his key across the counter. His fingers hovered over it for a second, his eyes darting from Jacob to the keys. Bill looked down, his mouth twitching, mumbling like he was talking to himself.

Jacob took the key from the counter. He continued to watch Bill closely, but at the last second decided to drop the conversation. Bill seem stretched too thin, like his ear lobes.

"Well. It's a good thing I won't be hanging around much, then."

"Uh. Yeah. Just turn the key in tomorrow. Jessica will be in at 6. If you need extra towels or deodorant or toothpaste, we have some, complimentary. But, the pool's shut down for the year. Sorry."

"No problem. I don't swim. Good night, Bill.

He looked confused and then laughed nervously and placed his hand over his name tag.

"Oh, yeah.You too, Mr. Barclay."

So, outside of his experience with Mrs. Vick, he hadn't really met any normal people since he left the bar in Lexington. Even Luke had been out of the ordinary. Disturbed, incredibly intelligent, clever and mature for his age, Luke was far from normal.

Even when he thought more about the Vicks, it seemed strange that a couple of their age had set up a camping supply business several hours from any large town and yet managed to keep one the best stocks of inventory he had ever seen. The farmer he noticed this morning had seemed normal at first but Jacob watched him closely as he met his menial tasks with an obvious lack of zeal. At the same time, he performed these tasks with determination and focus.

Jacob realized that maybe what these people all had in common was a resignation to a life of unhappiness. He stood there stunned for several seconds. Something about this revelation shook him. He couldn't put a finger on it.

Jacob could smell the rain. The light breeze had picked up to a steady whipping of the branches around him. Leaves careened crazily in the wind, blown uphill and over the small ridge there. He realized then why the beavers had scurried to cover.

If he didn't find shelter or at least make his way to a higher point, he would be caught in a low area with no real place to rest from the storm that was surely brewing and developing from the west.

His thoughts went back to the local people here in these mountains. Something about their reserved nature had bothered him.

As he dealt with his surface thoughts of protecting himself from the coming storm, he decided that what they had in common was a deep sadness. They were resigned to their existence. Here, on the edge of what many would call civilization, they were exposed to the two curses affecting society.

On one hand, they were vulnerable to nature and the difficulties of a mean, unfair life. On the other hand, they were easy prey for ordered chaos—the false sense of protection from the mean, unfair life that we call civilization.

His thoughts trailed off, recalling long-lost lectures by philosophy professors and literature teachers at Syracuse. Soon, with a stiff breeze blowing dampness ceaselessly into his eyes and the low, rolling gray clouds approaching quickly from the west, Jacob dropped all thoughts of lectures and people and focused on himself.

He had to find some shelter because he didn't have time to build one. He climbed the incline and followed a game trail as the sky darkened and the low limbs crashed about him. The moaning of the trees as the wind picked up was like a mournful opera, with bass voices sighing, a background harmony as tenors and altos screeched out alarming solos.

He hadn't experienced a storm like this before. He had of course heard about them, but was caught off guard by the ferocity of the wind and the quick development of the storm. He pushed against the wind and then decided to follow its flow as it seemed to want to push him north and upslope.

He crossed over a low ridge, the wind buffeting him and pushing at the weight that already had his muscles and joints screaming. He wasn't used to this much exertion for this length of time. Gritting his teeth and stumbling forward into the gray cloudbank that obscured the mountain ahead, he silently cursed the stair climber and elliptical trainer at home. They had ill prepared him for this journey.

No amounts of pushups and crunches and two mile morning runs could prepare a man to lug a seventy pound backpack, a fifteen pound rifle and an extra twenty pounds of weight he should have lost prior to the trip.

Then there was the wind. It swirled around him, invisible but substantive. It drove with it the leaves and dirt of the forest. The thick smell of moist earth and decaying leaves rose heavily on the increasing current of air.

Amid his flight up the hill, his lungs full of the earth-laden air, his ball cap threatening to fly off like a derelict kite on a March breeze, he crazily thought back to his childhood stories of Cyclone Pete. He imagined the two revolvers tied boldly to the beaten leather chaps, the Wild Bill Cody turn of his cowboy hat, the sides almost rolled into themselves and the personified cyclone that whirled around him. He thought maybe if someone would witness his wild scramble, they might mistake him for that legendary character.

He could envision himself brandishing the Remington .22 like it was a baton, held in both hands across his body swinging it back and forth to provide a balance so as not to allow the weight of the backpack to tip him over. Despite this flash of his imagination, he felt old and tired and ridiculous. He mentally chastised himself for ever making this trip.

His mind scanned over a dozen details as his body plunged ahead. Thankfully, the wind lessened as he climbed higher on this side of the mountain. He had cut himself off from the worst of it. It was a good thing, because he could already feel the fatigue.

The energy from his recent lunch already burned off. A deep burn entered the muscles in his legs, backside and shoulders. He slowed his pace, understanding that as he neared the zenith of this mountain, he would again be subjected to the fierce winds. At a higher elevation, the gusts would be even more severe than in the valley.

He took stock of his situation. Turning, he tried to assess the direction of the clouds above. They roiled and turned and he couldn't discern their direction. He could see through the canopy to the south, though.

All he saw was great sheets of silver rain, a mist emanating from the valley he had just escaped, and several streaks of bright lightning tracing their way from one cloud bank to another. A roar escaped the heavens and he could feel the rumble of the sound roll past him a split second after the sound assaulted his ears.

He knew that there was meant to be beauty in all of this. He remembered Janice comforting Clarice when she was a toddler, telling her the rumbling from the thunder was just God bowling in heaven. It was so quaint an image that Jacob had actually adopted it as a personal conviction. For years, to Jacob, God was just the heavenly bowler.

He could picture him in flowing white beard and a red and black bowling shirt with a neon green ball, licking his fingers as he lined up to hurl the ball down the lane. Jacob imagined God would never have to worry about a one-ten split.

But now, God was just plain ferocious. And Jacob was concerned. He recalled his thesis paper he prepared for philosophy class about how man was unprepared for nature. Compared to the forces of nature—the perfect storm, hurricanes, tornadoes, avalanches, earthquakes, tsunamis, lightning—man was inconsequential.

Now, the lightning traced fingers of death across the southern sky. In a land with which he was only familiar through a cursory knowledge of a topographical map, Jacob Barclay felt small and insignificant. He wanted to go home.

Phillip had tried to convince him several years ago that everything he believed about nature was true about God. Jacob had almost been persuaded and managed to satisfy Phillip temporarily by attending services for a month or so before he began to just not show up, always having an excuse. Somehow, now he regretted his stubbornness and wished that Phillip were here to experience this with him.

Jacob wanted desperately to shake his fear and enjoy the beauty. He kept thinking about Idaho and Saskatchewan and his failed trips of yore. The voice of Janice rang as a trident above the tumult of the thunder and the wind, over the moaning boughs and the shrill whistling of the leaves: "Jacob Barclay, you come back to me in one piece!"

At a time of great doubt and fear, it puzzled him that he thought of Janice. It dawned on him that ever since Luke had mentioned her (twice, in fact), he had thought about her several times. More than he had since their divorce. And now, he was worried that he would disappoint her by not returning home safely.

He didn't want to dwell on this inexplicable change of heart. He wanted to do the manly thing and deal with the danger at hand and fix what seemed to be almost certainly broken. That is how most men defined their roles in the universe: cosmic mechanics always tinkering with broken things to set them right.

He could feel the wind shift again and the breeze blew stronger at his left side. He pointed himself straight up the slope and decided to get to higher ground and reassess his situation from a better vantage point.

Maybe he would get lucky and find a cabin, a farm or a cave nearby. Anything to get dry, out of the wind and away from the deadly lightning that he feared the most. He began at a trot, leaning forward and adjusting the bulk of the weight over his shoulder blades.

Soon, his back was screaming from white hot pain. He could feel the knot of the muscle in his lower back and just above his hips begin to knot. He slowed his pace, but remained resolute in making progress, one agonizing step at a time.

He could do nothing, it seemed, to alleviate this condition. He resigned himself to gravity and an aging body, cursing himself silently again, gritting his teeth from the pain, and pushing through. He dared to look up, his breath coming in ragged heaves, his lungs splitting, his back feeling as hard as an ironing board.

He was nearing the zenith. He noticed that if he veered off to his right, there was a slight shelf that intersected the slope and ended at some boulders at the top of the ridge.

Desperate, he scrambled across the slope, wishing he could drop the rifle or (*please, God*) drop the pack from his strained back. Twenty yards later, the rain came in torrents. Leaves fell crashing about him as the rain slammed the dried carcasses to the ground without mercy. Jacob was blinded, the rain mixing with his sweat, the salt stinging his eyes, the silver sheets of moisture obscuring his view.

The boulders that lined the ridge appeared as hulking dark gray creatures guarding the muddy backdrop of the sky. All around him were the sounds of rain smacking the earth. Jacob had heard the patter of rain, had even experienced rain storms that sounded like an AM radio station that had gone off-air.

This rain was different. It seemed to punish his senses. It stung his skin, filled his head with a constant minute splatter, partially blinded him, and filled his mouth with the taste of metal. He could smell the moisture as it soaked his exposed skin and he drank it up as his breath came in heaves, the rain misting off of his nose, dripping off his unshaven chin, and soaking his feet and clothes.

In his hurried flight he hadn't thought to pull out his rain gear. It was still rolled neatly in a side pocket of his interior frame backpack. *Probably still dry, too. So much for being prepared*, he thought. His Scout Master would just shake his head in disappointment if he found out. He wished now he had thought of it earlier. He could feel rivulets of moisture tickle his spine as the rain drenched his underwear.

Finally, he made it to the boulders. He ran his hand across their rough surface and over the soaked peat moss as he moved around them. Soon, he found a spot between two of the larger boulders where the taller one had a lip that stuck out enough to provide some shelter.

He put down his pack and put his rifle in a dry stack of leaves. He quickly reached into his pack and extracted a 10' x 10' blue tarp that had built-in grommets. He dug out some rope and looking around desperately, found a place he could scramble up onto the larger rock.

The boulder was slick with rain, but his boots were adequately suited for the job. Plus, he was focused on his task. He made his way to the top and found some sizable rocks to use as anchors. He lined them up and then unfolded the tarp. He realized before he had finished with the second fold that doing this in the wind was a huge mistake.

He was perched in a compromising position, upright on a boulder eight feet from the ground. As he looked around, he saw that a fall from this height would easily result in concussion, a broken leg or a busted rib cage.

His legs weak from exhaustion and sudden fear, he dropped to his knees and scrambled as carefully as he could toward the overhang. He dragged one of the largest rocks with him and placed it on the middle of the edge of the tarp. Then, he unfolded one side and reached back for a second rock and anchored the right side.

He repeated the process on the left and then added some smaller rocks in between for good measure. The rest of the tarp was now wadded up in a near-folded mess. Not wanting the tarp to flap aimlessly in the wind, out of control and difficult to handle, he instead found a grommet from the opposite side of the tarp and tied a standard square knot.

He tied the other end of the rope loosely to a fist-sized rock and tossed it across the space between the boulders. It landed safely on the other side, trailing the rope with it. Smiling in triumph, his face glistening with rain, he turned on his knees, his soaking wet pants twisting on the rough surface of the boulder. He gingerly climbed down from his perch back the way he came. His boots sunk into the soaked soil at the base of the boulder.

More cautious now and understanding that he was nearing a personal victory over nature, he climbed the opposite boulder. It had fewer footholds and was rounder, but a large oak tree intersected the top of the boulder. He grabbed onto it so he could stand.

Finally, he retrieved the end of the tarp he had thrown across the gap between the boulders. Jacob pulled the tarp out using the rope he had tied to it and then promptly cut sections of the rope and tied them to four more grommets.

He secured one grommet to the oak limb; another grommet he secured using a flat rock he could barely lift. The other two he dropped to the ground on each side of the boulder. He climbed down and found some thick branches that he cut into stakes. He trod them into the ground with his boots and tied the remaining two ropes off to the stakes.

His body shivered as the wind pushed the temperature down at least fifteen degrees. What had begun twenty minutes before as a warming, sunny day was now a "gully washer" storm. He made his way back to his gear, satisfied with his impromptu handiwork. He looked up at the flapping tarp above him and hoped it would hold.

Rain still sprayed in from the sides, but he found if he hugged closely to the rock at the overhang, he had plenty of dry leaves. Knowing that he might be in for a long stay here, he began to search for dry branches close by that hadn't been soaked by the downpour. Soon, he had a stack of deadfall, a small amount of mostly-dry tinder, and had extracted his survival gear from his bag.

He laid out a new set of clothing and quickly stripped. He knew time was important because he didn't want to lose body heat. He also didn't want to stay in wet, cold clothes. It was still October, but in the mountains, it wasn't unusual to get temperatures hanging around freezing every now and then.

With a storm bringing currents of cold air, it would be foreseeable for the climate and the geography to mix a winter cocktail two months earlier than normal. He dressed deliberately, adding a layer of thermal athletic wear just in case. He pulled out his Frog Tog rain gear and unfolded the matching cap. He placed all of his clothes neatly on a dry pile of leaves, including his soaked Bills cap.

The wind picked up after a while and he felt it was too stormy yet for a fire. He was much warmer now, but the storm continued its rampage for another hour. He tried drifting off to sleep, munching on some nuts and raisins to get his energy back, and even pulled out the topographic map he had brought to see if he could get his bearings.

As he poured over the laminated map, unfolding it several times, he double checked his compass and tried his best to guess his elevation, direction and speed of travel. In the end, he gave up. Until he had better visibility and some landmarks to guide him—a river, creek, mountain peak, ranger station—he had no way of knowing where he was. He smiled. At least he wasn't lost. He was in Arkansas and he was pretty sure he hadn't wandered out of the Ozark National Forest.

He checked his Timex and noted that it was nearing three o'clock, yet it was completely dark out. Several times over the next hour, the flapping of the tarp would wake him and he had to put a new stake in. Once, he had to climb back on the larger rock and put some more stones on the tarp to secure it. But, by six thirty, he was completely exhausted and bored. He drifted off to sleep despite the rumbling thunder that eventually moved off east and north. By the time the last drops of rain fell at nine-thirty, Jacob Barclay was snoring loudly.

CHAPTER NINE

M olly didn't like to cry. It was silly and girly. She did anyway, angry with herself and ashamed at her behavior. She was only thirteen, but she had grown taller than her friends at school. She continually outpaced them in every game and even at school work. The only people that could compete with her were boys a year or two older than her. She proved that last summer in Little League Baseball; and before school started, the coach told her she made the AAU basketball team as the starting center.

She smiled through her tears as she remembered the coach patting her on the shoulder and looking in her eyes. That had been the first week of September—school had just begun, boys had started to flirt with her (*Yuck!* She thought) and it had been a full moon. She had remembered because Mrs. Ellis, her science teacher, had pointed out that the moon phases could explain the odd behavior of some members of the student body and even some of the teachers.

"The phases of the moon--its closeness to earth, its position in relation to Earth's orbit--affect the waves in the ocean, the mating habits of animals," a groan escaped from the girls, hearty chuckles from the guys. "And the emotions and actions of people. Your mother and maybe even your older sisters will have physical reactions to the moon sometimes. The moon is our clock, the Earth's partner in orbit with the sun and its gravity does magical things."

Mrs. Ellis smiled warmly, her tone and her expression tipping off the brighter students like Molly that she had chosen to leave stuff out. Molly hated when adults kept things from her. Her parents had done that and now look where she was: lost and alone.

Molly reached underneath her and pulled up some grass by the roots and threw them as far as she could. Destruction seemed to calm her in times like these. She had a pile of broken dolls and torn card games at home somewhere. They were victims of her temper and her desperate need to inflict retributive pain. She pulled another handful, this time getting some stubborn wildflowers in her grasp. Her grimy nails tore at the moist forest soil. She tossed it over her back, almost hitting her face with her bicep. She ran her forearm across her runny nose and pouted, suffused in self-pity and loathing. Everything she thought of, she hated.

The more she thought about it, the more she hated even thinking. It was wearing her down. She had made it pretty far, she felt, since escaping the cabin three nights ago. She hadn't even realized how hungry she was until this morning. Now, with the dew soaking her blue jeans and her stomach growling mercilessly, she looked around her for an easy meal. She knew she could eat the wildflowers.

They would be bitter, but had a sweet aftertaste. She had played doctor with her brother and he had taught her that

Indian healers had used wildflowers and other plants to heal and for magical powers.

Believing her older brother implicitly, she had eaten the nasty little yellow flowers that grew under their porch until her belly ached. He explained that she needed to eat different ones—some of the flowers the Indians used to make poisons to tip their arrows and spears. He told her that she probably had eaten some poison, but she was so strong it hadn't killed her or made her sleep for twenty years or made her drunk like daddy got when they were broke.

But what she really wanted was a steak, or slice of pepperoni pizza or a big juicy piece of blueberry pie with two scoops of vanilla ice cream. Just the thought of real food made her wince with pain. She could stand the pain from the scrapes and cuts on her arms and neck, but the pain in her belly made her nervous. The blood that ran from her various wounds caked over with dirt and dried.

Plus, she admitted to herself, they looked pretty cool. She probably looked tougher than ever. Even Bobby Calamore wouldn't mess with her if he saw her all her dirty and bloodied like this. She imagined herself as a warrior, a protector—a really hungry warrior with scars and a mean, "don't mess with me" look.

She got up and brushed some of the moisture from her jeans. The air was cold against her legs even through the jeans and she could feel goose bumps popping up on her thighs. Her brother would make fun of her and tell her she had goose pimples. Molly would tell him he had face pimples, so ha, and then they would both laugh and he would tackle her.

She didn't have the heart to fight her brother, and would mostly just laugh until she ran out of breath or he would give up. Her family didn't have much, but Molly and Brian had each other. She had always felt safe around Brian. Except for now, she thought.

She fought the urge to be sorry for herself. Molly wasn't keen on pity. She wanted to be brave and knew that if she was to survive her nightmare, she would have to be strong. Looking back now wouldn't change anything. She had read somewhere that regrets were pointless and Molly agreed with that philosophy. She could have thousands of regrets in her young life. Nothing would change the reality of what she had experienced.

Molly looked up at the mountain ahead of her and glanced back over her shoulder at the sun. If she tried really hard, she thought she could make it to the ridge of the mountain just out of her sight. It was misty with fog, but last night before it got dark she had noticed even at this distance that it had smaller trees.

She hoped to find berries, or at least make an attempt to set a trap for a rabbit or squirrel. Although she had no tools or weapons, she had faith that she would come across some way to survive. The one thing that dominated her thoughts, though, was food. She needed something to eat and fast.

She hadn't had anything to eat for three days. For a week before that, she had moldy bread and barely cooked rice. The skin clung tightly to the bones of her arms and legs and her hip bones were the only things that kept her jeans from falling to her knees every time she stood.

Molly clamored forward. She felt like she was walking on stilts. She had used some at recess when she was younger. She remembered the unbalanced feeling and falling ahead like a tree being chopped down. Her head was heavy. This feeling now was not too different. She turned again, shielding her eyes from the sun, and watched a hawk circle the hillside behind her. She blinked, unconcerned, and continued to walk up the mountain.

The leaves rustled loudly around her. *I must sound like a big herd of deer*, she thought.

Once, she and her brother had scouted the woods near their farm looking for mushrooms and ginseng roots. They had come upon a herd of at least twenty deer. They were milling around a copse of mulberry trees next to a field that had been cleared for a gas well. The deer bounded off, their hooves making a clapping sound, the leaves rustling like paper being wadded up in a ball.

She was startled at first at the noise and the suddenness of the event. She had smiled at the wonder of the spectacle of all those white tails jumping up and down as the deer blended into the cover and disappeared. Her brother had looked over at her then and gave her a meaningful look. She could see he was determined, his eyes wide and his crooked smile gave her the impression that, like always, he was motivated by the prospect of blood.

He raised his eyebrows and said, "I will get one of those this fall and we'll eat good."

And they had. Venison was as plentiful in their home as beef or chicken, even though they raised both. Her dad sold most of the cattle, milked the cows and sold it, and the chickens were abandoned after the third year. Her father said, "I can't compete with the big chicken farms. Arkansas is no place for chicken farmers, unless you's got one of them mills with all them workers."

Deer, squirrel, trout and boar were plentiful, in season and out. Her dad and her brother enjoyed hunting and they never were without food, it seemed.

Molly realized that she was salivating at the thought of deer meat.

As she climbed the hill, thinking, she conjured up in her imagination a plate with deer sausage, eggs and skillet potatoes with ramps. Her mother was from back east (Virginia?) and once a year, her family mailed them baggies with ramps and other green stuff that her dad took back into the bedroom without a word.

The ramps tasted like strong onions, and the next day at school all her friends would hold their noses and give her a wide berth in the halls. It made her smile. She'd even seek out opportunities to breathe on her friends Cassie and Lewis just to make them cry out to make her stop.

She wanted to go home. She knew she couldn't now. Not after what she had done. Not after what had been done to her. She felt angry and ashamed, but she fought both of those emotions off for now and just tried to move. *No time for feeling sorry for yourself,* Molly thought.

She set her jaw and grimaced as the muscles in her back and the back of her legs cried out to stop. She realized she needed some more water and knew where to get it. She glanced to the north and kept the stream in her vision. She wondered idly if maybe there were crawdads in there, but dismissed the thought. It would be too easy. If she were wrong, she might not be thirsty anymore, but would be faced with a tough uphill climb with an empty stomach.

She walked like this for another hour, her thoughts touching back on the agony and fear that gripped her the last few weeks. Just as she would be succumbing to the despair and the pain, the weakness that was besetting her body and tiring her mind, she would steel herself again and determine to change the subject and keep going.

Keep on truckin' on, she thought, recalling her uncle Larry's favorite saying. He would always laugh, take another swig of his Iron City beer he brought with him from back east and hitch his pants up and belch. His sleeveless shirts and sweat-brimmed hats made him almost a cartoon version of a backwoods character.

Molly always enjoyed it when her uncle would stop in on one of his long hauls across country driving his semi. Molly's mother always dreaded his visits because he had divorced aunt Liz and he never wiped his feet, his mouth or his butt, her momma had said.

Every so often, Molly would look back over her shoulder and note the location of the sun. It was hot on her back when she started, the morning frost began to gradually burn off, the spiraling mists made the woods appear like a fairy tale.

But, as she got closer to the top of the mountain ahead of her, she noted dark clouds rolling in from that direction. She narrowed her eyes and looked desperately at the bushes on the peak of the ridge. She hoped she could see the berries that lined the lower branches, a mulberry tree, a wild apple tree or anything that resembled food.

Disappointed, she continued on, and watched the clouds get closer. She had survived the storm yesterday and wasn't concerned. After what she had endured, fear was going to be an emotion that was rare. It made her cautious, but it also made her careless. *And*, she thought, *I may just be acting weird because of the moon.*

CHAPTER TEN

J acob moved along the shelf slowly, saving his strength. He had eaten very little this morning. He had snapped hundreds of photos of the beauty of the misty morning from the top of the mountain he still hadn't identified. He had turned the camera settings to black and white. He was confident that the exposures would be excellent material for his portfolio.

Although he wasn't completely lost, he had to admit he wasn't sure about his location. He knew the general locale and which direction he was heading, but many of the mountains around him had no official names on the topographic map he had purchased in Bexton.

Even though he wanted to stop soon, he forced himself to continue to climb again. He had left early this morning and felt refreshed from the extended rest. However, he had underestimated the toll the brisk walk up the steep mountain had exacted on his aging body. Despite this, he was determined to reach a point where he could view the surrounding valleys and mountains to see if he could get his exact location.

This exercise was more a point of pride than a matter of survival. He needed to be prepared. The older he got, the more he was compelled to push his physical limits.

Orienteering had been one of his least favorite merit badges all those years ago. Over three decades removed from that experience, Jacob struggled to master the skills required to not only determine direction but to read the contours of the land and identify land mass markings to determine location.

He winced as he recalled Mr. Vincent chastising him for his lack of understanding while the other scouts had naturally developed the discipline to complete the badge. In the end, he pushed through and finished it, just going through the paces so that he could get the stupid badge. Now he wished he had put forth more effort. It was so much more difficult to pursue these things as an adult, sometimes.

It wasn't that he always found it difficult to learn new skills. He had learned what it was to be a bachelor, a grandfather, a divorcee. Not that he was particularly good at any of those pursuits, but he felt that he had grasped their essence and was continually improving. He hoped that survival was the same way.

He paused for a moment to catch his breath and pulled out his plastic canteen. The water was soothingly cold on his throat and he realized just how thirsty he had become, breathing hard in the moist air.

He pulled up his binoculars, a lightweight, simple 10 x 20 set with rubber caps. He popped the caps off and glassed the hill ahead of him. The shelf ran along for another quarter mile and then intersected a point. He suspected that along that point he would find a better view of the valley because the trees seemed thinner there, farther apart and tall. Fortunately, this hill wasn't as rocky as the one he left behind this morning. The going had been rough.

Remembering the harrowing events of yesterday's storms, he pulled out a barometer and glanced at the readings. It had a temperature gauge attached and it read forty-two. He sighed, because that was unseasonably cool for this time of year. He glanced back over his shoulder at the shelf behind him and the growing cloud bank that was gathering there to the north.

He wasn't too interested in waiting out another storm. His tarp had torn and frayed and he doubted it would be much protection after the beating it had taken in yesterday's wind. The rocks he had used to secure it overhead had worn thin places in the tarp. A wind-blown branch had torn a four-inch hole in the middle.

He started off again and made his way along the shelf as it gradually climbed to meet the ridge. A few minutes later, he was perched over a magnificent view of three intersecting valleys below him.

The ridge and shelf met together to create a bluff that dropped at least a hundred feet down. Trees and bushes clung desperately to the steep decline, but traversing the bluff to the shelf below and then to the intersecting valleys would be dangerous if not deadly. Moss-covered deadfall, wicked-looking scrub brush and the occasional sharp-pointed boulder were strewn along the entire decline. Jacob shook his head and whistled low.

His gaze shifted to the other mountains. He resisted the urge to pull out his camera right the. He dropped his backpack to the ground with a grunt and retrieved his topographic map.

He proceeded to spend the next five minutes re-acquainting himself with his lost orienteering skills. After much deliberation, he decided he couldn't possibly be lost—he just didn't know exactly where he was.

He did narrow it down to three places: all mountains that overlooked three intersecting valleys with steep drop-offs and no visible water. He was surprised how common this feature was here in the Ozarks. Several patterns of topography repeated themselves. From the best he could figure, he was at least forty miles from civilization.

That, at least, made him happy. Maybe being lost wasn't so bad.

Finally, he put the map away and with a grin, got out his camera. He glanced then at his rifle, lying propped against a small sapling. He wondered if maybe he should have left it behind.

What if, at the end of civilization, gun powder didn't work? He had read a book by S.M. Stirling that depicted an apocalyptic vision of just such an occurrence.

Of course, his book was as much an exercise in historical preservation of medieval methods of war, agriculture, politics, colonization and society. However, it certainly appealed to Jacob because of the implications of survival, a monumental change in society due to a blow to civilization and the themes that mankind would bring about his own demise.

As silly as he sometimes felt as he thought about these deep concerns, his beliefs were constantly reinforced by the actions of others and by various events, conversations, videos, research and literature.

Sometimes, something as simple as a visit from Phillip would confirm that even God expected man to fail. And, if history was any clue, the cycle of destruction, survival, rebuilding and collapse could repeat itself endlessly.

Mankind could not depend upon itself for preservation because mankind was not in control of its own destiny. Forces beyond Man's control affect us despite attempts to prolong life, cure disease, prevent disaster, combat our enemy, please our ally and even create life.

He caught himself in a reverie. He realized he needed to get some nutrition. He was getting drowsy and his thoughts were straying.

He grabbed two protein bars from his backpack and a package of trail mix he had prepared himself. He munched on the granola, raisins, pumpkin seeds and yogurt-covered dates and soon felt his energy return. He gathered up his things and grunted again.

Jacob detested getting older. He didn't consider himself old, but as he aged, he was constantly disappointed in his inability to maintain his former physical prowess. Sometimes, he even felt he was getting dumber, not wiser. Of course, Janice would agree. She was a firm believer in his regression.

Jacob was sure he didn't want to go down the treacherous slope, so he backtracked along the ridge and then descended a shallow slope on the westward side of the mountain he had just climbed. His intent was to get to the valley before nightfall and then set camp in higher ground just north of his current location. The only problem was he had to backtrack and then circle back around to reach the point he wanted to check.

He shrugged his shoulder and readjusted the backpack to take the weight centered across his back. Soon, he was travelling more quickly than he had since he started. His strength returned soon and his body warmed to the exercise

His muscles adjusted to the strain and the jarring of crossing through rough terrain. He picked the best route he could without veering off course too much and within an hour, he had made his destination.

Upon reaching the point where he wanted to make camp, he noticed that the clouds he had noted earlier in the north had circled back south and were traveling north again and in an easterly direction that would put them over him within an hour. He was alarmed by the arcs of lightning popping across the cloud bank.

He needed to seek shelter. He glassed the ravine ahead of him—it was too steep and if a toad-strangling, gully washer came, he was sure the ravine would turn temporarily into white water rapids.

He turned back around and considered the ridge from which he had just descended and shook his head. The trip down had been easy with very few boulders to navigate and a clear game trail to follow. But, that meant that traveling back up it would be a strain on his weary body. He looked around him, trying to decide the easiest route and the one most likely to bring him to shelter quickly.

He chose to continue following the game trail. He picked up his pace as much as he dared. He didn't want a repeat of yesterday. *PleaseLord, just give me some time to reach some shelter and then you can let go with all you want,* Jacob thought.

With some measure of relief, Jacob found the path led to a large clearing with a collapsed barn. He considered it briefly but continued on. He figured it was too dangerous and he was confident that he had time to avoid another storm.

Besides, he wasn't convinced the darkening clouds would actually produce a storm. Perhaps, he thought, the storm would spend its fury elsewhere. Plus, he was encouraged by a sign of shelter so early in his search. Jacob made a mental not the wrecked barn's location in case he needed to backtrack.

Soon, the slope picked up again and he was puffing as the strain of walking for so long began to catch up with him. He needed to push himself, he realized, but feared his desperation would cause him to make a mistake.

He slowed his pace and concentrated on controlling his breathing. He drew in breath through his nose and then blew it out through his pursed mouth. It reminded him of the Lemaz technique he had been trained to use through those classes he took with Janice when she was pregnant with Phillip. He suddenly wished again he brought along a partner.

He had learned the value of a partner early in his career when Brenda Kacey had pulled his fat from a fryer in a domestic dispute. The husband had hid himself away when he saw the two Buffalo PD officers approaching

The wife refused to help because she had a change of heart after she had made the call to the police. After Brenda and Jacob argued with the wife for five minutes, the husband entered and stabbed Jacob in the elbow with a letter opener. He had yelled, "You are trespassing!" and cursed enough to make Jacob blush despite the sharp pain in his elbow.

Brenda grabbed Jacob just before he could turn and pull his piece from his holster and blast the guy in the face. She pulled the letter opener out of his elbow and said, "Janice is gonna love this story, Jake."

He had failed to laugh at the time, but when they settled everything inside and made their way back to the cruiser, Brenda had explained that her last partner had lost control and shot a ten year old boy in front of his three year old sister. The officer had lost his badge and the image of that girl as her brother fell down with two bullets in his thigh had haunted him. She didn't want another partner lost to knee-jerk responses.

He forgave her then. He never again forgot the value of a partner to "get your back."

Now, here he was, his body failing him and Mother Nature evidently holding a grudge. He knew one-on-one, he would lose any battle he fought against her. His only thought was to succumb to her power and seek to outrun her fury or hide away from it.

He was fairly certain that a repeat of the previous day was not likely, but he didn't want to gamble with his chances for a light sprinkle or a gentle mist. He had trudged well over two miles now —mostly uphill--and was nearing the limits of his body and will. He wanted to set up camp and possibly catch a short nap again.

But these wishes were to be deferred for another time. The rain came suddenly in a torrent. The wind was practically non-existent, but the lightning forked down from the heavens and struck a tree two hundred yards to his left. He could feel the hair on his arms bristle.

He jumped, stumbled and then fell forward. He skinned his hands on some brambles and looked wide-eyed as a thirty foot tall tree crashed, its trunk ablaze. The stump where the trunk had been just moments before was blackened.

Jacob scrambled to his knees. He used the rifle for leverage as he struggled with the weight of the pack and the weight of the fear that gripped him as he looked heavenward.

He realized with a jolt that even if he saw it coming, there would be no way for him to avoid almost certain death. Instinctively, he recognized that he had exposed himself to danger yet again.

Here he was, days from help with another storm dropping rain and spitting lightning at him like God was taking out his vengeance upon this soil or upon the silly middle-aged man that dared to test himself against the powers of nature.

Resigned to his fate and overcoming the initial irrational fear spurred on by the flaming tree and the ferocity of the cold rain pelting his face, Jacob found his balance and used the rifle like a walking stick to briskly walk up the slope. In the gathering gloom, he could see ahead of him a larger, dark shape against the backdrop of a low shelf above him.

As he came closer, he could tell it was not a natural feature. He did his best to ignore the blast of thunder as it rocked the hills and echoed through the valleys through which he had just passed.

As he squinted through the rain obscuring his vision, he could make out what looked like a roof. A sense of hope washed over him. He picked up his pace, bringing the rifle in front of him and sprinted up the slope. It felt like he was running through oatmeal. The dirt beneath the layers of leaves was soaked and every step was like sliding forward then back again. Still, he made his way toward the top of the slope onto a gently sloping shelf.

CHAPTER ELEVEN

V ictor Carothers knelt by the fireplace and stoked the embers there. The storm was rolling over them again and the temperatures were going to drop. He didn't mind, though because it meant that the farm would remain dark most of the day and that was how he liked it. The fire began to catch and he added a large log of oak. The growth of his beard felt warm and scratchy at his neck, but he enjoyed it.

He heard the scraping of feet on the wooden floor of their house and didn't turn around.

"Where's ma?"

He didn't answer his son at first. He still wasn't sure he wanted to trust him. He continued to tamp the iron stoker into the bright red coals. The color reminded him of his wife's eyes. It brought a crooked grin to his haggard face. He could feel his beard scratching the grey cotton hoodie he wore over the same faded shirt he had worn for a week.

"Dad, is ma outside?"

"She'll be back in a bit, Brian. Just hold your horses. Go out to the barn and get me some more wood. I think it'll be a cold night tonight."

Brian hesitated a moment. Victor looked back at him with hooded eyes, his chin brushing his shoulder.

"Sure, pa. I'll be back."

Victor turned back to the fire and listened as Brian tromped off. For a sixteen year old, he was already beginning to become independent. He had friends, girls, sports, hunting, his work in shop and spent time on a computer at the Bexton Library for as long as he could get away with it.

Brian wanted so much, it seemed. Victor couldn't remember being so ambitious when he was a kid. He recalled only work and more work. For he and his two sisters, Rose and Clarissa, play was relegated to Sunday afternoons and occasionally in the long summer evenings after chores were completed.

Brian would walk the ten miles into town just to have access to a computer. He would have his friends come over—during the day, nonetheless—and pick him up to go into town to watch movies, play sports or talk to girls. Victor couldn't object. It was one way that Brian could appear normal.

Victor wasn't sure he had felt normal in years. Certainly, it had been long before he had met Patricia.

Now, he spent most of his time in the house, waiting for her to come home. He didn't mind that she was the bread-winner. He just didn't like the waiting.

When the kids were younger, he had missed them. Now, he mostly slept during the day and tried to forget about them.

He figured that was as close to normal as he was going to get. When they talked to him, he was sometimes taken off guard. He thought he had been forgotten, left behind.

He took solace in Patsy. She always came back and she always gave him just what he needed. The only problem was that after all these years, the list of what he needed had narrowed down to three items. Entertainment wasn't on the list.

They had no television. The radio could only pick up a few country music stations out of Bentonville. The AM station only had talk shows all day and static at night. He would listen to those programs during the day if he needed to sleep.

Oddly, during the short summer nights, he would sometime turn the static down low and listen as stations the world over would fade in and out. He listened closely to see if he could make out a foreign language. It was a little game he played that worked better than counting sheep.

He looked around the drab room. An old couch slumped in the center of the room facing the fireplace. Two chairs, a rocking chair and a leather ottoman took up much of the room. Pictures in metal frames and small shelves with knick knacks lined the wall next to the fireplace. Below these was their only real treasure: a three-shelf book case full of books with black spines and gold embossed letters.

The opposite wall was mostly windows and stained wall. There were no curtains. Through the dirty glass of the windows, Victor saw Brian kicking the dirt in the yard as he headed for the barn.

He could hear the barn door slide open and he stood and watched Brian turn the wheel barrow up. Victor dusted off his worn jeans and watched the flames lick the oak. He could feel the heat warm his pallid skin.

He put up his hood on his sweatshirt, hoping to contain the heat and warm his ears and neck. He hunched his shoulders and rubbed his hands together briskly. Waiting was like this. He was contained within himself, his voice inside his head demanding action, his body unwilling to comply.

He was still standing there several moments later when Brian loudly bumped the wheel barrow up the porch steps. Victor glanced outside, more annoyed than curious. He could scold the boy, but for what good? He was tired of arguing.

Besides, he wasn't sure he preferred feeling left behind. He wanted Patsy to come back soon. He knew it was better to shut down until she showed up, but he wanted to see her walk through the door and smile at him. He wanted to hear her tell him she would make it all be alright.

She was the glue that held the family together, but all he cared about was that she could be there for him. It was an interesting arrangement, he and Patsy. He was in control but allowed her the run of things so he could get just what he wanted with the least amount of effort and management.

Brian opened the door then and poked his head in. His close-cropped hair was copper red like his mother's, but he had a premature growth of beard and Victor realized with a start that Brian had his face and could likely grow a full beard as coarse and thick as his own.

"You want to help, pa? I got a big load."

Victor lurched forward, irritated, but he realized he had nothing better to do. Anything he could do to relieve some of the tension would be nice, too. It wasn't that he cared how Brian felt, it was just that it helped if Brian was happy. Patsy would be more likely to come home early. With this storm, she might even be home before supper tonight. He grabbed the door and nodded to Brian. They hauled in the wood, large pieces of maple and birch.

"We'll need to cut down that stand over yonder if we want to make it through the winter," Brian offered at one point, his breath frosting and floating above his head like a thought.

"Sure. Sounds like something we should do as soon as it dries up, what do you say?"

"Sounds fine. I'll be willing to help if you will trade me for some time to go into town with Charlie."

Victor set down his load of wood on the floor beside the fireplace. He deliberately kept his back to Brian. He cleared his throat and pretended to think about it. Of course, he didn't care. At the same time, Victor resented his son and his ways. He wanted him to be direct.

"Yeah. I suppose that would be alright. Did you ask your ma?"

"She told me to ask you."

It was probably her idea, Victor thought. He tried to conceal that thought, because he knew if he weren't careful it would creep into his grin. He just nodded as if that were natural. He dusted off his hands and shook Brian's hand with a grim smirk.

"You want to rustle up a squirrel or two for dinner?"

Brian perked up immediately. Victor knew Brian loved to hunt almost as much as Victor did. The only difference was they enjoyed a different hunt. Victor preferred to hunt at night and was waiting for the day when Brian asked to go along. So far, he hadn't showed an interest, but Victor was certain it wouldn't be long.

"That would be fine, dad. How many do you think we'll need?"

"Three would be the best bet, I would venture. Make sure you get a grey for me, though. I like my meat tough."

"One grey and two reds coming right up then," he said. He crossed the room with a bounce in his step and took down the 12-gauge shotgun from above the mantel. He fished in his pocket for a shell and put it in his mouth as he broke the barrel down and held it up so that he could look inside. Satisfied, he popped it in place and snapped the barrel shut.

Victor watched as he thumbed the safety and looked up with a grin. "I'll be back before dark unless it starts raining."

Victor looked back at him, his arms crossed. He wished he were warmer. He allowed a prideful smirk to play across his face and scratched his beard.

"Just be careful. And watch out." This caught Brian by surprise and Victor watched as Brian's attitude changed as he remembered. Brian's smile faded and he nodded, serious and sad. Victor expected Brian to get angry, but he just turned and stepped through the living room, into the kitchen and then out the back door.

Victor grabbed his coat and walked out the patio door to the porch. He wrapped his arms around himself and looked back up the hill as Brian disappeared into a stand of oaks. He didn't want Brian to be too happy, but at least he was gone now. *Nothing left but the wait,* he thought, as he turned to go back into the house.

CHAPTER TWELVE

J acob's legs were weak and his lungs were burning. His hands, numb from carrying the cold steel of the rifle in the freezing rain, throbbed. But, as he neared the coal-black hulk of a shack, he felt a lifting of his spirits.

He hoped someone was inside. Recognizing instinctively that it was abandoned, Jacob peered in through the front window. He climbed up the two rickety stairs to the structurally questionable front porch and immediately was stunned to feel the hairs on the back of his neck raise in alarm. He recalled this feeling from his dozens of raids over the years.

He scanned the door and noted the frame near the handle had been broken. Curiously, it appeared the damage had been inflicted from the inside. The door was barely closed; the catch on the handle didn't meet with the recess it was supposed to sit in.

As he pushed the door open with his rifle, an odor assailed him immediately: rot and carnage like he hadn't experience in years. The darkness was palpable. The air inside was thick with mildew and humidity.

The constant pounding of the rain and the whipping of the wind made him nervous. Not seeing was one thing. Not being able to hear was disquieting. The two combined were unbearable. He felt his body resist. His every fiber wanted to turn around and seek shelter elsewhere.

Something evil was here. He could sense it. It was in the darkness, in that pungent odor, and in the cloying air. Jacob fought the urge to leave.

He remembered his flashlight and pulled it out of his pocket. He held it in his left hand and the rifle he held one-handed in his right. He brought it up to his waist and flipped the safety off with his thumb.

Quietly, he stepped forward into the room, his eyes adjusting as he moved. He could make out darker patches of color through the gloom on the wall ahead of him and a table over by the sink to his left. His flashlight sent a cone of light into the darkness. Dust and flies hovered in the air.

Another door led off to his right just inside the entrance. He glanced that way, but decided to let his nose lead him.

The smell of death was stronger toward the kitchen. He could see a linoleum floor and a faint gleam of the faucet. On the table were glasses, plates and what appeared to be knives and forks.

He noted the hulk of a refrigerator beside the table, then and saw another room just beyond it. He could hear the loud hum of the old refrigerator even over the racket outside and the pounding of the rain on the metal roof. The door to the room past the refrigerator was open and a faint red light emanated from the room.

Jacob swallowed hard. He was shaking, the rifle bobbing in his numb hands, his head throbbing with adrenaline. He knew from experience he needed to stop for a second and gather his wits.

He was certain he was at a crime scene, but he wasn't sure he was alone. What was that warning he got as he stepped on the porch? Had his subconscious detected a noise or a movement? Or was it the stink of human decay?

He listened now. He allowed his eyes to scan slowly while keeping his head still, knowing that his peripheral vision would pick up movement more clearly if he didn't turn his head.

Jacob could make out that the smears along the walls were dried blood splatters. A murder or murders had taken place here.

He licked his lips and took a deep steadying breath. The rain continued to assault the roof of the cabin. It created a cacophony that muffled most of the sound in the house. Unless someone was going to yell or talk loudly, he wasn't going to hear them. Or they, him, he reasoned.

So, he determined to move slowly and be alert. The room seemed empty. There was very little cover to offer a place to hide.

As he neared the table, he confirmed that it was indeed silverware sprawled across the wood top. The chairs were metal with cushion seats. Blood splatter covered the kitchen linoleum. Food scraps dotted the top of the table and Jacob watched, nauseated, as dozens of roaches feasted. He breathed purposefully through his mouth to minimize his nausea and turned his head to note the refrigerator.

Photographs were held in place by alphabet magnets upon its surface. He couldn't make out faces, but they seemed to be of a family. Grim, with a determination he hadn't felt since he retired, Jacob moved on to the room adjacent to the kitchen.

He deliberately ignored the sink and cabinets. The bedroom was his destination, and he was pretty positive what he was going to find. His mind raced through probabilities of victims, motive, and the murderer.

Who would do this? He didn't know many of the locals, but from the people he had met, he couldn't imagine any of them doing this. He had to admit, he had very little time to truly know them, and that bothered him even more.

He stepped into the room, and now, even though he breathed through his mouth, the stench was overwhelming. He became dizzy and with some alarm brought his sleeve up to cover his nose. He held the rifle out one-handed, extending his arm

The remains of a naked man hung suspended from railroad ties staked through his shoulders and hip into the far wall. Several limbs were missing, his abdomen was split from his navel to below his chest and the gore hung as low as his knees. His head was tilted forward onto his sternum. Jacob could see that the top of the man's head had been cut off. Inside his skull was empty.

His hands were nailed, driven into the wall. Dark imprints of other such holes dotted the brown plaster and lathe wall. Blood was everywhere. Maggots the size of rice pilaf squirmed in large lumps near the corpse.

Not an expert in forensics, but familiar with crime scenes, Jacob imagined that the scene of this crime was less than a week old. Flies buzzed around him sluggish and bloated. So he could see the cause of death and narrow down the time of death to "not recently," but what he struggled with was why.

The cool air was working its way into his bones. He could feel the cold black boards of the cabin collapse in upon him, rise up and greet him. He swooned there in the threshold into the murder room, the room of blood and guts, flies and eerie red glow. If evil existed, this would be its calling card.

Jacob gathered his wits. He glanced around the room and finally was certain he was alone. Then he recalled the first room off of the entrance.

With a final gaze at the scene, he turned to go back and check the final room. As he turned, he noted the bed for the first time. It was just inside of the entrance to his left. It looked out of place. The queen-sized bed sported a beautiful ironwork headboard and was odd here in this room of death.

Blood covered the sheets, the pillows. The pillows. The detective in Jacob sprung alive, his mind ticking off possibilities and running scenarios. He didn't want to think about it, didn't want to process the horror of what he was experiencing. It wasn't his job anymore. He had never been a crime scene investigator.

Despite his reservations, Jacob decided that this crime was unique. He gripped the rifle in his hands tighter, knowing that his search was not complete and his safety wasn't ensured.

His skin crawled as his mind dwelled on the scene even while his attention was riveted upon securing the cabin. He began the rudimentary process of creating a profile of the murderer and decided that he couldn't narrow it down to just one. Something about this set-up smelled funny and it wasn't just the corpse in the bedroom.

He made his way through the small house, still sneaking slowly and his senses alert. A bright steak of lightning lit up the interior of the house and he flinched. The thunder shook the small shack and rattled the refrigerator.

He heard glass clinking inside. By the eerie light of the lightning, he noted several papers lying about and made a mental note to scour the house. He listened at the door for a second before pushing in. He really didn't expect anyone to be in there, but he aimed his sights across the room at a dresser and snapped immediately to his left as he stepped through the door. He strafed back to his right, then from the floor to the ceiling. Finally, he dropped to his knees and checked under the bed. The room had no closet.

Satisfied that no one was around, at least inside, he made his way back out to the kitchen but kept his rifle near him. He took off his jacket. It had been dripping water all over the house.

Now that the situation was secure, he needed to keep as much evidence intact as he could. He wished then he had brought along a simple crime kit. But who would have thought to bring it? Who would expect to come upon a crime scene deep in the woods of Arkansas? Besides, he was retired! What was he doing here?

His heart had not stopped thumping rhythmically in his throat. His head throbbed and every muscle in his body was strained from the tension. He closed his eyes and forced several breaths.

He thought for a moment that he might think better outside where the air was clearer. He pushed that idea aside.

He needed to think about what he was going to do next. His instincts as a detective told him that this crime scene would be easy to decipher given some time and the proper tools.

He briefly considered the Sheriff. He dismissed the man before ever seriously including him in any plans he was formulating. Not only was the man barely competent enough to administer parking tickets, Jacob was lost and unsure how long it would take to regain his bearings.

No. He could not turn to the law if the law was not available or capable. Since he was either in or on the fringes of a National Forest, the possibility of a park ranger entered his mind. He quickly rejected that idea as well. He was sure that with all those thousands of miles of forest, roads and mountains a ranger would be as scarce as a town the size of Bexton.

So, he allowed his mind instead to dwell on the crime. He had no way to identify the victim. Something about the nature of the crime—a remote cabin, the brutality, the timing, the lack of alarm in Bexton of a missing person—told him the person was of little consequence. He mentally chastised himself for diminishing the life of another individual, but realized the truth of the situation.

He needed to concentrate on halting this act from repeating itself. From the signs he had seen so far, he deduced that this brutal crime had been repeated numerous times.

The wall of the bedroom was marked by other holes and darker, older stains. The bed itself looked a regular part of some sort of ritual. The bare floor was littered with bloody tracks, some still tacky, but others faded.

Judging by the layout of the room in which it took place and the remoteness of the area, he also suspected that it was a group activity. Just from his brief glance at the bed, he understood that the murder and sex had been intertwined.

Further clues would likely confirm his suspicions. He knew he needed to check the refrigerator, the sink, and any dressers first. He also needed to inspect the outside as soon as it was light and the rain stopped. The family photos on the refrigerator would possibly hold some promise, but Jacob wasn't positive. They could be of another family entirely, or of possible victims.

All these thoughts came to him in a rush as he pulled up the chair and put his flashlight on the table, scattering the roaches there. With a disgusted grimace, he swatted a few of the foul creatures onto the floor where they skittered on the dirty linoleum and scampered into cracks nearby. He ignored them, and put his head in his hands, his elbows resting on the table.

The light from his flashlight pierced the darkness and through his hands his vision was tinted pink. He let his weariness wash over him. He couldn't even think about eating to renew his energy, but sat there still. Soon, his heartbeat calmed and his breathing slowed.

Jacob shook his head in disbelief. He tried to shut out the world for a moment so he could focus. The rain continued to punish the roof of the home, the lightning piercing the darkness intermittently. He was far from anywhere, alone in house of death. His need for a strong cup of coffee was acute. He sat there with his hands cupping his face for several minutes and soon was dozing.

CHAPTER THIRTEEN

T he windshield wipers drummed methodically. Patsy Carothers hated driving in the rain. The road was a gray streak of nothing in front of her. She drove cautiously and listened to country music on the radio. It was mostly static since the late model Ford Taurus sedan had its antenna in the windshield. The thumping in the trunk had ceased about an hour ago.

It didn't seem right to her, but Victor had assured her that he would fix the cassette recorder so that she could play some of her favorites. She missed listening to Frank Sinatra and Bing Cosby. They brought back memories. Memories of days she mostly forgot until she heard a familiar tune.

She smiled despite her stress over the difficult driving conditions. The winding Arkansas highways were familiar to her, but only because she had settled here two decades ago. Also, she was from the Appalachians—Tennessee and Virginia. The winding mountain roads were similar to here in the Ozarks.

The only real difference she noted was that when night fell in this area of Arkansas, there was simply no light. Often, Patsy thought that the countryside surrounding their farm was the darkest area in the nation. But she didn't mind. In fact, she preferred it that way. It made things easier.

The wind whipped the vehicle and she drifted into the oncoming lane. She gripped the wheel harder and resisted the urge to overcompensate. There was no oncoming traffic, so she could take her time and correct naturally.

She drifted back over to her side, careful not run the tires over the berm because the ditch on her side was four feet deep as the road wound up to her right. She was only a few miles from home and as she was on familiar turf. So, she began to let her mind relax. Patsy was intent on making sure all her bases were covered.

She glanced up in the rear view mirror to check her eyes. They were their natural chocolate brown. Her hair was dyed a dark black, but it was luxurious and hung just above her shoulders.

Her slender figure and the unique set of her cheeks enabled her to appear six to eight years younger than the thirty eight years she already had put on this body. She ate right, worked hard and never allowed herself to indulge. Well, except on occasion; but who didn't?

Her concern about her hair and her eyes were well founded. Before she left Eureka Springs, she had stopped at a gas station, pulling around to the side and making sure she parked away from the pumps. She had to visit the ladies room, but mostly she wanted to make sure George was secure.

His hands were chafed from attempts to escape, but she checked his pulse on his bound wrist. His pulse was weak, but still ticking. She smirked and gave his still form a lewd look as she shut the trunk.

Victor was sure to be pleased about this one. George was fifty five, but he was fit and didn't appear to have abused his body. That meant prime real estate.

She licked her lips, savoring the taste of her strawberry lip gloss she had applied while in the bathroom. George had been one of her favorites. She had met him three months ago while playing black jack at Harrah's Casino in Kansas City. He had bought her a drink and they had talked for hours over cards. He was in the entertainment industry, a film maker.

She said she was a librarian. It wasn't too far off the mark. She won some, but gave more back to the house before the night was up. She tried to laugh it off, but it bothered her that she was so distracted.

Finally, just as she was ready to turn in, George encouraged her to try her hand at roulette. She declined, but he insisted. In fact, he put four hundred down on thirty and won twelve hundred. He gave her half and told her she was his good luck charm. He had been winning at the black jack table as well.

She did her best to turn on the old Patsy charm, lighting up the room with her toothy grin. Of course, her barbs were in and George had no chance of getting away.

Over the course of the next few weeks, they had met in various places, but mostly in casinos. They liked the simplicity of Indian Casinos and found that sitting next to each other pulling the slot handles for two hours were as much aphrodisiac as they would need to culminate their affair.

Victor knew, of course. It was all part of the master plan, all part of each of them getting just what they had agreed they needed. And, wasn't that what a happy marriage was about?

After the fiasco last week at the cabin, she knew she needed to come up with a remarkable catch to keep Victor happy. He had almost lost it after Molly had discovered them.

Brian's reaction to his sister's captivity compounded Victor's anger. But Brian realized that her decision to lock Molly in the cabin was as much for her daughter's protection as it was for punishment. She was positive that the reason Victor couldn't see eye to eye with Brian was because they were so much alike.

Brian was understandably upset. He wanted so hard to be a hero, to grow up, to be a man. But he was still a boy. Her boy. And she wasn't going to let Victor's selfishness destroy her family anymore. Oh, she would give him what he needed: what he thought he needed.

She wasn't delusional. Patsy knew she had led Victor down this road when they got married. She had grown out of it and he had grown more accustomed to it. Eventually, she went through the motions, enjoying seeing Victor happy and getting fringe benefits herself.

She dumbly and blindly allowed her entire family to become enamored with her youthful hobbies and ambitions. Instead of growing tired of them, they embraced them. Long after her faith and belief faltered, they carried it on and with relish. She continued to play along, but only because it was a way for her to meet her needs.

Patsy wanted more than anything to remain young. And so far, it was working. Everyone was happy. Her flings and affairs reminded her of her desirability and youth. Her snaring of victims (sometimes even willing) to sacrifice themselves to the appetites of her family satisfied their needs. Especially Victor's.

She guessed it had started in college. She had attended Middle Tennessee State University and as a freshman, her roommate Bernice had introduced her to the occult. It had blossomed into a wide variety of activities and she was exposed to the underbelly of society

All races and socio economic situations were fair game to the obsessions with death, dying, necromancy, witchcraft and other darker interests of the occult. She had even lived one summer with a Haitian student who had performed voodoo. But he had freaked her out when he started inviting other girls over to join them in bed. There were some things that were just taboo, even when someone is morally corrupt.

That was only the beginning of the corruption. By the time Patsy met Victor at a bowling alley in West Memphis, she was fully indoctrinated into the ways of blood. And Victor had seemed so eager to experiment with her that she found herself becoming more and more interested in him.

When he asked her to marry him, she couldn't think of one reason why she shouldn't. He was compliant, willing, and even had an appetite to rival hers. It was a match made in....well.

The road in front of her curved left again and she slowed down, knowing the next dirt road to the right was where she needed to turn. She had let her mind drift for several minutes and hadn't realized the intensity of the rain had picked up. As she made her turn, the confident feeling she had left her. She couldn't explain it. She had gone from congratulating herself and thinking back to her college days (when she had been so potent and attractive, she could bed any guy she wanted) to feeling that something wasn't right.

Cautious again, she pulled over onto the grass alongside the gravel road. She didn't want to get out and get soaking wet, but she wanted to be able to concentrate. She listened and watched the back seat through her rear view mirror. She did not hear anyone stirring.

She turned down the radio to silence the light static. She had been so intent in her thinking that she hadn't realized she had completely lost the station. All of this bothered her. It must have been the long nights over the last few weeks.

She was on edge, excited, nervous and something kept creeping at the edges of her consciousness that told her something wasn't right. Victor would call it precognizance (his own word), but she chalked it up to women's intuition. Little alarms kept going off in her head. Something was going to go wrong. Maybe it already had.

She realized some of her reaction was just natural jumpiness. She had just kidnapped a man she had seduced and now she and her family were planning on feasting on his organs, draining his blood and injecting it. That would make anyone nervous, she figured.

Satisfied that George was secure and quiet, she pulled back onto the gravel road and peeled out, gravel cracking loudly in the Taurus' fender wells. She enjoyed driving fast which was one of the big reasons she never brought Victor along.

She also liked to make him wait. It really got him in a lather by the time she got back. However, over the last year or so, they had only taken a few opportunities to feast. The kids were getting older and, well, even though they embraced part of the lifestyle, they were still resistant to most of the gruesome parts. Patsy had to admit that if she had been raised like that, she would have rebelled long ago. So, she didn't hold a grudge. Besides, Brian was just protective, she knew. Big brothers usually were.

But, that was just the beginning of the trouble if they allowed it to fester. Molly, she hoped, would be better in time. Patsy knew getting Victor right was the first order of business. Satiated with what he required, she could then concentrate on weaning her family off of their morbid appetites. She certainly had gotten her fill.

Now that she was nearing forty, she felt maybe it was time to put this all behind her. But Victor was going to resist, she knew. And if intervention and cold turkey didn't cut it, well, she knew where the 44 Magnum was and she certainly knew how to use it. And the shotgun. Yeah, the shotgun would be better. Less likely to miss.

But she was jumping ahead of herself. First, she wanted to try this plan. So far, she had even had some fun pulling it off. She just couldn't shake the feeling that she was missing something big. Did George have a wife after all? She couldn't imagine she would miss on a detail like that. After their first meeting, she had checked him out.

George was divorced and his ex-wife lived in Alaska. She had moved there shortly after they split up. That was five years ago. She wasn't even listed on his life insurance anymore.

He had lived in Fort Smith for a year and owned properties all over Arkansas, Oklahoma and Missouri. He even had part ownership in some companies in Bexton. At first that had set off alarms but she could see that he had not been involved in it for several years.

Patsy turned left onto a narrow lane with a single rut down the center. The car bounced and she had to slow down. It was extremely muddy. She didn't want to get the axle hung up on the center of the rut, and she didn't want to go skidding off over into the field. She managed alright, but her mind wandered and she glanced nervously in the rear view mirror every few seconds. She had a feeling; the hairs on her arms stood on end and she felt light-headed.

She gripped the wheel tighter and put the transmission into low gear to slow the engine. She knew from experience that the next decline would send her out of control if she went down in overdrive.

She bumped and bucked along, the wheel forced to each side as she rode the rutted the road to the bottom of the slope and then slipped it into an even lower gear as she started up the next side. She made sure to resist the urge to gun the gas. The Taurus, its tires badly bald, would not make it up the hill unless she went slowly. She used the momentum of coming down the hill to make it up the next.

She had almost topped the twenty yard run to the top of the slope when the car slid into a deeper rut. The back end slewed heavily to the right. She panicked, but turned into the slide. The car jumped the rut and the rear wheels left the ground completely. She could feel the Taurus lift slightly and she knew she was in trouble.

She cursed. She did not permit swearing in the house, but when alone or with her flings, she swore prodigiously. But, all the swearing in the world could not change her situation. The Taurus swung almost completely around and despite Patsy stomping on the brakes, the sedan slid down the hill to the right. Its momentum carried her into the thickets and the rear of the car hit a tree.

The car turned in an arc, its wheels off the ground, the engine screaming. She barely held onto the steering wheel as she was jerked the other way when the car hit another tree as it spun in the air.

The air bag went off suddenly, hitting her in the face hard. In fact, this was the only injury she felt. The white billowy bag smacked her lips and she could feel blood trickle down her chin. The explosion and the force knocked her head back.

Her neck muscles were tense and her hands were numb. She realized that she no longer had them on the wheel. She also could tell the engine had stopped. She cursed again, her lip swelling and her tongue flitting out to catch the blood there almost by instinct.

CHAPTER FOURTEEN

M olly couldn't sob. The rain had her nervous, but she didn't care. She had found no food. She looked across to a field about a hundred yards away. She knew it would be dangerous to be out in the open in a storm. She was deathly afraid of lightning.

She knew in her gut that there was food in that field. Something deep inside her willed her to get up and look. She was getting weak and colder by the minute. The temperatures had dropped, but she had very little energy.

Molly just wanted to curl up in a ball at the base of the big tree under which she sat for shelter and sleep. But she knew what would happen if she did that. She might never wake up, she feared. So, she stood on shaky legs. Her pants were heavy with rain and her shirt was clinging to her small frame.

She laughed at an image that came unbidden to her mind. She had hidden in the big dryer from her brother Brian when she was little. She needed a tumble dry right now. But, as she imagined herself tumbling over and over, her eyes went wide and her stomach flopped.

Coming to her senses, she braced herself against the tree and looked down for a long stick to use as a cane. She had seen Brian walk through the woods with a stick that he had shaved all of the bark off of and tied a leather cord along the top and through a hole he had drilled there. He would wrap the leather cord around his wrist and then scamper through the woods using the stick to give him extra leverage. Sometimes, he would even use it like a pole vault to leap over obstacles like brush deadfall or rocks.

She soon found a branch that would work. She didn't have the strength to break it off at the right length and it was a little skinny, but it would do. She grasped it and put it out ahead of her. Pumping her arms and legs, she pushed off with determination toward the field ahead.

Even through the rain Molly could see splashes of brighter color among the greens and early fall pastels. If she wasn't hallucinating, she might even swear she could see berry bushes over near the lower part near where the woods faded and the field started. But the surrounding grass was high except for some areas she knew were game trails.

Brian had shown her how to set a deer stand near places like this. Thinking of deer made her mouth water. She knew getting close to a deer in this weather would be easy, but felling one with her bare hands would be impossible. In fact, she was scared that it might charge her. She had heard stories. But she wasn't even sure if they had antlers this time of year.

These thoughts occupied her mind as her body strained beyond its natural capabilities to survive. She wished she had paid more attention in Science class or had joined the Girl Scouts. Maybe then she would know more about what plants she could eat. She had not found a flower yet that would satisfy her and she was scared she would get poisoned. She continued on, and as she got closer to the end of the field she could see that her guess had been correct.

She fought the urge to run ahead, but suddenly became very alert. If this was food, she might have competition for it. She was determined if it was anything but a bear or lion, she would be willing to fight for it. Her eyes darted back and forth and when she was satisfied that she was the only hungry creature on this stormy afternoon at this particular thicket, she lunged ahead, her walking stick held like a spear in her right hand.

Finally, she was there, the berries red and ripe. She was sure they were raspberries. When she raised them to her mouth she crushed them in her fingers. She sucked the juices from her fingers as she chewed. She ignored the scratches from the briars, but dove back in, grasping and feeding the plump, over-ripe berries into her mouth.

She noted that there weren't very many berries on the bushes, but all around the ground berries were strewn about, many of which were squashed or had been picked at. The rain had dislodged many of them, she imagined. This late in the year, it was unusual for them to still be on vine, anyway. Molly dropped to her knees, picking up the fullest berries one by one. She confirmed that the berries indeed tasted like raspberries, but at that point she did not care.

After about five minutes of scrambling around the base of the bushes and looking around for more in the narrow thicket, Molly rested against a tree with low-hanging branches as the rain subsided. She licked her fingers idly while she tied up a cloth torn from her shirt.

She had kept back several of the berries, the squishiest ones. She figured they would get smashed into a pulp and she could drink the juices through the cloth. But, as she worked, she noticed that the color of the stain of the berries on her fingers were similar to the blood that had caked the floor of the cabin. She couldn't help the image that came into her head. She just choked back a low sob and wiped her sticky hand across her nose.

Molly wondered what she was going to do. She wanted desperately to tell someone what had happened, but didn't know where to turn. She couldn't even tell Brian because evidently, he had known all along. Her mother had seemed sympathetic, but her father—how she hated him—acted as though she wasn't there.

She had screamed and ran from the room, her father hugging her mother under the sheets while the man dangled there from the wall. She had followed her mother and father earlier, but had lost them in the woods. She had thought at first that she had gotten lucky to have found the cabin. But, when she entered, she was confused by the sounds she heard and had entered the bedroom without knocking.

Her family was strange. She knew that and had accepted it long ago. In fact, she actually reveled in the attention it got her. Or the lack of attention, was more accurate. But now, she wished that she had a friend or a teacher or someone she could turn to. She felt so alone and so hurt. No one had offered an explanation, but she understood.

She had learned enough about the rituals of love and death from her mother reading to her. Her mother was proud of her collection of books, but if Molly ever felt the need to share the things that she had learned from them at her mother's knee, she would have been expelled from school. It was beyond witchcraft. Molly had giggled when one of her friends from school had gotten upset with her when she had claimed that Harry Potter was a wimp.

But, despite the knowledge that her family was strange, despite her admittedly odd upbringing in the remote woods of North Central Arkansas, Molly was not prepared for the strange scene that met her in the bedroom of the secret cabin hidden away in the woods just miles from their home. She understood implicitly that she was not meant to be there, but she also knew inside that her mother wanted her to see and her father could have cared less. But the argument that ensued and her eventual imprisonment was a slap to the face.

They expected her to accept her family's "appetites"-- whatever that meant. All that Molly knew was that the whole scene and the subsequent fight assaulted her senses. She was completely horrified.

At first, all she could do was cry and rock, her head between her knees, curled in a ball. Her mother had refused to hold her. She demanded that she stay. Molly was hurt and confused by the imprisonment more than the body.

But after three days trying to ignore the cadaver in the bedroom and with very little food to eat, she finally broke down. Brian had come then while she was curled up in her room sobbing. He had held her and apologized. She didn't know for what, but suspected that he had known for a long time and regretted not telling her sooner.

In the end, he told her he loved her but she needed to stay a little longer. He said it was for her own good. She guessed that he meant their father. That would figure. He assured her that he would be back.

After two more days, she grew tired of waiting. She broke the door by pounding a butter knife into where the door latch went. After she did it, she stood on the porch and listened. She was worried she would get caught and punished even more severely.

Then she had turned and chastised herself as she noticed that the window in the front would have been big enough for her to crawl out. It had never occurred to her during her whole captivity to break the only window in the little shack. She had shrugged, and left without looking back. That had been three days ago.

She wasn't even sure if anyone had been back to check on her since. She suspected that they hadn't. Somehow, she had been discarded. She searched for a reason.

Had she been a bad daughter? Had she been rebellious? Well, she had been curious, that was for sure. And she resented her parents keeping things from her. She knew that they kept the basement locked and that they would go down there.

She knew that every once in a while her mom would leave for several days and her dad would pace around the house. He reminded her of the monkeys in the cages at the Little Rock Zoo. He wouldn't shave, he wouldn't cook, and sometimes he wouldn't bathe. The house would go to rot if it weren't for Brian.

Molly also knew that much of what ailed them as a family could be traced to her mom's library. Her dad would peruse the titles, pull one out and read it for hours.

Sometimes he would stand up all of a sudden with a smile on his face and sweep Patsy up in his arms.

Molly could see the excitement in her mother's eyes when her father behaved like that. But, recently, she had noted that her mother was more often exasperated at her father and seemed unhappy. Molly was too young to read too much into those weary stares and occasional sighs under her breath, but she was quite sure her father didn't notice. He seemed to become more distant every year.

And when Molly had interrupted their ritual, her father had looked over at her and it appeared as though his eyes bored right through her. They didn't accuse her, he wasn't surprised, he just simply didn't care that she was there. Her mother had thrown back the covers and slid out. Molly didn't pay that much attention, but through the throbbing in her head as she processed what she was seeing, she had heard her mother's bare feet hit the wooden floor.

All the blood. She could see several old milk jugs, their metal handles tinted red with blood. They were opaque, but blood lined the rims. Blood was on the wall, on the spikes that held the man's shoulders. Bone and blood. Blood was on her father's beard and all over her mother's chest and arms.

She had wanted to scream, thought maybe she had, but had managed only a quick high-pitched breathing. She had collapsed there on her knees, but her mind wanted her to turn and run away. Then her mother had her, and she lifted her up and brought her out to the kitchen, holding Molly close.

She could feel both of their hearts racing, her mother's sweat in her mouth as she buried her face in her shoulder.

They sat in the kitchen, her mother alternatively stroking her hair and growling at her for being foolish.

After several minutes, her father had come in, fully dressed now and sat down opposite. Victor had stared at her mother, directly past her with his brow down over his eyes and a deep frown on his face.

"What are we gonna do with her, Patsy?"

"Hush. You're gonna scare her."

He had chuckled at that.

"Too late. Done had the bejesus scared outta her already, dontcha think?" His speech was slurred like he had been drinking.

Molly hadn't noticed any of his beer bottles. She didn't smell it on his breath. In fact, what she smelled frightened her even more. She could smell blood. It was a musky scent, one that alerted her, one that stirred something in her. She was repulsed and excited at the same time.

Her face tingled then and she turned in her mother's arms. She was compelled to look. She couldn't help it. She knew that her father was grinning. And in that grin she had confirmation of her fears. She suddenly looked back up at her mom's face, hoping it wasn't true. But it was there, a blackish red stain at her lips, the same blood that coated the teeth of her father like chocolate milk or Oreo cookies.

She shut out the memory the best she could. It was time for her to move on. She was angry at herself again. She had almost fallen asleep. Her stomach wasn't full, but it no longer growled at her. She had more energy, but her hands still shook.

Her eyelids were heavy and she felt an overwhelming insistence to lie down and sleep. She almost listened to the voice that convincingly told her that she would be alright and would wake up refreshed. She knew that to be mostly true, but the reality was she would wake up cold and hungry again. *At least you will wake up,* the voice reasoned.

She sat like that for several minutes. She wrestled with herself and scratched her matted hair. The rain was gone now and the darkness was descending upon the woodlands. She understood that soon the temperatures would plummet and unless she was moving, she was likely to get very cold.

It was a wonder she hadn't already gotten sick as wet and cold and under-nourished as she had been. Something was keeping her alive. She didn't wonder what it was, because ever since she was nine she had suspected she was special. Her mother had told her so. But this feeling was different.

She looked up at the clearing sky. She looked up to be comforted. She looked up and beheld the last sinking of the sun. To her right, up high in the sky and closer than she had ever seen it before, the full moon greeted her as the dark violet sky turned a navy blue and then to black. She stared at it until its image burned itself into her mind. She blinked away the sleep and with legs steadier than they had been in days, she stood up. Using her hiking stick, she navigated the edge of the field, picking up the last of the raspberries before she headed back down the mountain.

CHAPTER FIFTEEN

T he State Trooper said he'd be by this afternoon to visit with you. He wants to meet you over at the café and get some coffee," Estella said.

Sheriff Shoemaker nodded and sipped his coffee. The stuff at the station was bitter, but it hit the spot. He needed a quick wake-up. His eyes were still crusty and his voice hoarse. It was all the moisture and the dropping temperatures, he figured.

Estella looked at him over her thick glasses and had a superior smirk on her face. He glared at her, sour and uncomprehending.

"I hear you been spendin' a lot of time with that boy, Tommy. You tryin' to hone in on his ma?"

Billy Joe realized for the first time that her hair was dyed red. He could see the silver and white roots of her hair. He smiled, despite himself. She wanted to keep up appearances, he guessed. Estella was a gossip, but she was as interested in making news as delivering it.

"Nah. Just like Tommy is all. He's a good kid. I think he'll make a good Sheriff someday. I'm just showing him the ropes."

He hitched up his trousers by the belt and expanded his chest as he said this with false bravado and a sly smile.

Estella didn't seem convinced. She dismissed him with a wave and began to turn and make her way back into the dispatch room.

"Ahh. I know better. I think Liz could do better than you, but after what that woman has been through, you might be a steal."

That was as nice a thing as Estella had ever said to him. He had no interest in Liz, really. Estella had put the thought in his head, nonetheless.

He shook his head. He was fairly sure a woman like Liz would find nothing about him attractive. She was young, pretty and wasn't divorced officially. Still, her husband wasn't coming home from all accounts. Billy Joe didn't even consider it any further.

He idly picked up a donut from Bell's Bakery and nibbled on it, allowing the crumbs to dust the tile floor of the break room. He took another bite, wrapped it up in a napkin and headed out to his cruiser. He wondered as he strolled through the little office what Trooper Nunez wanted with him. It must have been somewhat official or he would have shared it with Estella. Rather, Estella would have bugged the Trooper until he relented.

He got into his cruiser and backed out, thinking about the Junior Varsity football game last night. Tommy had played wide receiver and worked hard, but not one pass sailed his way. He blocked, ran ghost routes and played on special teams, but never touched the ball all night.

They were defeated by Cave City who ran the ball unmercifully down their throat. Bexton had an option offense and only threw the ball maybe ten times all game. Half of those went to tight ends on slant routes and the other half went to running backs on various screen plays.

He was disappointed, but not angry. He knew Tommy would be disappointed, too. Tommy wouldn't admit it, of course. He was too much of a team player. It was among Billy Joe's favorite things about Tommy.

Billy Joe knew the coach. They had gone to school together. He thought about it for a minute and decided to cruise on up Holland Road and have a visit. He decided he wouldn't mention names, but just talk offensive philosophy.

Coach Gruber had played defensive back and running back when they were in high school and Billy Joe had played line on both defense and offense. Gruber had gone on to college and Billy Joe had enlisted. They came from two different paths, but similar backgrounds. He thought maybe he could influence Coach to include some more pass plays in the repertoire.

The drive was a short one. He noticed Gruber's car in front of the Board of Education building and pulled in alongside. He got out, hitched up his trousers again and glanced around the little sleepy town. It was mid-morning and barely a soul was stirring. The rain had drenched the streets, water pooled in areas along the sidewalk and in the potholes along Third Street. School was in, but the Coach taught Physical Education and Health on every day but Thursday. It was his day off and his only day to get game plans ready for the Friday's Varsity Football game.

Puzzled, Billy Joe climbed the wet concrete steps up to the heavy metal double doors. He went in, conscious of his image in the glass. He needed to cut back on the donuts. Gruber wasn't much better, but he had more muscle and more hair on his head. Sheriff Shoemaker touched his hat and considered removing it inside the building.

It smelled like pine cleaner inside. He looked up the hall and saw the receptionist glance up at him with a wan smile. He removed the hat and her smile brightened.

"What can we do for you today, Sheriff?"

He held his hat before him, more or less covering his hefty gut.

"Well, I just thought I'd drop in and talk to Coach Gruber."

154

She blinked twice and frowned. He didn't know Alice very well, but if she was like most receptionists, at least good ones, she would be adept at guarding the gate. Receptionists were as much filters for executives as they were greeters.

He understood this, and knew that flattery would get him nowhere. Dogged determination would be effective: once. He decided to play it cool. He could always catch the coach later.

"I'm afraid Superintendent Johnson is in a meeting. Coach Gruber is in attendance as well."

He raised his eyebrows and appeared surprised.

"Oh. I see. I guess I'll catch him later..."

He heard voices and Johnson and Gruber walked out of an office behind her. Their tone was serious and he could see the receptionist drop her eyes and look away. She cleared her throat. He could tell it was a warning. Johnson looked up, perturbed. Then he noticed Billy Joe.

"Ahh.Sheriff. How nice of you to drop by. Is there a problem? Did I park illegally again?" he asked, smiling.

Dr. Johnson was a man of means that had moved back to Bexton to take on what he thought was a failing school district. He didn't plan to stay, but had not found a better opportunity once he got here three years ago. The big turnaround he had imagined that would make him a hot commodity never happened. In fact, the school district took a nose dive.

"No, Dr. Johnson. I just wanted to visit with the two-time All-State defensive back, that's all."

Coach Gruber looked at him, his brow furrowing. He seemed like his mind was elsewhere. He perked up at the mention of All-State and then the compliment finally hit home.

"Oh. Sheriff. Sure. I just need to wrap things up here. You have the cruiser parked out front?"

"Yup."

"I'll join you in a second, OK?" He asked. It was more like an order, but Billy Joe didn't mind. He could tell he had interrupted a tense moment. He didn't want this to taint his goal. He wanted Gruber in a good mood. Timing was everything.

"Sure. I'm right by your Blazer."

"Right."

Billy Joe spun on his heel and tipped his hat at Alice as he replaced it on his head. She smiled a condescending smile.

Why am I so backward, he wondered. He popped back outside and noted the dark clouds. He wished it would stop raining

That would probably be Gruber's excuse: raining night, slippery ball, high percentage plays, yada, yada, yada. But that would be alright. It wouldn't rain every game and so maybe out of the last four regular season starts, Tommy would rack up some catches.

He slipped back into his cruiser and turned on the radio. He switched it over to the police band and considered getting out his *Sports Illustrated* while he waited. Just as he was reaching for it, he noticed the coach come down the concrete steps. He smiled at him and unlocked the car.

The coach grunted as he folded himself into the seat. He was shorter than Billy Joe had remembered, but his hair was the same as in high school: blonde, feathered back with long sideburns. His face was heavier with worry lines at his eyes and temples, and his shoulders seemed wider, but he was essentially the same Drew "Crash" Gruber he had grown up with.

Drew smiled. Billy Joe could see through his plastic smile that he was merely tolerating his presence. He probably got this type of speech all the time and was expecting what was coming. Billy Joe almost decided to drop it and just make some small talk and invite him over for dinner.

"What's on your mind, Sheriff? I kicked that Blake boy off the team for that prank he pulled. You don't have to lecture me."

Relieved, Billy Joe determined that he would broach the subject after all.

"Nothing like that, I assure you. I just wanted to talk. I watched the JV game last night."

Drew looked out the window, seemingly un-interested.

"Yeah. Got our backsides handed to us on defense. Those boys down at Cave City must be eating a ton of beans and cornbread."

"You got that right. But that's not what I wanted to talk about."

Drew turned.

"You want my permission to date Sally?"

Billy Joe was taken aback and shook his head. It was all he could do to not laugh out loud. Sally had been Drew's girlfriend for fifteen years.

They had lived together for the last five years. Gruber had no idea that she was making soft porn movies down in Fort Smith since she got out of college. He found out, went ballistic, and broke up with her about two months ago.

Most everyone in town had known. Even Mr. Spencer. But, everyone figured Estella had told him. Which wasn't too far off base, he figured.

Sally was bad news. Her dad ran the car dealership in Mountain Home and lived in Bexton because it was quieter, it was said. After Sally got out of college, her mom and dad split up and her father moved to Fort Smith. He had convinced his daughter to come down there and star in some of his internet movies.

Sally figured she would cash in on her looks and her acting to maybe break into the big time. She never made it. In fact, it wouldn't strike Billy Joe as unusual if she wasn't mixed up in drugs, too.

"Of course not." He desperately wanted to turn the conversation back to football. "I wanted to talk about our offense. I mean, it seemed we were pretty conservative and predictable out there, don't you think?"

Drew looked sour for a minute, as if the thought of Sally was still there on the edge of his consciousness and the Sheriff's question had not been uttered.

"Predictable?"

He scratched his chin and looked out the window across the street to the cleaners. "I don't think the option can be predicted. That's why we run it." He sounded defensive, but hardly convinced of his own answer. His mind was still somewhere else. Billy Joe could tell he had made this argument before. Now he wished he had picked a better time or not said anything at all.

"Come on, man. We played together. You know that I'm qualified to say it was predictable."

Drew turned to look at him, his eyes were sunken and his lips trembled. Billy Joe noted that Drew was trying not to smile. Instead he raised his eyebrows.

"You're qualified to criticize my coaching, Billy Joe? Really?" He huffed and turned away. He grabbed at the handle as if he were ready to get out. "Half this town thinks they're qualified. Far as I am concerned, you all can sit your carcasses out there and coach. I don't care anymore."

Billy Joe reached across and grabbed Drew's arm. Drew turned back, his eyes threatening. He didn't let go.

"Don't leave just yet, coach. I didn't mean to tell you how to coach. I just wanted to offer some advice. Sometimes we forget lessons we learned when we were younger."

Drew shook off his arm and opened the cruiser door. He slid out and stood up. He started to shut the door, and then leaned in and looked Billy Joe in the eyes.

"How long did you know Sally was a whore?" His voice was raspy. Billy Joe realized for the first time that Drew had been drinking heavily and he finally put the puzzle together as to why Drew was visiting Dr. Johnson on his day off.

"I didn't know. Honest. Estella told me after you discovered it and kicked her out. I haven't talked to her since."

Drew stared at him and nodded.

"Sorry, Sheriff. I'll look into what you said. But I've been coaching for a long time. You've been a law man for a long time. Neither one of us like being told how to do our job, but since we both work for the public we are beholden to what everyone else thinks we should do. I think I'm shut of it, now."

Billy Joe met his gaze and he could see despair and resignation.

"I understand," was all he could manage to say.

Drew stared at him a moment longer and nodded.

"Yeah, I think you do. You just might, that's for sure." He smiled grimly and winked at him. He stood back up and turned away without shutting the door.

Billy Joe just sat there for a second. He hadn't realized that he wasn't the only one that was in agony. There were other people in the world just as unhappy as he was. He thought briefly about running the coach down and giving him some real advice. He discarded it, though, because it would likely be advice that he hadn't followed himself.

CHAPTER SIXTEEN

J acob sat on the porch to clear his head. He was fully awake now and his stomach had settled enough to eat some jerky. His hands shook as he opened the package. He looked down the lonely hill, lit by the bright moon. He had slept for at least two fitful hours at the table.

When he woke he had finished the job he should have started before he sat down. In fact, he chastised himself for improperly managing a crime scene. He wouldn't be held accountable for his lack of procedure, but it gnawed at him. Besides, he could have left evidence that would leave him open for suspicion.

He came outside to get some perspective and to escape the cloying scent of death. He had to make sense of all that he had seen. It appeared that at least four people had been in the building including the victim. He still held the belief that the victim was a vagrant of some sort.

Bloody footprints still dotted the room where the body rotted on the wall. Some were narrow, appearing to be female. Others were wide, with a large big toe and a high arch. So, he guessed, two adult perpetrators, one victim and one *(what, spectator?)* other.

The only thing that had confused him was the bedroom off the entrance. The door had been jimmied. The bed had been slept in. Markings on the bed post led him to believe the person there was young. They had drawn little moons in different phases and several balls: baseballs, footballs, soccer balls, basketballs. It was odd and he couldn't link the timeline of those drawings or the unkempt bed with the murder.

But all clues led him to deduce that someone else had been in the house and had been left behind as a prisoner and then had subsequently escaped. He couldn't hunt around outside in the dark for prints and doubted that he would find any. Most of the prints inside were scuffed and he didn't have the tools to tell them apart or get a sample.

But the refrigerator was different. He was a bachelor and he could easily judge the shelf life of most perishables. The few things left in there were inedible. Some had been experimentally picked at before: a meatloaf, a jar of what appeared to be congealed soup that had been left uncovered, and a pan of moldy cornbread.

So, he sat on the porch watching patches of clouds pass by the bright moon. He hadn't realized how dark it was on the mountain. But, the moon lit the trees with an amber glow. A harvest moon, Neil Young would call it. It still wasn't enough light by which to hunt and he was worried he would ruin or bypass an important piece of information. He wanted to methodically cover the ground surrounding the cabin to discover as much as he could before he finalized his plan. He really had no idea what he would be up against.

He stared into the night, soaking up the moisture and listening to the sounds of the forest awake. The rain was gone for awhile, he could tell, but it had made its mark. He could hear the soft patter of water dripping from leaves and from the eaves of the cabin. He wished it would keep raining and just wash him and this forsaken shack away.

He stared at the wood of the porch. It looked a dark gray by the light of the moon, but he knew it was closer to a coal black. The shack had been painted at some point with a flat black paint. He guessed that it would naturally blend well into the foliage here. But, over time, the trees here grew taller and what once was a camouflaged house was now a sore thumb, a blight on the landscape.

It's one window had thick, dirty glass. Its door was solid, but not centered properly. When it swung out, it stuck on the porch floor halfway open. Generally, it was built well despite its dilapidated condition. It certainly had withstood the elements. He figured it was at least a decade old and had served as a hunting cabin at first, then abandoned. This mountain was crossed with deer and boar trail, but it was tough sledding. There was plenty of good hunting elsewhere. Besides, if he wasn't mistaken, much of this wilderness was protected from hunting.

He thought again about the crime itself. He wondered about the type of monsters who would take organs from a corpse. He was reminded of Luke's parents. He remembered as Luke recounted his story, he hadn't felt moved by sympathy. He figured organs taken from a coroner were from bodies being explored and taken apart in the course of the scientific process of discovering the cause of death. In this case, he couldn't keep from shivering at the possibility that the cause of death was entirely about getting to those organs. What would be the odds of meeting someone with a story like Luke's and then coming across a scene like this in a place this remote? Jacob shook his head. He couldn't believe it was coincidence. Something here was out of place.

Or exactly in place. He couldn't shake the feeling that he was meant to be here. This flight up the mountain, this remote shack in the middle of nowhere, Luke, this whole trip: they were tied together. He couldn't deny the feeling that sometimes his life felt like it was all culminating to one event.

He knew people could deal with murder, floods, lightning strikes, homicide, and other plights in the city. They had all the benefits of technology like hospitals, support groups, police, courts of law, neighborhood watch and cell phones. Here on the edge where all that someone had most times was a good knife and common sense, abuses of humanity were more intense. Survival was paramount and most every waking second was spent in endeavors that improved the likelihood of that survival.

In the city, people would watch the nightly news, read the newspaper, shake their heads at the atrocities and maybe go as far as locking their doors or calling the cops if they saw a suspicious person. But, they would return to the coffee shops, the bars, their churches secure in the nature of their safety and survival. Moral indignation in the city was a luxury.

Because of these thoughts, Jacob had always had a special place in his heart for the homeless. That was why when he looked upon the corpse in the other room, he could easily slip into a prayer for the man's soul. The homeless, the underprivileged and the handicapped were as close to the edge of civilization as someone could be and yet right in the middle of it all—shut out to its benefits, its nets of safety, its mental state of security.

Now he was here, and it was up to him to deal with this crime against humanity. It was his test. He could feel the responsibility keenly. He wished that he was imagining all of this.

He sipped some water from his camel pack. He noticed how many more stars were visible out here. He was always amazed at the beauty of the universe and how it was always more evident the further he got from the big cities. He heard the cries of a rabbit, probably escaping a fox far off on the ridge above the cabin. He could hear the dripping of water hitting leaves almost a foot deep.

It was still hard for him to place the scene inside the house with all this natural beauty. It was on the fringe of his thoughts rolling through his inner self. He couldn't shake the feeling that what had happened here was out of sorts with its environment.

It reminded him of his trips to Idaho and Canada. Every time he would get enamored with the natural beauty, God's creation. Then, he would be reminded of the cruelty, the underbelly of violence and happenstance that lay under all which seemed pure and natural. It was separate and yet an integral part.

It was moments like these, feeling depressed, disappointed and alone that he felt the simultaneous pull of belief and frustration in God. He wanted to believe that all this had a greater, bigger meaning. He had been assured by

Phillip that no matter how lofty the greatest thought of the
most brilliant man on earth could be, it would be
insignificant to the lowest and basest of the thoughts of God.
But, how could a God, all-knowing, all-good, all-powerful,
all-seeing, allow atrocities like this to happen?

It wasn't that he felt compelled to deny there was a God.
Jacob recognized that God existed. He just couldn't connect
the nature of God with what happened around him in the
world, his own sense of what was right and good.

Phillip would probably say something about free will.
That was too pat an answer for Jacob. Evil had to play a part
somewhere. He was not immune to the feeling. He sure
wanted to punch Sheriff Shoemaker in the mouth, had
wanted to hurt Janice before he left, had wanted those
women at the bar in Lexington to ask him to go back to their
house.

Free will was a broken concept. It was as much an
excuse to fall prey to our basest most selfish feelings as it
was an inspiration to do what was right. It fell back to the
essence of each person: their individual goodness or lack
thereof. That was how Jacob saw it.

God was just the grand puppeteer that steered the weather
and laughed as the puny humans cursed him and blamed him
for the ills of the world. Or worse, God sat on his throne
clucking his tongue at the pathetic worshippers always asking
for more money or for Aunt Bessie to survive the cancer
treatment or Uncle Joe praying for a promotion at work.
Jacob was glad he wasn't God. He didn't know how He did
it.

He wished then that he had held on to that copy of the
Bible that he had found in Lexington. He thought that he

needed direction now more than any time in his life. He was on the precipice of falling or progressing as a child of God. He understood this and resented it at the same time.

He didn't like the idea that he could be unredeemable. He determined that he could pray without the help of a directing passage. He wanted to do what was right, was that not enough? He had never even considered partaking in an act as heinous as the one that had played out in that remote cabin.

Didn't that put him a leg up on someone who did? Somehow, he thought it didn't matter. He didn't know a lot about God, but he was pretty sure he didn't have a sliding scale of sin.

It hurt Jacob's head to wrap his mind around things like this. He really just wanted to take the facts and digest them, come up with a suspect, hunt him down and in the end have justice rule out. He was positive that whatever happened tomorrow, it wouldn't be that simple. He knew something would come to him. It always did and that was the biggest reason he believed there was a God. Beyond anything else, Jacob did not believe in coincidence.

What was it that the clues so far had told him? One person did not do this alone. Someone had been left behind. They escaped. They did not live here regularly. The person that was killed was part of a ritual that was tied to sex and the consumption of the human body. That usually meant some sort of vampirism or cannibalism. Bottle rings left in the pools of blood in the room probably indicated some sort of storage of fluids or vessels to carry organs.

Other clues led him to believe that the perpetrator or perpetrators were not affluent. Everything pointed to expecting that they were near poverty. They would not be able to afford the services of Luke's father and therefore would have to look for alternatives. Dangerous and criminal alternatives.Deadly circumstances.

His plan of action was to get back to civilization and contact the authorities. The Arkansas State Police or a branch of the FBI possibly would handle this case. Jacob wasn't even sure of the jurisdiction here on this remote mountaintop. He gazed out across the tree line that was illumined by the glow of the moon. Somewhere out there was someone qualified to address this. Somewhere out there was justice for the ones that had committed this act of violence and hate, this blemish on humanity, this atrocity to God. And Jacob realized that being God's instrument, for better or worse, was an awful responsibility.

His mind was wandering and he realized he wasn't going to get much done tonight. Relieved that the rain had gone, he laid out his sleeping bag on the porch and decided to sleep out under the stars tonight. The ceiling of the porch was full of cobwebs, so he took the time to sweep them away. He didn't want a spider to drop on him in the night.

CHAPTER SEVENTEEN

T he car wasn't on fire and that was a relief. Patsy was tangled up in her seat belt. Her arm was numb and her face stung.

She wanted to bite her lip but realized it was foolish. Blood trickled down to her chin. She glanced into the rear view mirror and raised her face to see the damage.

Remarkably, the air bag had added some color to her otherwise chalky appearance and the blood on her lip was sensuous. She could see that her sunken eyes were going to be darker soon. She forced herself to focus. She blinked away tears and sucked her lip.

Patsy regained her wits slowly and decided that the first order of business was to see if the car would drive. She looked for something to puncture the confounded air bag. She extracted her arm from the seat belt and reached over to her purse on the passenger side. She grabbed a ballpoint pen and popped the top off with her cherry red fingernail. She pointed the writing end downward and reached up as high as she could, her elbow near her ear and stabbed forward.

The popping sound of the air from the punctured bag still made her jump. It reminded her of the biscuits in a can. No matter how many times she peeled the wrapper off, the popping would make her flinch, like a bakery jack-in-the-box. White powder filled the car like flour. She was too angry to laugh.

Clear snot ran out of her nose and she wiped her forearm across, not caring about womanly decorum. She looked down and unstrapped the seat belt. The keys had fallen in the floor during the jolt. She hoped that was why the car had stopped running. She could see now the steam coming from the front end of the car without the airbag in the way. But she wasn't going to lose faith yet.

"Ah, that stinks!" She could smell some sort of fluid, like from the radiator. She snatched the keys from the seat and put them in the ignition. It clicked consecutively, but did not start. She bit her lip despite the pain. It was raining hard and she didn't want to get out. She looked out of the window as the windshield wiper finally decided to work again. Through the warped view she could see that the car had slid about twenty feet before hitting the tree. She wasn't far from the road. It was a good thing she had been going as slow as she was or she may not have survived.

Patsy tried to calm her mind and center on the here and now. She was usually prepared for events like this, but she struggled. In the back of her mind, she saw disaster. Her daughter, innocent, walking in on her and Victor, the body of the hobo hung like a gory scarecrow on their bedroom wall. Having sex in the red-tinted room while the corpse hung on the wall had been Victor's idea. He had read that the effects of the ingested blood could enhance the experience.

The hobo was Victor's idea as well. Little more than a lure of food and shelter had brought him to their shed. Victor hadn't cared when Molly had entered while they were in the act. He was more perturbed when she had ended it prematurely. The whole plan had been a disaster and yet Victor had only wanted more. He had even insinuated that Molly could watch.

Patsy felt her skin crawl. She had let everything get so incredibly out of control. Control was her only tool. Now, she thought it was all unraveling, falling apart in front of her eyes. She began to cry, her tears falling into her lap, staining her cotton gown with moisture.

She was as concerned about herself as much as she was for Victor. She cared more for her diminishing role in their family than she did the corruption of her children to ideals she no longer held dear. She had lost her faith in her lack of faith. She could no longer pretend she was not conscious of the wrong she was doing. She chose not to dwell on it now, though. Wrong time and too late to have regrets. Regrets were for the weak. Hadn't she drilled that into the kids enough?

The acrid smell began to sting her eyes. She sighed heavily and closed them. She imagined walking the remaining two miles to the farm house. Two more hills, a long stretch of field, two winding areas surrounded by woods: she had driven this road so many times that she could do it without looking. But was that the only answer? What if she left George here? She didn't like the idea, but realized she could run most of the way home and Victor and Brian could return and secure the body before she could drag him all that way in the first place.

But, should she finish the job first? What if he woke up? What if someone came along (although that thought was preposterous, she wasn't foolish enough to dismiss it) and discovered him? If that happened, it would be better if he was dead. It would be easy to connect her family with the vehicle.

In that case, it would be better that they had only kidnapped him. But it was all relative. What was most important was that she regained control. She had to decide what to do on her terms; terms that would put her firmly back in control of her family. That would mean she could regain Molly's innocence and Brian's trust. That wasn't going to happen, even if she made Victor happy.

Something in her was awakening and she was scared of it. She thought it might be heart.

All these thoughts mixed up in her mind in a few moments, though she was not aware how long she had closed her eyes. She opened them with her hands clenched, the pen still in her right hand. The rain beat at the hood of the car and splattered, the windshield noisily and rhythmically did a poor job of clearing the rain from the windshield.

Despite the noise, she heard George groan for the first time. That was when she made up her mind. Something in her rose up, something she only felt when she was focused.

The urge within her was an element of her nature that she tried to deny, and yet had nurtured for so many years. It came forth now and took hold of her and she shuddered and a wicked grin came upon her bloody lips. She confidently opened the car door and stepped into to the torrent of rain.

She didn't notice the cold drops pelting her face. She didn't notice that the fender in the back was severely broken.

With her chin on her chest, her cotton dress already soaked and clinging sensuously to her narrow frame, she opened the dented trunk with the keys she had extracted before she exited the vehicle. The trunk popped audibly and the light came on.

She looked down at George lying bound in the dirty trunk. A wrench and a jack lay under his legs. Grease, dirt and discarded trash lay all around him. She shook her head and clucked her tongue. She had stripped his shirt at the hotel. His grey chest hairs against his weak pasty chest looked pathetic. His balding pate and the flap of extra skin under his chin rendered him insufficient.

She wondered now what she had seen in him. He groaned but she was fairly certain he was still unconscious. It didn't matter. She wasn't taking any chances. Better to kill him now and worry about this whole mess later. She could care less if Victor was happy. It was his fault that she was losing control, she had decided. And now, they both had to go.

She almost laughed at the simplicity of it. She had been weak. As soon as Victor came to her as she held Molly in that dingy cabin kitchen, looking at her like she had abandoned him, she should have put a knife in his eye and then across his throat.

In her mind, she did it now, knowing that it would make her feel better if she believed she had done the right thing, the heroic thing in the first place. Instead, Victor had forced her to imprison their daughter in that cabin to protect her, trapped in there with only a corpse for company and no food to eat.

The dangerous look in Victor's eyes and the lascivious grin across his face had served as sufficient warning to her that the end justified the means. Molly would be safe, but scarred. That would have to do.

The look on Victor's eyes that night had not been different from the look that had attracted her all those years ago. He was someone without fear, someone willing to do something marvelous. Well, she had gotten that right and wrong at the same time.

Victor had always been willing for her to do the dirty work. It suited her because she felt in control. She controlled his appetite, she controlled her fantasies, she controlled the exposure of her family to their desires and activities. She knew that it was all a lie.

She had been duped into a false sense of all that she had believed was true. Victor had to pay. She would take it out of his flesh. She would languish in his blood on her hands and in her mouth. She would taste the river of life in his body flow into hers and taste his thick iron-rich blood coursing through her. She would taste victory. And then she would put all things right again.

She stopped for a moment. Something about the cold rain and standing over her moaning ex-lover made her pause. She could feel warmth leave her as she came to her senses for a moment. She was herself again, but something had changed.

She considered all that she had been contemplating, the complex and corrupted feelings that were coursing through her heart and mind. Normally, she would ignore these episodes and allow them to happen outside of herself, as if it were someone else that thought these things, did these things.

She allowed herself, her normal self, to listen to that other, malevolent self.

Now lucid, she realized for the first time the inability for her to be redeemed. She shrugged and with a purpose and a resignation to her destiny, she pulled the tire iron from under George's arm. He began to open his eyes.

"You men think you have us all figured out," she said through clenched teeth.

He didn't react much, a little fluttering of his eye lids, a shuddering of his body as he moaned again. She began to tremble, as much from rage as from the bitter cold that was seeping into her bones.

She raised the tire iron above her head with both hands and brought them to bear on his head. She continued to smash the iron into his head, his torso, his limbs. She cried out with each hit, and felt her body warm, her mouth screw up in a bloody grimace, part smile and part pain.

CHAPTER EIGHTEEN

S he had never felt so tired. She couldn't tell how far she had walked, but she was grateful that the rain had stopped. The moon had been her guide and had been true. But, now she sat on a log overlooking the cabin she had escaped.

She had traveled in a circle and now she sat there stunned. She couldn't believe her eyes. She had stopped to rest her legs and through the lifting morning fog, had seen the vision of a roof barely obscured. She had blinked, wondering if she had come upon another house. The shelf she was on was higher up the ridge, but even from a hundred yards away, she could easily tell the haunting porch and the blackened wood.

She sat there and shivered in the morning cold, her clothes still damp, her teeth chattering. She hated that place. She had hoped never to see it again. She hoped never to see her parents again. She wanted to put it all away.

God was so mean. Why couldn't she have walked until she found a nice old family looking for a little girl to take in?

Why did her life have to be so hard? She was so mad, she couldn't cry. She didn't feel loss, but only a galvanizing of her spirit. She looked up then to the waning moon, its image barely visible through the haze and the bright blue sky of the clear Arkansas morning. She asked the moon to take her home.

Molly closed her eyes and imagined a warm house with a big fireplace like the one at the public library. She pictured stockings hung, she could smell cider and pine and see a Christmas tree with old-fashioned garland and taste hot chocolate and pumpkin pie.

She dozed then, caught up in the way things should be. Desperately, she clung to her dreams, concerned for what she had become, what she was becoming. Deep inside she yearned for a different life. But, that which had changed in her over the last week held her back. It kept her an arm's reach from her dreams, taunting her, reminding her of her wretchedness, recalling her family's morbid and sick reality. She was part of that. It was her heritage, and the evil voice in her head teased her that it was her destiny, her legend to fulfill.

Confused because she really didn't know what that meant, she opened her eyes and stared at the cabin with determination. She wasn't going to let the stupid cabin ruin her day or her life. She would confront She wouldn't back down.

There was something there that was drawing her, but she wasn't sure it was the cabin itself. There was an air of expectation, a feeling of something that needed to happen and was waiting on her to step forward and allow it to happen. Was that destiny? She wasn't sure. All she knew was that something made her butt itch and her legs twitch and she felt compelled to get up off the damp log and slide down the leaf-covered bank to the cabin below her.

She steadied herself with her new walking stick, bent over and tied her second-hand Nike's for the third time this morning. She then took off over the hill with more energy than she was actually feeling. She slid down the leaves, actually exhilarated by the rushing cool wind of the morning whipping her short-cropped hair and whistling in her ears.

She fought the urge to let out her customary whoop, but enjoyed the slide nonetheless. Finally, she reached the bottom and using her walking stick, she skipped up toward the cabin. She tried to feel more confident. She made an attempt to appear fearless: a quick skip, a false smile, a firmer grip on her stick and she narrowed her eyes to vicious slits. If God could be mean, then so could Molly Carothers, daughter to filthy vampire wannabes and sister to Brian, a confused and selfish young man.

She continued, putting on a face that she imagined would make an ogre pause. She stepped over a log in her way and that was when she saw the yellow sleeping bag on the porch. She stopped, worried and confused. She let out her breath in a rush. Molly let her thoughts gather around this strange phenomenon.

She knew instinctively that this was not her family's sleeping bag. It looked like something from Vick's, not something they would have bought at a yard sale. Her senses were attuned to the natural noises of the forest now and so she listened for anything out of the ordinary. She heard a rustling around the other side of the shack and froze.

Dark Mountain

A man, dark-haired with a narrow scraggly beard and a dark, long-sleeved shirt and jeans moved toward her, his eyes glued to the ground. He seemed to be walking gingerly and his brow was furrowed as if he was trying to solve a particularly hard cross word puzzle. He looked like Brian doing his Algebra homework.

Something about the man set her at ease. Maybe it was his eyes. They looked sad and yet appeared intelligent and confident. But he was worried now. If he had been inside the shack, she was sure she knew why. Maybe that was why he had slept on the porch. She hadn't realized how bad the body smelled until she had escaped. It had been like breathing again for the first time. She had been so excited to get away, she had barely noticed, though. Now, looking from the man to the dark, eerie sight of the shack, she knew that despite her best efforts, she would not be able to go back in there.

She wanted desperately to run up to him and feel his arms around her. She blushed at that thought. But, she couldn't deny how her heart beat, how she could barely contain her emotion. She needed to feel rescued. She fought the shame she felt at herself for being so weak and out of control. She sniffled, barely stopping the flow of tears that were dying to burst from her eyes.

It was then that he looked up at her, his eyes registering fear and something else. She wished she could be an adult so that she could understand all the emotions she could see on people's faces. Some she understood easily like anger and hunger, but sometimes, the mysteries that were revealed to her through people's eyes were only partially open to her because she didn't fully comprehend. Like her father's eyes the night she discovered her mother lying above him and the bloody corpse on the wall behind them. Her father's eyes dark with a creepy red glow. The way he had looked at her had scared her as much as anything else in the room.

But, the look from this man was different. In that moment, she stored away that image. She wanted to remember that look, his eyes intent, his mind switching quickly from one puzzle to another.

"Well. Hello." He said. He sounded cool. Like a movie star. But that was probably just her imagination. She wanted to be rescued, after all.

"Hi to you." She said, her voice hoarse from disuse. She realized with trepidation that she had just spoken to a stranger. But her common sense chimed in that maybe today a stranger could be safer than the people she had loved.

He looked around behind her like she had appeared out of nowhere or she had some contingent of friends that had joined her.

"Why, I didn't hear you approach. You live around here?" There was caution in his voice and she could tell there was danger in the question. She decided to not hold back.

"Sure do. In fact, I spent almost five days cooped up in that cabin there with a dead man. My mom and dad killed 'em." She pursed her lips and dared him to argue. He didn't respond--not verbally; he just stared at her. She got nervous.

"You don't believe me," she said. She knew he did.

He slowly shook his head.

"No. From what I've seen, you just confirmed my theories. I just can't believe you appeared here and answered all the questions I have been pondering for the last fourteen hours."

He looked stunned and dropped his hands to his sides. He turned away from her for a second and started to walk away. She panicked and began to follow him. She took him by the hand and he turned suddenly, pulling his hand away.

"Give me a sec. Okay?"

She looked up at him, hurt. *What kind of rescue was this*? She nodded, though. She didn't want to lose him, so she trailed just a few feet behind him. After a few moments, he turned around and got on one knee. He was tall, but so was she. He looked her directly in the eyes and she thought she would cry.

"You alright?" He asked. She bit her lip and nodded.

"I'm just hungry. But I don't want to ever go home again."

He looked at her grimly and she understood that was exactly what she was going to do. She was going to lead him there. God wasn't just mean, he had a lousy sense of humor to boot.

"I have some things you can eat. And some water if you're thirsty." That was all he said, but his eyes betrayed his intent. He was going to win her over to taking him there. All he was debating now was if he should take her with him or not.

"Take me with you," she blurted. He looked confused, and maybe just a little angry. She knew it appeared as though she had read his mind, but she didn't have time to wade through the games adults tried to play to manipulate kids.

She was beyond them and she had no tolerance anymore. She was tired and she really didn't want to go back, but if this man could destroy her nightmare, then she would do whatever she needed to do. He didn't have a halo, but Molly could tell that she could trust this man. She had made up her mind before he finished talking.

"What do you mean? You just said..."

"I know what I just said, but I know you want me to show you how to get there. You'll be lost here without me. I might even be lost. I only came back here because I traveled in a circle. Please? Let me come with you?"

He looked at her intently and got up off his knee. He gestured to her to come with him. She moved forward and he spoke again.

"What's your name?"

"Molly Carothers." He nodded and when he got to the porch he reached into a large backpack and took out some bags. He extracted something and then handed her two strips of beef jerky.

"Molly, it is nice to meet you. I wish it was under happier circumstances. My name is Jacob Barclay."

"Thank you Mr. Barclay," she said, nibbling on the jerky. It was salty, but she didn't mind. Her stomach growled and she did her best not to look like the biggest pig in Arkansas. She saw a gun leaning up against a baluster. It looked familiar, like one of Brian's hunting rifles. She looked at him, still nibbling. "Will you kill them?"

He scoffed lightly. He looked sadder.

"I'm not that kind of man, Molly. But, if I have to, I can." She nodded. She understood. In fact, that answer felt more natural than a *Heck Yeah*! She wanted to hug him. He handed her a bag with a tube.

She looked at him, questioning. He took the nozzle and put it to his mouth. He drew in the water and then showed her. He wiped it off with a paper towel and handed it to her. The water was cold and fresh.

"Mmm. Thanks. I didn't realize how thirsty I was."

"When you feel your stomach lurching, often you are more thirsty than hungry. Everyone thinks they need food, but water is more important." He smiled at her, a warm friendly greeting.

"Drink all you want. I have more."

She obliged without shame. Now this was what being rescued should feel like. As she watched him gather his things together and set out some more food for her, she realized with some fear how bedraggled she must look. And she was sure she smelled awful. He hadn't batted an eye or turned up his nose yet. She wanted to take a bath more than anything now.

She looked down at her dingy fingers, her ragged nails, her boy's jeans and t-shirt and was embarrassed. She knew it was petty and vain, but she couldn't help herself.

"Do you know the way back? You said you were lost." He appeared comfortable and calm. But, she could tell he was preparing himself. He probably had a mental checklist.

"I know it's not that way." She looked up the hill where she could still see the log she had sat on just moments ago. "And I know when I came here, I crossed behind the cabin." She pointed with her left hand off at an angle from where they sat on the porch.

"Good. That's what I thought. I couldn't make out individual tracks, but I could see that a path had been slightly worn. Do you come up here often?"

"No." She shook her head. "This was my first time. But I think my parents come up here from time to time."

"Do you have any brothers or sisters?"

"Just Brian. He's older than me."

"Does he know?"

"Yeah." This was one subject she didn't want to share with Mr. Barclay.

"I see. He didn't tell you until it was too late, did he?

She just shook her head. She pleaded with him with her eyes to not ask her any more questions about Brian. She was pretty sure he didn't get it.

"How far to your house, Molly?"

"I dunno. Not far. Less than an hour walk, if we don't get lost."

He nodded and put on his serious adult look. That look that meant that an adult would brook no argument. It was a kinder countenance than she was accustomed, but still carried all the import of her father's aggressive stares after dinner when he wanted her to go to bed.

"I may be forced to deal with this situation in ways that will put your family at risk. I can tell you love your brother very much. Can I count on your help or are you going to get in my way?"

She knew what he was really asking and it offended her a little. She tried not to be insulted, though, because he was being honest. He didn't need a little kid under his feet hindering him when he came to the farm and confronted her parents. She was sure it would get sticky.

He was right. Even though she resented that last meeting with Brian, she still loved him. If it came down to Brian or this strange man, she was pretty sure she knew who she would choose. That thought bothered her. She wanted to be rescued, but it was a conditional feeling. She suspected most adults had similar feelings.

"I won't get in your way, Mr. Barclay. But, I think it will be best that when we get to the farm, I need to get some stuff and get out of there. Can we wait until they leave or something? I don't want them to see me. It might go better for you if you surprise them."

He nodded at that. He hadn't thought of it. He hadn't planned that far ahead yet. He was still making it up as he went.

"I appreciate your honesty and the help. I hadn't considered them being home. If they are home, we can wait and I will let you get what you need and see that you make it safely." He stopped. He almost said home. "Do you have someone you can stay with you can trust?"

She shook her head without thinking. "I don't have family near here and even those back East aren't likely to take me in. Besides, I don't trust them any more than I do my family."

She remembered her uncle and the strange looks he gave her. Molly also remembered that her father had gotten drunk and they had all sat on the porch smoking marijuana until four in the morning talking about pentagrams and explosives.

"Well, let's talk about our plans and maybe get to know each other better before we head out. You full?"

She nodded shyly.

"Great. Well, I can't tell you how glad I am I met you. I imagine you want to get away from this place as badly as I do. Let me get some things and we'll be off. We'll talk on the way." She nodded and waited patiently for him while he rummaged around in the cabin. Shortly, he came out and they trudged off together up the hill behind the cabin. The sun had risen in the east and was at their backs as they crossed the ridge. Soon, they were comfortable with each other and talking naturally like they had been friends for a long time.

CHAPTER NINETEEN

E stella came across the radio, as irritating and grating as
ever. Who married women like that, anyway?

"Billy Joe? Come in. You hear me?"

"Woman, do you not know proper radio protocol yet?"

"Learnt it and forgot it the same day. Anyway, did you
forget the meeting with the Trooper over at the coffee shop?
I just saw him pull in."

"I'm on my way there, Estella," he lied.

"Good. He ain't the patient type. He'll probably make
you pay."

"Thanks. Unit One out."

"Whatever. Get me a day old donut and bring it over a
let me in on the gossip."

He shook his head and turned around. He had been
headed in the other direction. He waved at Mrs. Harrison as
she passed by and Lucy Albrightson, the senior high track
star running down Main Street. Then he saw the café and the
state police cruiser with its oddly old-fashioned lights and its

mismatched colors. Ugliest police cruiser in the country, he thought.

Subconscious, he put his trooper hat on and pulled in. He wasn't actually late yet, so he didn't know what the fuss was about. Then he saw Dr. Johnson's Cadillac. Puzzled, he got out and bumped his head on the door frame. He cursed loudly, drawing the stares of some shoppers across the street. He tipped his hat at them, trying to cover his wince and doing his best to figure out this turn of events.

He didn't like the feeling he had at the pit of his stomach. Ever since he had left Coach Gruber, it had gnawed at him that the coach was a desperate man. He wasn't sure of the nature of the conversation Coach had with the superintendent, but he didn't have to work to hard to guess.

Drew's personal life was encroaching on his professional life. He felt badly that he had gone there to badger him about offensive philosophies for Tommy's sake. That was the last thing his former teammate needed.

He opened the door and its chime rang obnoxiously, warning of his more than obvious entry. He failed to understand why small town folk felt compelled to put a bell above their door. The place was so small, if he opened the door, he could see all the way to the back office and watch Paula washing the dishes in the kitchen.

He saw Charles Nunez, the Arkansas State Trooper in a corner with Dr. Johnson. Neither had looked up when he entered and somehow Billy Joe thought that was a bad sign.

He got the waitress' attention and made a sign of a cup of coffee and pointed to the table where they sat. That was the extent of ordering at Max's Café and Donut Shop. It had ten tables with four chairs each and two booths at the back where

Doc Johnson and Officer Nunez sat. Most were clean and the regulars had their favorites. Several of the chairs were dangerous at best, just one big man like Billy Joe from being firewood. But, the homey atmosphere and dark interior lent themselves well to quiet conversations. There was only one other client in the café at the time and she appeared to be waiting for an order to go.

Charles saw him coming and stood to greet him with a grim smile and a quick glance to his belt. Billy Joe knew what that was; the trooper was interested to see what the sheriff was packing. The glance was quick and he seemed satisfied.

"Sheriff. Thank you for agreeing to meet me and thank you for getting here early. I have business off in Mountain Home in the morning so I appreciate it." Dr. Johnson cleared his throat and stood up as if he were leaving.

"Oh, Dr. Johnson. You can stay. I think the Sheriff here can handle this matter sufficiently. I don't want to intrude on his jurisdiction." Billy Joe was wary. He didn't like the sounds of this. It felt as though he was being set up.

Trooper Nunez didn't care about jurisdiction at all. It sounded like he was trying to pass the buck. He hoped this didn't have something to do with Coach Gruber. He wasn't sure he could be partial. After this afternoon, he had more sympathy for the man than he had for anyone but himself for a long time.

"I think that would be sufficient." He sat down like he was unconvinced. "You want some coffee, Sheriff?"

"Done ordered some from Colene when I came in." It arrived just as he finished. He took it from her with a grin.

"Could I get a dozen donuts for Estella to go? She likes the filled ones."

"Oh, don't use Estella as a scapegoat. We all know you like your glazed, strawberry filled donuts," she said, teasing. Trooper Nunez smiled too as Billy Joe squeezed into the booth, trying not to look sour.

"You just run on back and get me some of those donuts and I'll make sure not to leave your tip under the water glass this time."

"You never could take a joke, Billy Joe," she said, teasing. He usually wasn't embarrassed, but now he could feel his face flush. He sucked in his gut and tried to put on a smile.

He turned to Dr. Johnson who appeared as if he'd been to a particularly rough proctologist.

"So what's up?"

"Well, we'll talk about Dr. Johnson's concerns first. That isn't why we were meeting."

"Alright. Shoot."

"Well," Dr. Johnson began, "we have several students who have not attended school over the past two weeks. We have contacted most of the parents and confirmed everything from illness to family out of town and one family that decided to suddenly home school their children. But, two particular students have not been located. We have been unable to reach their parents and they live in the remotest part of the county. We, and when I say 'we,' I mean the county school district, cannot and will not investigate if we suspect criminal activity."

Billy Joe turned to Trooper and sipped his coffee.

"Well, you are right. It doesn't sound like your jurisdiction." He glanced at the superintendent and gently blew on the coffee. He had burnt his lip. "You gonna tell me who it is and why you suspect criminal activity?"

Dr. Johnson cleared his throat. He was clearly uncomfortable. Billy Joe glanced over his cup at Trooper Nunez. He had a thin smile and was picking at a Danish pastry on his plate.

"They are brother and sister: Brian and Molly Carothers. We aren't sure about the criminal activity part, but Coach Gruber refused to talk to Victor Carothers. He seems to think the man is a militant. We might have a David Karesh on our hands here." Billy Joe saw Trooper Nunez roll his eyes and stare down his coffee. The sheriff learned a valuable lesson right then: don't assume too much. He had been completely off on his guess about the coach's conversation with Dr. Johnson.

"Well, I'm not sure it's that serious," he looked meaningfully over at Nunez, who nodded back, "But it certainly warrants looking into. I can go out there with one of my deputies in the morning. School truancy is a serious matter. The kids are our future."

"Ahem. Gentlemen, I am afraid I am aware that you are pandering to me. The situation is much more serious than a mere truancy problem. Molly Carothers is a good student who is greatly missed by her coaches. She plays three sports at Benson Junior High. And Brian has a project due in wood working shop that Professor Milton had personally helped Mr. Carothers complete. It meant a lot to him and so their extended absences are very curious, to say the least."

Billy Joe concentrated hard and wanted to sound defensive. He came off as phony and dismissive. "Well, Mr. Superintendent. We'll make this a matter of the law and investigate it as thoroughly as we can and use appropriate levels of county resources. If you deem it necessary, we can treat it as a missing person scenario and call in township resources as well."

"That won't be necessary. It is enough that you take me seriously. If there is criminal activity, I assume you will do your duty. I just felt that the State of Arkansas should be appraised of situations where the stockpile of weapons and the solicitation of minors were involved."

"And that would be appropriate, under normal circumstances in a verified situation. Until then, we will revert to jurisdiction." Nunez turned to Billy Joe, "You will immediately update me if the situation requires State or Federal procedures, right Sheriff?"

"Yes sir."

"Good. Now, if you will excuse us, Dr. Johnson, we have some pressing matters of some confidentiality to cover, if you don't mind."

Dr. Johnson rose, seemingly miffed and ready to leave the two self-important men to themselves. Important person that he was himself, he didn't leave a tip or pay for his coffee. Billy Joe noticed Colene hold up her hand as he walked out the door and then put her hands on her hips and huff. Billy Joe chuckled quietly. She noticed and sauntered over to refill his cup.

"Keep your silly chuckling to yourself. I'm putting his coffee on your tab, you big lug." He just smiled and tipped his hat.

"Don't worry about those kids. Family is just probably keeping them out of school because it's fixing to be hunting season, or they are gathering wood for the winter or something. You never know. I've heard theories about old Victor going on two decades now. His old woman drives about the county every once in a while. She's still a hot piece of tail, if I do say so myself. But they're no Karesh or McVey."

Billy Joe shrugged. "If it's all the same, I'll go check it out. Coach is an old friend of mine and I trust his judgment. I think you are right, but if the kids aren't going to school, I need to straighten them out. They are never going to amount to anything if all they do is stay cooped up on that run-down farm."

"If you say so. I think the worst you will find out there is an old guy holed up with a shotgun guarding half an acre of shriveled marijuana plants, if you ask me. But, it's your call."

"Yeah. So you have something to talk to me about?"

"Well, yeah, a couple of things. First, I want to give you this." He pulled a file out of his briefcase on the floor. It had a stamp that said "Official" in red. "You want to glance that over. It shouldn't concern you, but I'm giving copies of that file to every county sheriff in north Arkansas. I would e-mail or fax it, but it seems some of these backwater places don't even have a modern computer."

"Hey! That hurts, Charles. I can't help they won't upgrade the computers.

"Yeah, but you have a nice shiny new squad car."

"It'll outrun your ugly piece of Detroit scrap."

"I don't doubt that." He laughed and then slid the folder closer. "Take a look."

He flipped the folder open and saw several reports. All of them were missing persons and all them were from southern Missouri towns except for one. The missing person on that report was from Fort Smith. He saw the name and froze. It was George Foster, Sally's dad. Evidently, he had been missing for three weeks.

He swallowed hard and felt perspiration form on his head. Confused, he looked up at Trooper Nunez who was leaning back and sipping his coffee again. He had finished the Danish, Billy Joe noticed. Nunez appeared nonplussed. This was routine for him and he didn't count on a reaction from him.

"You recognize any of them? They been through here lately?"

He didn't respond. Billy Joe just looked back down to the folder and shook his head. He read the other names just in case. No one remotely familiar popped out at him. He stared at the picture of George, taken several years ago before the divorce.

George wore a flower print Hawaiian shirt and a bead necklace with an earring in his right ear. He had always maintained a little hippie in him, even wearing tie-dyed shirts and wearing his hair long and back in a braid from time to time. Now he was missing and Coach Gruber was acting depressed.

No one had seen Sally in weeks, but was that so unusual? His mind raced over the possibilities and failed to make a connection with his greatest fear. He could not suspect Drew of murdering George for a thousand reasons. The biggest, though, was that Billy Joe doubted that he, personally, would have ever killed a man over Becky Chastain. That alone was the center of his theory of Drew's innocence and he knew with a growing frustration that it was a weak hook on which to hang his hat.

"Well, let's just say there's been a rash of these in the area. As you can see, some criminal mastermind in our local FBI think tank feels there is a common thread in these 'abductions,' as they're calling them. I think they're drinking too many Red Bulls, but a man's gotta do what a man's gotta do. I don't want to alarm you and I don't want to set you too much at ease because these psychics, or criminologists or whatever they're calling themselves, sometimes hit a home run. I personally think they strike out more, though and puke down their leg doing it. But, hey, who am I, right?"

"Umm. Sure, Charles. So, is this all the info they have on these folks? I mean, do they have full dossiers on them?"

"Sure, why?"

"I just want to have as much information as I can as I make the files," he lied.

"Well, that's just a mock-up and summary, for the sake of the investigation. The FBI is carrying on their own investigation and asking for our help to get the information out locally. Heck, it's been in circulation a week. I was asked to put that one into the file just yesterday before I called you. Seems like he's been sought after by the FBI for a while, anyway." He pointed at George. Billy Joe just stared at the file, a frown drawing his face down.

"You look a little peaked. Are you feeling alright?"

"Yeah. Just feel a cold coming on. That time of year, you know?"

Nunez nodded. He grabbed the file, took the extra copies out, straightened them up, pulled out a small stapler and stapled them together with a whack. He pushed the copies over as Billy Joe sat there numb, his coffee cooling on the table.

"There, you keep those. Let me know if you have any information."

"Yep." The trooper put the file back in his bag and stood up to leave. He left two dollar bills on the table, smiled at the sheriff and started to leave.

"Charles."

He turned, a questioning look on his face.

"You said there were two things you wanted to talk to me about. What was the other one?"

Trooper Nunez laughed, his head going back and his hand going naturally to his baton.

"Yeah. There was that other thing." Nunez leaned over and put a meaty hand down on the table and lowered his voice. He glanced from side to side as if he didn't want anyone to hear. Problem was, he did, Billy Joe realized. "You know that porn star from up here, what's her name?"

"Sally?"

"Yeah. That's it. I've got a guy up at the station who is getting married. You think she'll do a bachelor party?"

Billy Joe swallowed hard and tried to keep the disgusted look off of his face. He didn't need this kind of trouble. Several seconds seemed to click off and Billy Joe desperately reached inside of himself to come up with the right answer.

"You know, I think she wouldn't. Ever since the coach broke up with her, she has taken to the straight and narrow."

"Hmm. That's too bad. Well, she was just a back up anyway. Tom over at Fort Smith said he could hook us up with some of the club girls. I was just trying to save a buck on a local gal is all."

"Can't blame you. Have some fun."

"You, too you old tub o'lard." It hurt, but Billy Joe laughed and watched as he left.

"He's the biggest jerk in the state," Colene said as she poured some more coffee in his cup. He looked up at her, sympathetic. She blew him a kiss and walked away.

He sat there a little longer, nursing his coffee and waiting on Colene to bring the donuts. He wondered how Charles hadn't noticed the connection between George Foster and his daughter Sally. Maybe it was because the trooper only knew her by her last name, Sails. It was the name she adopted after George's divorce. It was her mother's maiden name and served double duty as a stage name for her movies. He shook his head and pulled a wadded up ten dollar bill out of his wallet.

He believed the next day or so might prove to be interesting. He wasn't sure he was ready for this much drama.

CHAPTER TWENTY

B rian sat under the shed porch, a limp squirrel in his left
hand, his Old Timer pocket knife in his right. He
stared out into the pouring rain and listened to the rhythm of
the downpour on the tin roof of the porch.

He glanced down at the squirrel, the fourth one he was
skinning, and grimaced. Its head was tilted back, its two
front teeth protruding from its mouth, its front legs splayed to
either side with blood speckling the fur on its back, sticking
to his palm. He placed the blade at its throat and pretended
to slice across its windpipe. He imagined how easy it would
be to do that to his father the next time he fell asleep on the
couch in the den. He imagined the trail of dark red that
would flow as he awoke, choking, his arms flailing and his
eyes wide with horror.

He had seen this grisly scene played out in his mind for
the last three years. He had only recently known that
someone could be capable of actually pulling it off. He had
witnessed his father murdering a man in just such a way.
The man was a burly, hairy guy with a full beard and straggly

clothes. Brian figured he was a hobo. It didn't matter. Brian remembered the gloves the man wore. They looked hand-knitted like someone would get from their grandmother for Christmas.

At the time all he could only think that this man had family somewhere. In thinking about family, he was inevitably reminded about the state of his family. Brian was smart enough to realize that his parents were sick. Despite all she had done, he loved his mother and wanted the best for Molly, but he couldn't help think that maybe that all of this sickness was to be his legacy.

He had read about families like his and knew that other sons in his position were doomed. They became mentally unstable, tried to become the hero and died in the process or eventually repeated the ugly cycle. It was either in his blood or it wasn't.

When he was reminded of blood, he remembered the wolf cub he had kept two years ago. He had killed its mother out on the mountain one cold winter, the snow falling around him and his twelve gauge still smoking from the three shots he had pumped through it in rapid succession.

As he was gathering the mother wolf's carcass with numb hands and numb heart, he noticed the cub huddled shuddering at the mouth of a small cavern in the side of the mountain about twenty yards away. He had lured the young female wolf and had kept her as a pet for a year. Molly had become attached to the cub and had named it Vixen. Brian was opposed to this, knowing that the wolf was still wild at heart. Plus, he didn't want his parents to find out they had been hiding it in the shed for the winter.

One day the next fall, Brian arrived home and the wolf was hanging over the entrance to the shed, its pelt stripped and the animal's muscles and skeleton exposed. He knew that his father had suspected something. He instinctively understood that his father was sending a message in his usual sick and twisted way. If he didn't bury Vixen before Molly returned, he would have to console her for weeks. It was going to be hard enough to lie to her and tell her Vixen had returned to the woods.

He had been right. Molly wandered off several times over the next month looking for Vixen, calling for her until it got too dark and returned home with her eyes red and swollen and breathing in heaves. Over the next year, she had gone farther and farther afield, skipping school and traveling far off at night with only the light of the moon to guide her.

It was on one of these treks recently that she had happened upon the cabin. Brian knew in the back of his mind that it was all his fault. Despite what he knew about his parents, he felt that the awful truth was that in the back of his mind, what had happened to Vixen didn't really register as a tragedy to him. He was emotionally unaffected by its death. He was only mildly concerned about his sister and her reaction. Even though he blamed himself indirectly for leading her into stumbling upon the cabin by telling Molly a lie, he didn't regret it the way he thought maybe he should.

So, sitting there holding the cold, stiffening corpse of the squirrel, Brian wondered why he wasn't affected by all this death. In fact, it all seemed to be leading him to one thing. He was consumed by thoughts of murdering his father.

With a pall in his cheeks, Brian realized that all could be made better. Somehow making his father pay for all the pain and turmoil that he had caused seemed...right.

Brian spent little time worrying about missing school or how Molly was faring in the cabin. He could care little about her fascination with wolves and the moon. He could care less about his mother and father's sadistic, glorified cannibalism and vampire worship. He didn't care that he was abandoned, mistreated, malnourished, beaten, molested, or that his youth had been stolen. He was obsessed with the blood. The blood he knew needed to be spilled, the blood that would make his world right.

He felt strongly that events were wildly spinning toward a culmination. He could feel the hand of fate pushing him, could feel the heat in his chest at the conviction that was growing in his mind and soul. He must be a tool of his fate. He must accept the legacy that had been successfully handed to him by the blood that he shared with his parents. It was this blood that would make retribution for the sins of his entire family. A flicker of hope blossomed in his chest and he felt relief and purpose wash over him.

And then he looked down again at the poor rodent in his hand. He had squeezed its neck and its head hung loosely by a flap of stubborn skin and fur. He felt the wetness of tears fall down his cheek. He was wondering if he were crying for the squirrel, for himself or for his fate. That is when he heard the wet patter of feet in the yard and a woman's sob. He recognized the sounds as his mother despite never having heard her cry or run. He dropped the squirrel and raced to the front lawn.

He saw her just as he rounded the shed. She hadn't noticed him and in that instant, he saw his mother in a different light. It was as if time was frozen and he was able to note everything he had missed about his mother. She was completely soaked. Her hair was plastered to her face and her mouth was drawn in horror. But her eyes were different. She looked scared and angry at the same time. Her eyes burned with a flare of hatred and malice.

It was a side of his mother that he had never witnessed. She had never been a doting mom, but he didn't recognize this woman. Sure, it was the same clothes she wore every time she went "hunting." But, the way they hugged her form, she seemed older, more vulnerable than he had ever seen her. Yet, her eyes did not seem to convey this weakness of spirit.

He felt like he had caught her in a revealing moment. She appeared deliberate, like an actress who knows her next lines are the most important in the scene and she is steeling herself to emit the emotions that the lines require. Her gaze was strange mix of confidence and fear.

It was the same stare of the mother wolf as she had crouched near the cave entrance, her teeth bared in a snarl, her feral eyes daring Brian to come closer. He had shot her, knowing she was being protective, knowing she was dangerous. It had proven he was worthy, taking the life of another hunter. At that moment, he knew that his destiny included another hunter. He felt the strong pull at his chest. He could not look at his mother the same way. He realized that her weakness was that she had never stopped it; she had let it escalate. She had been selfish and careless. And Brian could not let her live.

This realization came in a rush of shame, regret and conviction. He was a hunter. It was in his blood and he had proven his skill and cunning before. Now he had to muster the heart to do what he must do. He turned his grimace into a look of concern and called out.

"Mom! You alright?" He could already hear his father's clumsy clodding approach.

The door to the living room burst open, the hinges creaking.

"Oh! The car! I need help!"

His father cursed and rushed up to her as Brian came around and flanked them. He could hear their pulses. He could feel their heat. He could smell their fear. They cursed each other and his mother explained in a rush of words and sobs what had happened. Brian listened, not caring. He just stood there numbly, hoping he could be brave when the time came. He was afraid he would not know when the time was right. He may only have one chance. Something in his gut told him it would be soon.

He stood there, the rain pelting him, soaking his flannel shirt and making his jeans feel like they weighed ten pounds. His hands were loose at his sides and he could feel how ready his body was to act. That was strange because in his mind, he was still struggling with doubt and insecurity. What would the future hold? What would happen to Molly? Where would he go? But his muscles were ready. He could feel the steady beat of his heart, a beat that belied his turmoil.

Of course, his parents barely noticed. Their anger and disappointment with each other was boiling over. He was sure the pelting rain and the blowing wind did not help the situation, either. They snarled at each other. He could see the veins on his father's neck pulsing. His mother was trying to be soothing, but was bungling the attempt. Her hatred and anger kept her from articulating her logical statements. She spoke through clenched teeth, her voice seething, her chest heaving with the effort to keep herself under control.

This distraction would prove convenient, he was sure. He just had to know when it was the right time. He knew he would need something deadlier than his pocket knife and was searching mentally for the best way to maneuver back to the house to get his dad's revolver, or possibly the Model 1911 he kept hidden in the drawer above his closet. That would be tricky.

As he anxiously planned these things, he forced his body to relax. Although they were engaged in a heated discussion, now was definitely not the time to start a ruckus. He might catch them off guard for a moment, but when they were this aggressive, it wouldn't take much time to unleash their anger on him. He decided it would be wise to pay attention and wait until he was beckoned to go to the house or to help in the rescue efforts.

He took the time then to observe his parents. He noted the color of his Mom's skin. It was whiter than usual, and her lips were almost black. Her eyes were tinged red with desperation, lack of sleep and blinking away the rain. He noticed his father as well. The skin on his face sagged in a way that told the story of the years he had spent frowning. He had only seen his father smile occasionally and he always seemed sadistic and cruel. The frown he wore at most times was preferable to his smile. It creeped Brian out.

"So, what do you want me to do, then?" His father had his hands on his hips and his gut was protruding over his belt. His mother smirked.

"Whatever you want. I don't care anymore, Victor." The ice from her steely eyes almost made Brian shiver. Something was changed about his mother and he thought he could tell what it was. But his father seemed not to notice.

"Well, I suppose Brian and I can go and fetch the car. The tractor is running again and we can haul it on in and put it into the garage." Victor glanced at Brian, his eyes hard, a warning. "Go put some diesel in the tractor and get it warmed up, boy." Brian hated him more, but nodded obediently and shuffled off toward the barn, his ears alert.

He could hear the catch in his father's breath. Something Patsy had said had gotten through to him. As Brian turned away, he could noticeably see a change in his father. His stance changed and he licked his lips.

"You got me a present, huh?" He seemed calm, but wired. He was no longer angry at Patsy, but his head was bowed forward and his mouth drooped slack, spittle coating his thick beard. Brian recognized that gaze. It was hunger.

"It depends. We have to talk first. You need to have Brian go fetch Molly from the cabin and we need to sit down and hash this all out." Brian trotted through the rain toward the barn. His mother sounded sane for the first time in years. But behind the words, interlaced with her voice, Brian could hear the threat, the evil intent.

Brian's mind worked hard over his plan and the more he pondered his actions, the more his mother figured prominently in his freedom. She just wasn't going to be aware of it.

CHAPTER TWENTY-ONE

T he distance to the moon was ingrained in her brain. Not such a funny thing, she felt. She thought about as many mundane items as she could. She had to take her mind off of their destination. Molly trotted along, trying to keep up with Jacob. He didn't say much. He would glance back from time to time, his eyebrows raised, to ask her if she was alright. Well, she was and wasn't at the same time.

Her gut wrenched at the thought of seeing her father and mother again. As much as she wanted to be away from them, she needed them, too.

She couldn't explain it, but being around Jacob made her feel safe. He exuded calm, an invisible sense of peace. She looked again, half expecting big white wings to spring from under his jacket or a halo to don his baseball-capped head.

But, he just turned again, smiling mischievously.

"You need to stop?" he asked, his breath pluming in the brisk mountain air. Molly shook her head.

"You need something to eat?" Molly loved the way his mouth turned up at the edges when he spoke. It was such a happy face, the face of an angel.

"No. Just thinking, that is all."

"Ok. Well, we should stop up there around that shelf and get our breath." He pointed up the slope they were on. Over the melting mist of the morning, Molly could see a bare spot through the trees. "If you need a rest before then, let me know. Ok?"

They had spent the first hour or two talking. She wasn't interested in sharing any more. Every question was sensitive; every thought reminded her of why she didn't want to go back. The sooner they got to the house, the better. She wanted to get this nightmare behind her. Jacob needed to know what he was up against, she knew, but she had given him everything he needed.

The only thing she had left out were details about Brian. She realized that she had forgiven Brian already and felt like she needed to protect him. If the two of them could make it out of this together, they could start over. It was time for them to start looking out for each other.

Her long-term hope was Brian. Her immediate hope was Jacob. She couldn't afford to risk one for the other. As far as she was concerned, she needed both. She needed a concerned stranger willing to risk his life for her and she needed a family member that she had always looked up to.

*　　　*　　　*　　　*

Jacob trudged along, his mind going over details, his spirit uneasy with the way things were playing out. He wished he had his phone. Jacob had a tickling feeling down his spine and his brain kept telling him that he didn't need to get involved.

Something in his heart told him Molly wasn't telling him everything. He knew that instinctively, of course, but he didn't have a compulsion to put her through more agony. Sometimes the truth hurt more than was necessary. He kept telling himself that he was capable enough to see this through.

The problem was he didn't know what the end would look like. Often, he would try to visualize the outcome of a situation and backtrack from that image to arrive at steps he needed to take to get there. It was a positive action technique taught to him by Lieutenant Bingham.

But here, in this place and in this situation, Jacob struggled to visualize how his role in this drama would be beneficial. He no longer was an officer of the law. Although he was qualified, he had no business being here. He was a foreigner, an outsider with nothing at stake except ethics and morals; and his life.

Plus, the doubts kept creeping in, no matter how hard he tried. He pushed them away and focused on the next step. He supposed that was why he felt so uncomfortable. The hike was making him sweat, but it was the realization that he was marching ahead into unknown territory that was giving him the chills.

He glanced back again, aware that Molly was watching him closely. He supposed that she was scared of being left alone. He knew she trusted him, but certainly a young girl exposed to the things she had experienced would naturally have doubts about the intentions of adults. He had tried to assure her he wanted only to make sure what had happened in the cabin wouldn't happen again.

He considered that for a second and realized with a jolt that his actual intentions were much darker than that. He knew if he needed to kill Molly's parents, he could. He had not needed to take a life in the line of duty often. It wasn't something he readily wanted to repeat. He understood that he would despise the outcome but he would not regret the action.

Still, Jacob wanted mostly to get out of this alive and to bring this murderous family to justice. He was out of his jurisdiction and out of his comfort zone. What had begun as an exercise in survival had turned suddenly and irrevocably into a bad horror flick.

Jacob felt sympathy for Molly. However, he could not shake the feeling that she was behaving strangely in some way. He couldn't put his finger on it. She seemed adjusted, had seemed frank and mildly disturbed, but had taken all the horrific events and terrible experiences with maybe too much aplomb.

He didn't know if that was a coping mechanism or was indicative of her de-sensitivity to such atrocities. For the third time in a week he wished Alice had tagged along. He needed her to sort these things out. His instincts were good, but sometimes not enough.

Molly labored behind him. She was tired, but determined. She was what he and his childhood friends would call a tomboy. Even though she seemed tough and adjusted, he could tell that under all that veneer, she was scared. At least that was what he hoped she felt.

He couldn't imagine what it would be like. When she had recounted the story of finding the corpse in the room with her parents, he was struck at how much detail she recalled without a hitch in her voice or a tear in her eye. Her recollection had been almost clinical. It was as if she were chronicling an episode of a Billy and Mandy cartoon.

"Hey, tough stuff," Jacob turned his torso as he continued to climb. He noted that Molly was leaning more heavily on her staff. "What are your favorite cartoons?"

She looked up, her eyes bright but distant. Her mind was elsewhere.

"Cartoons? Those are for kids. I watch baseball and basketball when I can. We don't own a television. Dad said it is just propaganda." She had used the past tense, he noticed. She really *did* want to distance herself.

"I see. What do you think?"

She shrugged.

"I don't know. Other kids watch television and they don't seem as messed up as me. So, I dunno. Maybe propaganda isn't that bad. I never understood what he meant, anyway. Besides, the only thing I'm interested in watching on TV is sports and only when it's raining or I can't play."

"Gotcha."

They continued to trudge ahead and soon were resting at the clearing they had seen from down the hill. Their breathing was ragged and both took long drags of water from Jacob's camel pack. He had considered asking Molly to bear some of the extra load, but decided quickly against it.

She was certainly tough enough, but would be too proud to complain when it got to be too much for her. He needed her fresh. She already had enough burdens weighing her down as it was.

As Molly rested against a tree, her head back and her eyes closed, Jacob decided to give her some space and moved off to the edge of the clearing. He took out his binoculars, the map and compass. As he was glassing the northern slope opposite of them, he saw a road that curved around the side of that hill and into what appeared to be a large pasture. He could see tall grass waving off in the distance between the gap between the hill closest to them and the next.

He was sure that road would lead them to the Carothers' farm. It was getting close to noon and he decided to get things straight before heading off that way. He noted the sky and realized with a start that the weather might be turning against them again. Taking note of some landmarks and orienting himself on the map, he put away his gear and trotted back to where Molly waited.

"Hey, you wanna keep marching on or do you need a break?" He regretted the question as soon as it came out. He saw her brow furrow and her mouth turn down. He had wounded her. Just a small wound, under normal circumstances. Though, in situations like this, any nick in the outward veneer kids put up to convince themselves they are tougher than they are would hurt them deeper than usual.

Molly dusted off her trousers as she stood up, her shoulders straightening and her eyes narrowed.

"Sure. You need some rest? I mean, you're carrying all the stuff. I can carry some, too if you need me." It wasn't an offer but a challenge.

"Of course. I could use some help. How are your eyes?"

Molly shrugged. "Pretty good, I suppose."

Jacob handed her the binoculars. "I need you to keep your eye out for that road over there and plot us a course to get there before that storm." He pointed to both.

"That's not much. You want me to carry more?"

"No. That thing has been chafing my neck and my eyes aren't as good as they used to be. It will give you a chance to be my navigator."

"That would be great if I knew where I was and how to get back."

Jacob smiled reassuringly. "You will do just fine. So, you ready, then?"

"Yeah. I suppose. Can I have some more jerky to chew on while we walk?"

"Want to carry the canteen, too? The jerky has a lot of salt in it and it will make you thirsty."

"That would be great." She looked up at him with gratitude as he handed over the canteen and the plastic bag of jerky. Jacob was relieved that he had seemed to smooth things over so quickly.

He wondered again at the fate that had brought them together. It was an odd circumstance and he couldn't help but to feel a heightened sense of responsibility for this young girl who was so fragile and yet so resilient.

As they started off down the slope toward the road up ahead, Jacob glanced at Molly as she took the lead. He knew it was wise to allow her to set the pace. He wished he had thought of it earlier. When it came to being considerate for other people, he had gotten out of practice. Possibly, he had never developed the knack at all. Maybe that was his problem all along. Again, his thoughts drifted to Janice and his children. Perhaps it was too late for some revelations to make a difference. Maybe he could find a way to make it all up to them someday.

The rain came moments later as they wended their way along the side of a steep embankment. The road ahead was lost in the haze of the rain and the fog that rose out of the valley below them. Jacob knew that if they kept the slope to their right and made their way down the valley, they would come to a small draw between the two hills and that would take them directly to the small meadow and the road.

He wiped away the rain and tried not to step on Molly. The visibility was terrible. He could see her wet hair hanging in strings down the t-shirt plastered to her back. He reached into his pack and withdrew the top of the rain suit. He cursed himself silently for not considering that sooner. It seemed he was learning all sorts to things today. As he reached for her shoulder to let her know she could use the jacket, he felt the world slip out from under him.

The world spun as he slid. He was looking up at one moment, the rain pelting his face directly. Then, so quickly, it was absurd, his nose was buried in mud and leaves.

He managed to grasp a root as he fell, instinctually reaching out for the earth to stop his spinning and sliding. His body was buffeted as his knee struck sharply against a large rock. He let go of everything to grab hold of something to save himself. The rifle slid across the bank and was perched precariously just above him.

He hung in the air suspended above a small cliff with several sharp boulders in a ravine below him. He kicked himself mentally. He hadn't seen this washout earlier. In the rain and fog he had slipped right over the edge.

The end of a stick poked him in the head. He looked up to see Molly offering him the end of her walking staff. She had a strained look on her face, but was smiling. He couldn't imagine why. The binoculars hung from her neck, pointing at the ground as she leaned over to extend the staff within his reach.

"You gonna take the stick or am I going to have to jump over the cliff and catch you when you fall?"

Jacob laughed. It came out like a bad cough. The strain of holding himself by one hand was wearing on him. He took hold of her staff with his left hand and put his feet against the wall of the cliff and climbed up onto the embankment.

He had one moment of slipping and worried he would go back over the edge and take Molly with him. Soon, he was on the bank, seated, his head between his knees.

Molly sat beside him chuckling softly. She was nibbling on a piece of jerky. He looked over at her and marveled.

She winked at him. "Here I thought you were saving me. I guess we're even, huh?"

Jacob smiled. The fall would have been disastrous, but not fatal. But she was right. He needed her strength and her courage as much as she needed him. Remembering his father's one gesture of care and camaraderie, Jacob reached over and ruffled Molly's wet hair.

"Yeah, you're right." He looked at the rain jacket on the bank. It was covered with mud and the sleeve was ripped. He pointed at it. "I was going to give you the jacket when I slipped."

Molly looked across at him, affection softening her features, a dimple and tear punctuating her smile. "I know. I don't need it. I'm already wet. But thanks."

Jacob looked away and sighed. It was an awkward moment. He heard Molly get up with a small cough and when he looked back, she was offering him her hand.

"You ready to go already?"

"I'm ready to get out of this rain and change my clothes. I feel yucky. I think I could sleep for a week straight." Jacob smiled.

"I know what you mean."

"You want me to lead again, or should I watch your back?" Jacob couldn't suppress his chuckle.

"I'll be fine."

They trudged off with purpose and conviction. Forgotten in the excitement, Jacob's rifle slid down the embankment and tumbled to the shelf below. No one noticed.

CHAPTER TWENTY-TWO

S herriff Shoemaker put the file on the passenger seat and sat back. Pursing his lips and exhaling sharply, he regretted he had lost sleep thinking about what may amount to the largest criminal case he had ever undertaken. He felt woefully underprepared. All the television crime dramas in America didn't help him deal with the possibility that he might actually face at some point in his career an actual homicidal murderer.

His career had been marked by policing minor criminal activities: underage alcohol consumption, thievery, illegal firearm discharge and the all-too-common domestic abuse. He had never even dreamed he would ever be challenged by a homicide case that was both this foreign and familiar.

He *knew* George. Billy Joe was aware he was involved with criminal activity: pornography, minor drug solicitation, gambling, and prostitution even. All these crimes were tied indirectly or implicitly to the large crime syndicates out of Hot Springs.

These were the same folks that had overseen criminal activity all the way back to Chicago, New York and Las Vegas. The cliché mob bosses were an actuality even in Arkansas. George wasn't Sicilian, but he knew how to turn a buck whether it was legal or not. His connections had always provided opportunities and his lack of conscience was exactly the vehicle that was required to pull off illegal activities.

Most of these crimes had been carried out in his county, under his nose. He had let George slide, thinking they were, in essence, petty. Besides, for as greedy and unscrupulous George was, he was also generous. He donated to the local health clinic, the First Methodist Church, the Diabetes Foundation, and supported the local high school sports teams.

Everyone realized, surely, George wasn't altruistic. His every move was designed to give legitimacy to his car dealership and his other smaller businesses. For every Little League team that got their uniforms and post-game ice creams donated by George's Chevrolet dealership, an eighteen year old girl somewhere in Northern Arkansas was being prostituted with the promise of a movie contract. For every golf tournament sponsored by George's Farmer's Insurance branch with proceeds going to the new Science wing addition to Franklin Junior High, a fourteen-year old kid was buying his first dime bag of weed grown on one of George's partner's farms.

Sooner or later, the joke went, George would bite off more than he could chew. As debts mounted and his candle burned at both ends, George moved on to greener pastures. His wife left him, his daughter became addicted to drugs and his "legitimate" businesses couldn't sustain either his lifestyle or his creditors.

He left his car business to a long-time friend who shared what little profit was left over. George then moved to Fort Smith. He hoped that he could compete with the west coast porn companies by offering the girls in the south the same opportunity without having to move to Los Angeles to compete. At least, that was the talk at the coffee house.

George had fallen so far he had even convinced his meth-addicted daughter to come be his main starlet. The movies sold online for $16 and came in brown manila envelopes with Arkansas Razorback decals. Billy Joe had seen one passed around at a city hall banquet with smiles and winks and avid nods. He tried to ignore all this but it was there.

Now, George was missing. Perhaps he *had* bitten off more than he could chew. Maybe that was it and it would be up to some police chief in Fort Smith or a federal officer in Hot Springs or Little Rock to get to the bottom of it. Maybe that was what he deserved.

But, Billy Joe couldn't get the sour taste out of his mouth. It had all gone down under his watch. He hadn't been involved, hadn't overtly condoned it, but he hadn't stopped it, either. He had known. When opportunities arose for him to investigate, what had been his excuse to look the other way? He remembered. He had thought *Who's the victim? If no one is calling and complaining, why should I poke my nose in?*

Why indeed. He had been an accomplice. Most of the town had known and done nothing. But, he was the biggest sinner of all, perhaps bigger than George himself because

George had no guilt. Billy Joe was riddled with it. And now it paralyzed him.

He could feel his back pressing into the leather seat, could feel that small circle of sweat at the small of his back despite the cool weather. He watched the windshield, mesmerized by the falling rain and the rhythmical cadence of the wipers. He blinked rapidly, held his hands up to his face and tilted his head back until it touched the headrest.

He sat like that until the morning sun rose and the rain dissipated. He hated sleeping in his vehicle but he couldn't go into the house. He knew what he would do. He was ashamed at his weakness; he was aware that the bottle was winning.

The one way to overcome, to conquer Jack Daniels, Jose Cuervo or his old friend Bud was to let them have their space. They had their dwelling and he had his. The squad car had become his home, his sanctuary, his one place of purity. In it he could uphold the law, could solve world problems and overcome the urge to drown his fears and disappointments in alcoholic stupor.

He shook his head and wiped his face violently. He picked up his hat from the dash, knowing the little hair he had left was sticking up rakishly. He wanted to be presentable when he entered the coffee shop, sleep crusting his eyes, his uniform wrinkled and smelling faintly of the muskiness of his skin. He needed the coffee to feel right again. He needed it to clear his mind and get his plan straight.

The engine revved and he pulled away from the curb. The town was just coming to life. The rain had scrubbed away the grime of the small town. It would soon be replaced by the mud from the farmers coming to town for their usual

Friday business dealing, the kids throwing away their wrappers, the occasional dirty diaper alongside the road or the inevitable skunk smashed flat by every vehicle that passed.

It seemed this was a metaphor for his town. Even if he cleaned up this county, someone would come back and just trash it all up again. It would never end. So why bother with the small stuff?

Suddenly, he felt sorry for that cop he had met four days before. At the time, Billy Joe had felt resentment and a strange feeling of envy. Now, he understood that maybe living here where almost nothing happened was a blessing. Billy Joe was sure he couldn't handle the depression that would haunt him in a big city where the realities of the seedy parts of society would eventually wear him down. There wouldn't be a squad car big enough to contain that kind of hurt, that kind of guilt and disappointment. It wasn't a wonder that so many professional lawmen needed regular psychiatry.

The Buffalo cop had deserved some respect, not a bogus "warning" that only served to stroke the ego of a small-time, self-pitying, Podunk America county sheriff. He wished he could do things differently, the least of which was give a stranger a hard time. He considered these things as he passed the Faith Beginnings Christian Church. He saw the minister climbing the wet steps carefully, his corduroys sweeping against his old legs in the light morning breeze.

Repentance had been a theme the Sheriff had heard several times when he had warmed a pew. He would do his rounds: the First Lutheran over on Grand, the Apostles of Christ on Virginia Avenue and the Faith Bible Church out on

Robert Michael

Dawson Creek Road. He had gone to his mother's congregation, a withering old Church of God, for several years. He had tired of the same sermons, the same antiseptic-smelling folk, the same pot lucks, the same softball league. None of it seemed to dent him. He always felt above it or beyond it, somehow.

Now he strongly felt the draw to make things right. He couldn't do things over but he could do things differently. Surely, God would understand that.

He had always held the pistol of death steady. He had just never pulled the trigger. He was driven by the pain of his life of disappointment. His head would be filled with the rage, the pain of loss, abandonment and scorn he had received. Billy Joe felt he deserved more. He wanted more.

It was only in small moments that he felt right. He had experienced enough pleasure from life to be enraged by the rest. Times spent with Tommy or when the Cowboys won a big game or when the sun fell just right over his porch were offset by nights where all he could remember was the smell of the cigarettes on her breath and the feeling of her hands draped absently across his midsection. It was at moments like these--more common of late it seemed—Billy Joe was tempted to keep pouring the warm caramel whiskey until he passed out, until it replaced the blood that pumped through his corrupted, wounded heart.

Only two other cars were parked at the diner. He shut the door and ducked his head as he entered numbly into the coffee shop. He tipped his hat to Bucky Spencer and smiled wanly at Ned Becker and made his way to his usual morning table. Sylvia, assigned the early duty on Friday's at the coffee shop, gave him a warm glance. She raised an empty cup and her eyebrows in a wordless question.

"Yup. And a cream-filled Danish, if you've got some," he called back. He sat down without bothering to take off his hat. The folder fell open on the table and he began to leaf through it again.

When Sylvia returned with a steaming cup of coffee the color of mud and just as thick, Billy Joe barely registered her appearance. He nodded and kept staring at the document. It was all there. The feds had compiled a pretty accurate picture of George and it seemed that half their interest in the man was to find out if his connections had finally come to cash in their chips.

Billy Joe could deduce that the feds believed that George's disappearance and those of the others in the dossier were connected to mob activity out of Hot Springs. It wasn't overt, but enough references were there in the document and Billy Joe was intelligent enough to read between the lines.

Billy Joe looked again at the other faces. None were familiar. He took out his regional map that showed southern Missouri, northwest Arkansas, and eastern sections of Kansas and Oklahoma. He had marked the residences with red marker. It was easy to see that the majority of the locations of the victims were in a fan shape across southern Missouri and into Kansas. It wasn't his job to solve the crimes. But, George was *his* problem. The others were somehow linked, evidently, and if he could figure out how, maybe he could figure out if George was truly gone or just hiding.

And then there was the Carother family. He had made a commitment to investigate mostly to assist the coach. The superintendent was paranoid and Trooper Nunez was probably right. Billy Joe expected to find a family that was covering up some secret stash of illegal drugs or some domestic perversion. They didn't want prying public eyes near their farm, he was positive.

He was familiar with Victor Carothers, but only cursory. No one had seen the man in several years. He didn't attend his children's events, didn't come to town for groceries, farming supplies or hunting gear. Although his behavior was strange, hermits and folks that just wanted to be left alone were not uncommon in northwest Arkansas.

Billy Joe shut the folder and downed the rest of his coffee. Sylvia had dropped off the tab. It read "No danishes today. Sorry. Coffee on the house." The smiley face at the bottom of the tab gave him an odd pang.

"Thanks, Sylvia. I owe you one," he said as he picked up the folder and started for the door. She winked at him and he left the warmth of the coffee shop and came face-to-face with the moist, chilly Arkansas Friday morning. The fog had begun to clear and the wind had begun to push the remaining wisps into the dark gray sky. He decided that he should turn over some stones and see if he could find some of George's connections. Then, tomorrow morning, he would make the trip to the Carother place to perform what he was sure was to be a fruitless investigation. At least he could say he had tried.

CHAPTER TWENTY-THREE

V ictor sat in his recliner, smelling the mustiness and the layers of years of accumulation of dust. His senses were finely attuned to his surroundings. He felt a tingle at his neck. He assumed what he was feeling was anticipation of his hunt. Patsy had promised him an opportunity to turn a victim loose so that he could track him through the dark, damp woods. He wanted to feel the beauty of the hunt, feel the heat of victory as he stood hunched over the steaming body of his victim, his sacrifice.

He wanted to do this and he realized his whole body was shaking just considering the prospect of it. The time was close now and he silently prayed for the darkness to come. For with the darkness came immense power. He could feel his pulse quicken at the thought of how he could snap the victim's neck as he poised over him, his teeth tearing at the tender neck, his eyes wide and hungry.

He realized he was grasping the sides of the recliner so hard his fingers were buried to the wood beneath the cloth. Victor was not prone to emotion, but his eyes brimmed with tears at the thought of how loving a provider his wife could be to him. He was gracious, but his sentiment was tinged with the lust for the hunt. He listened for Patsy's footsteps as she came down the stairs behind him. He glanced up to see her boots.

He got up as she came around the bottom step to greet him with a lascivious grin. She and Victor stepped out the front door, the screen door slapping shut behind them. She had his hand in his and it was cold. Victor could feel his strength come, feel the calm and warmth of his convictions. He noted the clammy coldness of his wife's palm, but looked into the moist air around him as if he had come out of a dream.

He could hear Brian bring the tractor around to the front yard. Victor watched from the porch as Brian parked and dismounted. Brian walked toward the shed and Victor could see the animal grace, the sway and posture of a predator. Victor had been like that.

A hand was on his shoulder and Victor tensed. Discipline kept him from moving. He turned and looked down at Patsy, her face cleaned, the blood from her lips wiped away. She looked scrubbed and pasty. It made her appear as a mannequin, a fake. He imagined he could see right through her as if she were a slightly opaque glass doll.

"You want me to come along with you two? I feel better now that I've had time to get into some fresh clothes." He noticed she had put on some jeans, boots and an old blouse. Strangely, she was wearing his old hunting jacket as well. It was wool.

"Suit yourself. It looks like the rain is gone, but a chill is in the air. As wet as you were, you're likely to get ill."

"I'm as tough as leather. Besides, maybe it's not a good idea that Brian sees too much of what I got." Victor noted the sensual intonation. He felt like a rabbit, the carrot dangling there by the cage, knowing something was wrong, but tempted nonetheless. But, he wasn't a rabbit. Not by a long shot. He smiled lewdly and took her hand. It was still cold.

As he looked toward the shed, he glanced back at Patsy. A smug, satisfied look played at her features.

"Brian's got the tractor running. We better get back there soon. I'm not sure we have enough diesel to make the trip. How far back did you say you wrecked it?"

"Um. It's just after that last hill where the oak sits below the road. I spun the stupid thing on those bald tires and ended up smashing into the oak."

"Well, don't worry. It could happen to anyone in this weather. We'll go get it back and see if I need to get us a new one. Bart down in Fox Glen owes me a favor; maybe we can work something out," he said, doing his best to console her. He owed her for this. The least he could do was to be civil, despite the gnawing feeling he was getting in his gut. He forced his mind to focus on the impending hunt. It is what he lived for.

Patsy nodded. "Thanks for understanding."

Victor smiled. "Why wouldn't I? It's easy to roll a vehicle on a dirt road in the rain, even for a seasoned driver. Sometimes things just get away from you, that's all. We can't control everything all the time, right?"

Brian walked past them and then noticed them on the porch. He looked perplexed and guilty, Victor noted. He made a mental note to watch him carefully from now on. It was exciting to him to be a part of this game. "Your ma's coming too. You're walking, just so you know."

Brian nodded, hate pouring from his eyes. He managed a shaky grin and put his hands in his pockets and turned up the road, his head bent.

Victor looked at Patsy and stepped down into the muddy yard. He bowed like a gentleman, straight at the waist, his left hand behind his back, his right hand sweeping in front of him.

"Madam, your chariot waits." Patsy chuckled and held out her hand. He took it and led her to the tractor. It rumbled and sputtered and spewed forth oily filth. He smiled at Patsy as he hoisted her into the bench seat.

She scooted back, adjusted her jeans, wiped her boots on the fender that covered the tall back tires and patted the seat in front of her. He jumped up and allowed her to straddle him from behind as he stomped on the clutch and put the ancient John alongside the road to their house.

"It's just up around the bend just over a mile. See you there!" Patsy called after him.

Again, he nodded and Victor could see murder reflected in his eyes. He wondered who the target of that malice might be for a fleeting second. He chuckled softly.

The boy was dangerous, but Victor knew how he felt. He knew that in his heart grew the seed of violence and blood that would mark him, set him apart from his friends at school. Victor thought he could contain it. He felt that someday Brian would stand over a victim, his teeth bared and victory shining on his face as Victor stood by beaming with pride.

The thought of that was too delicious for him to dwell on for long. He sat up straight and could feel an odd weight, solid and small prodding his lower back and hip. He recognized the object to be his 44 Magnum. Patsy had come prepared. He was puzzled and curious, but the idea of his own automatic .38 tucked away in his jeans brought a red tint to his vision. The thought of torturing his prey with the gun made Victor mad with desire.

He continued to drive along in third gear, the tractor bouncing along as he imagined holding the gun to the man's groin and whispering in his ear as he pulled the trigger. The smile on his face was part grimace and part pleasure. He was not a monster, he thought, but the hunter incarnate.

*   *   *   *

The sun parted the clouds overhead and the chill that was brought on by the dampness of the rain gave way to clinging, humid warmth. Within minutes, Brian's shirt was drenched with sweat. Victor and Patsy—no longer "Mom" and "Dad"—had disappeared into the fog over ten minutes earlier. He expected the hate to grow keener, his resolve to carry out the necessary deeds to culminate into a tangible being. However, he was surprised as he walked and the distance from his parents increased his doubts and concerns mounted.

Now, he wondered if it weren't better just to run away. Maybe he should go back to the cabin. Retrieving Molly--if indeed she was still alive after over a week of imprisonment-- would certainly be the right thing to do. Brian acknowledged this fact, but his heart wasn't in it. Maybe he was too ashamed of his cowardice. The truth was, he didn't care. He didn't care what happened to Molly, or to his mother, or to some extent to himself.

Despite the doubts, the regrets, the options present before him, he continued to put his feet forward, his back slouched, his head down. He could feel the sun in his hair, his scalp hot and the sweat rolling down the small of his back. He stared at his shoes, and watched as grey pebbles were kicked forward as he scooted his toes into the gravel road. Thoughts rolled through his head in waves.

His fingers kept drifting to the butt of the shotgun in his jeans. He had found the Magnum gone and when he noticed the ammo cabinet open he had known then his mother's game. Perched behind his father on the tractor he had seen her smile and her joking with Victor. But her eyes were cold. He had seen the whiteness of her hand as she put it upon Victor's shoulder, and as she waved to him absently. Brian was nothing to her now, was probably nothing to her all along. But they seemed to have a common goal. He would let her play out her end and then decide where he would fit in.

The shotgun was comfortable to him. He had used it the most and was adept at it. He had sneaked it out of the house this way several times before. It was shorter than most shotguns, its barrel cleverly sawed off two inches. His father had then fixed a choke to the end of the barrel to cut down on the spread some to compensate for the shorter length. It had its limitations in hunting squirrel, but up close, the thing was deadly. He could peel a sixteen inch section of bark off a tree at twenty yards.

The shotgun rubbed against his knee and pinched at his waist, but it was better that way. It seemed to remind him of the pain he should feel, of his punishment for his sins. He kept the extra shells in the opposite pocket. For the first time, he was thankful for owning mostly second-hand clothes. The baggy jeans concealed the bulk of the gun. It was only obvious if he bent his knee too much. As he rounded the bend and could see the Taurus against the tree just below the road, Brian took shorter steps.

Victor was down from the tractor and his mother sat astride the tractor seat, smoking a cigarette. Brian noted the oddity but didn't bother considering why. His attention was too distracted by the body Victor was dragging from the trunk of the Taurus, water and blood spilling out onto the rusted bumper. Brian absently stopped in the road, his hands loose at his side.

He could see the strained look on Victor's face. He appeared shocked. His eyes were rimmed red and he stared at the body as he grasped the man's armpits and dragged him. The man was dead. Brian couldn't tell if his father was going to cry or kill.

"Ooops. Looks like we are caught, Vic." His mother's voice was brittle, scratchy and condescending. He deliberately didn't look at her. He knew his thoughts would be betrayed.

The man in Victor's arms was shirtless, his gray chest hairs sticking up strangely, matted with a dark brown sticky mass. Brian realized it was blood from the wound on the man's face. He couldn't see a distinguishable nose and the man's brow was sunken in over his left eye. It was a grotesque visage that made the bile in his stomach lurch to his throat. He could feel it burning there and his eyes water.

"I see that." Victor answered woodenly. Brian noted that the nails of the man's feet were yellow.

"Brian, have a seat in the grass, honey. You look like you're going to pass out." Patsy put her cigarette out on the frame of the John Deere and hopped down with an athleticism that betrayed her age. Brian felt the dizziness come on him. He forgot the shotgun. He forgot Molly. He forgot the mother wolf in the winter cave. He forgot he was the hunter.

Brian just wanted to run. It was more than the body. He had seen his father murder a man before, had seen the gleam in his eye, had watched as his mother looked on with pride and haughtiness...and approval. The overwhelming urge he felt to run, to turn around and abandon all he had known, to forget this life altogether came from the danger he felt.

The hairs on his head crackled, his heart was racing and the intent of evil was thick in the air. The hills around him, the trees, the waving tall grass, the blasting sun and the waves of moisture rising from the gravel road all were witnesses. They were backdrop and distant.

He felt heavy in his clothes, grounded. It was the feeling he experienced every time he ran track. He would plant his feet in the ground and prepare his body for flight. He was ready to run, to act, to move. But he stood rock still, his fingers tapping a rhythm on his legs. The feel of the shotgun firmly against his thigh seemed a memory.

Victor dropped the body to the ground, and stared down at it as if looking at a broken vehicle or a bad pet.

"I thought this was my kill?" Victor sounded sad. His tone was accusing, but petulant. Wheels in Victor's head were turning. Brian could see it. He watched, paralyzed as his mother flipped another cigarette into the wet grass. He could hear it sizzle quietly. Brian could feel the heat of the intent of the moment. Three hunters were circling each other, their weapons concealed. He realized his folly. It was impossible to hunt a hunter.

"You lied." His voice was flat. The accusation had no effect. "Did you hear her say this was to be my kill?" He looked at Brian, his eyes desperate and focused.

Numbly, Brian nodded. He couldn't speak; he felt as though his lips were caked shut. He wanted to lick his lips, wanted to swallow, but failed to do either. He just grinned a skeleton grin, his lips parting painfully, his teeth sticking to his mouth.

Out of the corner of his eye Brian noticed Patsy move gracefully forward, her hand caressing the tractor. The John Deere sat there quietly, not acknowledging her acid touch, its rusted green metal heavy and warm. Brian watched as his mother held a lighter in her other hand and played with it absently. The flame would flicker and disappear and she stared at it. Her act was convincing. Brian could feel her counting, could hear it in his head. *Flick, flick, flick, four, three, two, one.*

Victor kicked the body, its rigid limbs succumbing to his brutality. He stood over it, his hands on his hips, his protruding stomach peeking out from under his too-tight faded gray t-shirt.

"Brian. Your mother has lied to me. You just stand there. I know you what you mean to do. I can see it on your eyes. But it is your mother I am worried about." Victor continued to stare at the middle aged man lying helpless and dead in the grass. His voice was level and he spoke as though Patsy was not there.

Victor challenged him, his hands on his hips, his eyes expectant.

"Brian. Don't be scared. It will be alright. We just all need to get a good kick in on that old man. I didn't mean to kill him. I just got carried away. Let's just all get our jollies and I will work on getting a new one soon. C'mon."

She motioned to him as she walked toward the body and Victor standing there looking sick.

"It will free you up. Trust me. Watch. I'll do it first." She continued to walk; her boots seemed to barely touch the grass. Brian watched, his eyes followed her, processing all that was happening. She winked at him over her shoulder.

Victor noted her for the first time since Brian had showed up. His eyes tracked her and he could see Victor's guard go down for a moment. He could see some of his confusion lift, but the anger was still there. Brian could tell he was torn, conflicted. Brian wondered if his father truly understood the depth of the betrayal.

As she got closer, she brought her foot back as if she were going to kick a football, her aim obviously intended to strike the man on the ground in the head. Victor stood by, his look approving, his smile taking in Brian. At the last second she brought her foot around and kicked Victor in the groin.

The look on Victor's face was agony. Brian couldn't react. He couldn't believe what he just saw. Victor obviously was just as surprised. Briefly, he could see the confidence, the Sandman grin, the grit and vinegar that was Victor completely stripped away. The coward, the murderer, the abusive father and husband, the sinner, the man with evil intent and a deal with Satan was exposed.

And then it was gone. In its place were hate and turmoil, anger and murder. Brian remained still, just a spectator in this awful scene. He didn't see the punch, but watched as his mother's smug grin disappeared. She picked herself up, a dark wet stain on the knees of her jeans; a long rivulet of blood dripped from the corner of her mouth.

Patsy looked up at Brian and smiled, blood coating her teeth. She looked wounded and triumphant at the same time. Brian could see the red tint at the corners of her eyes, could smell the fear and hate in the air.

"Your father thinks he is such a BIG MAN! He didn't see THAT coming!" Her words were mush, "such" sounding like "thutch." She reached for the pocket of her jacket, a jacket his father wore hunting in the spring--a long, red wool jacket that hung from his mother's shoulders like a cape.

Victor shouted, "Don't even think about it! I know what you think you're gonna do and there's no way I'm gonna let that happen. You need to learn your place."

He punctuated that statement by pounding her kidney with his fist. He watched his mother grimace and fall awkwardly to the ground. She rolled to the side and came up in a crouch like a caged animal. Her eyes flashed and her grin had turned to a menacing snarl, her red-stained teeth bared.

Victor appeared to gain confidence. He wiped his mouth, a froth of white formed there and he brushed it away with the back of his hand. He stomped the ground, kicked the body of the old man. His laugh was sinister and cold.

"You all think you are better than me, but you are just dirt. Dirt! And I'm going to put you in your place." He looked at Brian again. Brian knew his eyes were wide, knew his brows were raised. He was stock still, scared and confused.

"You gonna just watch, huh, Brian? That's fine. You need to see your momma put low. Put in her place."

"Shut up!"

Patsy rushed forward and slashed out with the tips of her fingers. She struck like a cougar, her leap and her aim flawless. Her nails ripped four lines of red across Victor's face. Ragged pieces of flayed skin hung from Victor's face.

He recoiled and when Patsy slashed with her other hand, a piercing howl screaming from her lungs, Victor caught her hand roughly. Patsy tried to bring her left hand across to smack him in the head and Victor just ducked.

Victor jerked her right arm and sent Patsy flying over his shoulder. She landed with a grunt and a whimper. She rolled over again, but slower this time.

"Don't mess with me. Don't disrespect me." Victor turned to Brian, his eyes pleading, his mouth screwed up in a grim expression of hate. "You see that, Brian? That's what we do to dirt. We put it back in its place. Dirt to dirt right Patsy?"

Brian knew the moment to act was upon him. Victor was feeling confident again and his mother was getting punished. It was time to set things right. He tried not to consider the possibilities. He knew he had not planned well. His gamble was great.

By concealing his weapon he had bought himself time but now he would be exposed. How would he get the shotgun out? How would he aim it? What if he missed? Would a slug at this distance kill or just injure him? He had not considered these things before and he hesitated.

As he reached inside his jeans and grabbed the butt of the Winchester single shot 12-gauge, Victor's eyes shot back to him. He knew. Brian lost another split second as he processed this truth.

The hammer of the shotgun caught on his underwear briefly. He pulled it up, the barrel sliding against his leg, his elbow rising above his shoulder, his body twisting to accommodate the length of the gun. It felt like a year to Brian but he focused on acting, not thinking.

Then he had it out. Victor looked at him with a grin. Brian hadn't noticed the barrel of the pistol pointed at him until the bead of his shotgun was trained on his father's chest. The sharp report he heard was not the sound of his own gun. He had not pulled the trigger. He had hesitated again. Now he watched as Victor's body jerked to the right, his pistol dipped and his body slumped.

He glanced to his right and saw his mother crouched in the grass, blood on her blouse, a grimace on her lips and the 44 Magnum held in both hands. She was now pointing it at him. A thin line of blue smoke rose from the barrel of the revolver into the humid air.

"Put the gun down, Brian. I know. I know. Just put it down. It's over now."

Brian shook his head and lowered the shotgun. He dropped it at his feet and stepped back. Moving was liberating. It was momentum, it was escape. His mind reeled against the impulse. *She must pay. She must be punished.They both needed to be brought to justice.* But he couldn't resist the temptation to flee. His body overwhelmed his thoughts; his heart wasn't committed to the ill-conceived plans of his brain.

His feet pounded the gravel as he fled. He could hear Patsy cry his name. But he ran, his mind quickly re-assessing his options, hope cropping up like a new bud from the spring soil. The air was charged with energy; his head was thumping a staccato rhythm to the beat of his sneakers on the grinding gravel of the road home. That was when he heard another shot.

Brian spun around, and watched as his mother toppled over heavily just yards away from where she had crouched earlier with the Magnum. Victor rose up from the grass, his .38 auto in his hands now, dark blood staining the shoulder of his shirt. His progress was sluggish. He stooped to pick up the shotgun. Victor tucked the handgun behind his back with one hand and raised the shotgun level with his other.

His mouth was contorted in a grimace of anger, pain and determination. Pain was etched on his face. Pain and victory. Brian had never been so afraid of his father.

Without thinking about it Brian backed up, staring crazily at his mother lying face down in the road. Her hair was splayed out around her head like a starburst. An ugly wound covered the back of her neck. Brian was sick, his stomach churning, his face burning red with shame, fear and grief. Patsy was dead. Mom.

He put the back of his hand across his mouth to fight back the urge to wretch.

"Go ahead, boy. Cry now. It's your momma, but she pushed me too far. She's gone now and paid the price for crossing me, betraying me." He limped forward as Brian continued to back up. Victor lowered the gun but kept staring after Brian, kept moving forward in spurts.

He was hurt but not fatally. "If you're smart, and I think you are, you'll let this pass and move on with your life. We can do this together you and me. Brian, you know we have always been the ones destined to live in the blood. To tear the marrow from the bones of life and throw away the trash!"

Victor spit on Patsy's back as he passed her. Brian realized he was shaking his head, left hand still held palm-out at his mouth, his right hand pressed firmly against his ear. He was moaning softly. His voice was hoarse, but the moan quickly became a growl and then a scream.

"NOOOOOOO! Never! Leave me alone!"

Brian turned and ran. He heard the report of the gun, felt the heat of the shot as it passed by him on his left. He darted the other way and fell, his hands skidding on the gravel.

He felt the white heat on his hands, the bone-jarring pressure in his shoulders as he tried to break his fall. His chin hit with a thump, and he tasted the blood as he bit his tongue. It filled his mouth and he was only barely aware that his body had crashed to the road and he had rolled over.

Briefly, he was caught off guard by the simultaneous revulsion and lust he felt at the taste of his own blood. He spat it out and it covered his chin and his shirt. He cursed himself but was determined to escape. He scrambled to his feet, his hands agony, his head heavy and confused. He heard the shotgun drop to the ground. His father probably figured out he had no more ammunition.

Brian wheeled around and ran again, his breathing coming in ragged bursts at first, a feral, guttural growl coming from his throat. Soon, he fell into the familiar rhythm of pumping his arms and legs in tandem, his lungs drawing long, deep breaths, his heart adapting to the combination of fear and flight.

Victor yelled at him, cursed but did not pursue.

Brian had no plan. He had no idea where he was going, but continued to run toward the only place he knew: home. It was dangerous, but he knew if he could make it there, he would think of something.

As he ran, he blamed himself for his foolishness. He should have done something sooner. He should have called someone. He should never have brought that wolf cub home. He should have been less selfish. He should have loved his family more, should have told them that he was horrified at the nightmare his life had become. But he hadn't and he was ashamed. His family was monsters and he had let them get away with it.

His teeth rattled as he ran; his mouth was hurting, his lungs burning. He fought the temptation to look back. If he thought for a second that he was safe, had put distance between them, he was doomed. He wouldn't be safe until he reached the house.

Brian sprinted faster, his lips dry from breathing through his mouth, his hands squeezed into tight balls. He could feel the grit of the dirt that had gotten in his mouth and he tried to spit it out. That was when he heard the tractor's engine start, the loud report from its exhaust. He felt the fear grip his heart again and struggled to keep his pace. He could see the house, the barn, the shed through the haze of the burning fog and he hoped he was right. He hoped it wasn't too late.

CHAPTER TWENTY-FOUR

H is hunch had been correct. Molly practically beamed as she had pointed through the clearing ahead at the smoke coiling about the ragged shingle roof.

"There it is," she said. She was breathless with effort and success in finally reaching their destination.

"I was afraid of that." He regretted saying that as soon as it left his mouth. He didn't look back at Molly, but he could feel her tense from a yard away.

"We can do this. I am ready. I know what we can do. Brian can help."

He didn't answer. He wasn't sure what his response should be. The nagging feeling that something with Molly wasn't quite right came back stronger. The hackles on his neck were up. He couldn't tell if this was from Molly or her home ahead of them, dark, foreboding and solemn in the morning fog.

Jacob was relieved and apprehensive. He could feel fate unfolding around him, could sense a purpose, a direction. He felt as though he was guided and a lacked control. It unnerved him and left him weak in his knees. He wasn't sure if he was in awe of his role in this impossible drama or merely scared.

Jacob wanted to rest, but knew it would be best to push on. The house was only about a mile away and with the goal so close, he was sure that events would speed up soon. Danger and purpose charged the air around him and he could see the determination on Molly's eyes and in her posture. He knew it would be impossible to stop this charging rhino that was his fate, his calling.

Why else had he come here? He had considered this question several times since discovering the horror in the cabin and hadn't come up with a logical explanation. He had forgotten his motivations, his reasons for leaving Janice behind, for running from his life, escaping his responsibilities. Perhaps he had a greater responsibility and it was here.

Jacob hesitated to embrace this theory. Something about it felt out of balance and otherworldly. Yet, it felt right. Was it a universal truth: each person is where they are for a reason? Not just where, but when.

These deep and heavy thoughts bore him down. He could feel it free him and bind him. He felt stronger and yet imprisoned within that truth. Molly didn't seem to notice. Her focus was insurmountable. He envied her.

Soon, the path narrowed and they were on the back stoop of the house. The sun was burning his neck and he welcomed the cool dampness of the covered porch. He could smell wood burning and hear the chatter of birds from the trees surrounding the house. Molly opened the door quietly.

"Stay here. They won't expect me, but they sure won't expect you."

"Gotcha. You be alright?"

"Yeah." She turned and started to go in. She glanced back. "You'll come if I scream, right?"

"I got your back, Molly."

He tried to sound more confident than he felt. She took a deep, nervous breath. He could see the worry etched on her face.

"I don't think they're here. I can't smell them," she whispered absently as she entered the dark entry.

Jacob stooped by the door and listened as Molly walked about the house. She was gone for several moments and returned, her eyes big and her chest heaving.

"They're gone. The car's not out front and the tractor is gone, too. This is strange. Dad rarely leaves. I don't know what this means," she said.

"Slow down. It's alright. Let's think this through." Molly stared at him as he stood and she looked down at his hands, her eyes bulging.

"Where's your rifle?"

Jacob looked down at his hands, incredulous. He was stuck; his mind was tracking several thoughts at once. He wondered about the last time he saw the Remington .22. He considered his role again: maybe violence wasn't required. He questioned his resolve and his courage. He also had a moment of flashback to Idaho: the ravine and the bear. He couldn't escape the feeling that he had been at this place before, this junction between danger and peace.

Molly looked distraught. Her mouth hung open, her eyes begged him to produce the rifle. It was at the ravine, probably stuck in the mud or possibly it had fallen over the cliff when he tumbled over the edge.

Regardless, he was without a way to effectively defend himself. He didn't know how to console Molly. Even worse, he felt even more challenge. Now he didn't even have something to even the odds of their survival. He only had his hands, his wits and his faith that he could meet any challenge.

"What are you gonna do? You lost the gun and now how are we gonna get out of here? We should have never come!"

Molly's emotions took hold of her for the first time and the fear and the shock came forth as she spoke so quickly Jacob could barely understand her. He almost panicked then. They were in a real spot. Molly was right. They should have never come. Jacob could feel his morale wane, could feel the insecurities that had been haunting him come back.

He had been running away all his life. He needed to stand and face his challenges. He couldn't fall back on a vacation or solitude. He had agreed to protect Molly, had become entangled in the improbable drama that had befallen him.

Fleeing now seemed prudent, but Jacob knew he would never forgive himself. His conscience reminded him that the law here would deal with this, matters as gruesome and twisted as this should be handled locally. They would hold a trial here, would expose all the perversions, all the murders, the entire wicked family history laid bare. The children would be put in protective custody and need some serious counseling. The entire future spun out in Jacob's mind, showing him that all could be put right without him involved.

But, his nature was stubborn. He didn't want to be a hero. He didn't feel this was his place, his fight, his responsibility. That was what he had told himself his entire life. It was exactly the type of logic his father would have used.

Jacob grabbed Molly by the shoulders and looked her straight in the eyes.

"Molly, we can't turn back now. We have to set this right. I know we are taking risks, but you were taking a risk by escaping the cabin. You were taking risks when you found the cabin in the first place. You don't strike me as someone who runs away, Molly. I have always been that person. I have to be honest, now. I am no hero. I have been brave in my life, but mostly when I am needed most I disappear. Not anymore, Molly. Not today, at least."

Molly swallowed hard, looking up into Jacob's eyes. She frowned, and he knew she wanted to cry. He couldn't blame her. She looked down and then surprised him by punching his shoulder in one quick motion.

"Ow!"

"You shouldn't have lost the stupid gun! Why did you do that? You are the adult! I'm just a kid. I know that gun was our only way to stay alive. If you want to play cowboy with no pistol, then go ahead. I'm leaving." She started to turn away, a disgusted look on her face.

Strangely, Jacob felt hurt. Molly walked off the back porch and headed back the way they had come. She walked with her hands tight to her sides, her fists balled up and her steps rigid and determined.

"Molly. Stop."

She did. Her shoulders slumped and he saw she was sobbing. She had tried to hide her disappointment and fear in a tantrum. His daughter, Clarice, had done that when she was young, had never truly grown out of the habit, really. Molly stood rock still, her fingers clenched hard, her breathing ragged, her head bowed.

"Don't go. I need you to come with me. You know your way around and know your parents better than me. Plus, I don't have any other proof than you."

He could see her thinking, could see the arguments forming above her shoulders, could feel the heat of her hate from a dozen yards away.

"You've got the cabin. That's probably 'nuff." She said, and sniffled.

"Possibly. You'd be able to see them go away in cuffs this way, though."

"Yeah. I know. I've thought about that all the way here. I can't get the pictures of them in my head, though."

Jacob jumped as a heard a shot. Then another. He could tell they were a mile or more away, but that didn't matter. Molly almost bolted. She turned and looked past the house.

"That came from down the road." She looked at Jacob, her eyes red and swollen. "What do you think it was?"

"I don't know. But we should get moving." Another shot rang out, louder this time.

She ran back to the porch and went into the house without hesitation. Jacob, startled at her change of attitude and her swiftness of movement, took a second to pick up their gear and followed behind her into the house.

It was dark in the entry. Sun spilled through dirty windows into the living room. Molly disappeared around the corner and he slowed down and checked corners. He didn't like the eerie silence of the house. Shadows slid across furniture into corners. He could sense furtive movements, could feel eyes trained on him.

He knew it was his nerves. He barely registered the worn spots in the ragged carpet, the broken furniture, the stale smell of bodies and beer. He could hear Molly shuffling around in the next room. Then she appeared in the doorway and whispered.

"All the guns are gone. I got a knife from the kitchen. You want it?"

Jacob looked at the long, thin knife and shook his head.

"I don't take knives to gun fights, girl." He inclined his head toward the front lawn. "We need to go out there and find some cover. Maybe we can hide out until dark and then surprise him."

Molly just shook her head. She had quickly changed apparently. She had on new sneakers, a pair of shorts that went to her knees and a St. Louis Blues jersey. "You don't understand, do you? He's not as strong during the day. He feeds off the night. Darkness and blood: those are his power. We can't waste any more time. If my mom is here, we might be able to confuse them by making them fight. I've gotten out of whippings that way before. And maybe we can get Brian to help us."

Jacob took advantage of her sudden bravery and trusted in her instincts. He still felt he was in some foreign country in someone else's dream. Molly started for the door and he followed close behind, scanning the porch and the yard for movement.

Molly ducked under the porch rail and scooted on her backside across a wooden box in the front yard. Jacob snake his way around, running to keep up. He stopped when he got to a small building by the front lawn. Then a thought struck him.

"Molly. How many guns were in the house?" She didn't answer for a second. She crouched by a tree a few yards from him, her chest heaving as she stared down the road into the bright sun. She turned to him and gave him a meaningful look.

"Two pistols and a shotgun."

Jacob cursed under his breath. He mentally chastised himself. He looked west toward the direction of the shots and couldn't see anything but a gravel road that continued for about a mile before it turned around a bend.

Jacob wanted to stay near the house and the barn. He knew how to maneuver and defend himself in these conditions. He didn't feel comfortable hunting the Carother family down in the woods or out in the open. He looked around for something he could use for his advantage. An ax in a block of wood by the barn, an old Stihl chainsaw with missing links in the chain and oil dripping from its housing.

He took mental stock of the backpack at his feet. A whole lot of good all his survival gear now. Not much he could do with a water purifier, tent stakes and dried food rations. A dim memory of a *MacGyver* episode floated to his conscience. He smiled despite himself. It was just what he needed to get grounded.

'"Molly. Is there a phone in the house?"

She looked at him, her chin tilted down and looked at him scoldingly. "Are you kidding? Don't you think I would have thought of that first? No. Mom and Dad don't have phones, TV's or internet, ok? We are secluded out here. It's at least ten miles back to the main road and then another ten minutes back into town. The lake's ten minutes the other way, the ranger's office about two miles into the park. No one's gonna hear, no one's gonna know any of this went down. We are alone, Jacob. You're going to need to re-think what we're doing here."

Jacob nodded. She was right. He continued to watch the horizon and saw a figure running toward them. All that was visible was a head bobbing up and down at first, then a man appeared just over the horizon. Molly saw him too. Jacob could hear her breath catch.

"That's Brian!" She almost screamed.

"Shhh!" Jacob could hear something in the distance that sounded like a boat motor or a semi truck.

"That's Dad's John Deer. We gotta help him." Before he could stop her, she ran for Brian. Jacob chased after her, leaving the backpack by the shed. Molly's hair bounced back and forth and her sneakers slapped the gravel of the road. Jacob knew he wouldn't be able to keep up; she was quick and he was getting old and out of shape. She was excited about seeing her brother and he was cautious.

He could feel events getting further out of his control. He didn't like the feeling. He was going to have to trust Molly and probably now Brian, too.

"Brian!" Molly called.

Brian didn't seem to notice at first and then he saw her. He looked confused for a second and then yelled clearly.

"Run, Molly!"

He flailed his arms and waved toward the house.

Molly never lost stride. She didn't see the tractor's mirrors flash in the sun and its rear wheels break the horizon. Jacob saw it and noted the look of madness upon Victor's face even from over a thousand yards. He almost stopped and turned to run.

They were in the open and the tractor was barreling ever closer at a faster clip than Jacob had considered possible. It was as if the tractor was responding to the demon that was driving it. It spit diesel smoke into the thick, humid air, the black plume rising in the air like an inky dragon spewing its foul breath. Victor drove the tractor with both hands on the wheel. Jacob didn't have to see the pistol in Victor's hand to know it was there.

Molly continued to run toward Brian.

"Molly, what are you doing? Can't you hear me? Run! Get that man and go to the house!" It registered with Molly then and she saw the horror that was her father overtaking Brian.

"NO!" she screamed and skidded to a halt. She turned and ran back toward Jacob who had already slowed and intended to let the siblings pass him and take up the rear. He would just slow them down.

"Jacob, run! He's gonna kill us all!" Molly screamed.

Brian kept running and caught up with Molly and grabbed her hand. Together, they passed Jacob and he saw Brian's eyes glance at him as they raced by. He could see the questions there.

He could also see a madness that Jacob couldn't refute. Confused, Jacob turned and looked at the oncoming tractor. He saw there the bond between father and son. Their eyes held the same ephemeral glow, the dancing manic and bloodlust nature of the truly mad.

Then he ran, too. He pumped his fists at his side and tried to keep pace with Molly and Brian. Their backs were drenched with sweat and the dust that rose from the gravel road as they raced back toward the shadows of the house.

Jacob noticed for the first time that the house looked like a dirtier version of what may have been a painting of a typical farmhouse. The trees around the house had grown unhindered and almost swallowed the house in their shade. The shed was closer to the thick undergrowth of the forest and a cliff face that climbed twenty feet straight up.

The whole place was a trap. They could only go in the direction of the barreling tractor or up the path into the woods toward the cabin. The house was the only sanctuary close that made sense. The hay spikes at the front of the tractor gleamed in the sun, as menacing and dangerous as the look on the madman's face that drove it.

Brian was the first one through the door. Molly jumped up onto the porch and turned around, the knife from the kitchen in her right hand, her damp hair clinging to her forehead.

"Run, Jacob! He's coming!" Jacob hadn't even noticed how hard he was breathing until he tried to answer. Only a ragged sound escaped his chest, sounding like a yelp more than an intelligible answer.

He heard the boards of the stairs groan as he sprung up onto the porch and grabbed Molly by the shoulder and shoved her into the house. He could smell the diesel now, could hear Victor shouting something. Jacob couldn't make it out over the roar of the engine and his heart pounding in his ear.

"In the house! Lock the door! Get upstairs. We'll hold him off."

He turned around to see the tractor bouncing across the yard, its rear wheels leaving the ground and the Victor fighting to keep the dreaded nightmare of machinery moving forward. His shirt was covered in blood and dirt, his beard flecked with dust and spittle. Fear gripped Jacob's heart as he saw clearly the intention of the madman. He backed into the house and slammed the door shut.

The house shuddered and Jacob could hear the wood porch splintering, the porch roof ripping away from its frame. Scared more than he had ever been, he looked around the room for answers. Molly and Brian were standing in the living room, their eyes glued to the door behind him.

"Back away!" He shouted as he dove under a table just as the whole wall caved in, shards of plaster stinging the back of his neck. Jacob was engulfed in an explosion of sound and the force of something slamming into his back. He closed his eyes as dust flew all around him. Through it all he could hear Molly scream, "GO AWAY, DAD! I HATE YOU!"

CHAPTER TWENTY-FIVE

T he Sheriff tapped his leg impatiently and stared at the plywood walls of Trevor Martin's office. Trevor had been the manager of Bexton Chevrolet for over two years now, but George's plaques still lined the walls: 2001 Elks Business of the Year, 1997 Best Dealership NW Arkansas, and several awards for softball championships, chili cook-offs, and milestones. Trevor's wife and two kids grinned at Billy Joe from a digital photo frame on the desk. He stared as the picture changed to a fishing trip and then to Trevor kneeling beside a large deer, his bow across his lap, the bloody arrow lying across the poor animal's carcass.

Trevor was busy with a customer. Billy Joe could still hear his booming, insistent voice through the wall as he escorted a young couple through his 2009 closeout model sedans. Trevor was a good salesman, a terrible manager and a terrific sportsman. He single-handedly had won the state championship for Bexton in basketball his senior year.

His popularity had won him over to most folk, but anyone who spent too much time with Trevor soon learned how shallow and self-concerned he could be. No wonder George had trusted him with his business. A keen sense of self-preservation was what had kept George out of trouble for so long.

So Billy Joe sat in the leather chair and stared at the traffic outside the plate glass windows behind Trevor's chair. He counted cars, checked his watch, adjusted his belt and put his hat on his knee. Eventually, Trevor walked back in, a nervous grin on his face.

"They'll be back," he said gesturing to the clients as they walked to their car. The wife was obviously irritated at her husband, the young man gesturing. He was oblivious to his wife's mood and Billy Joe wondered if all men had this blind spot. He looked back at Trevor who had put a set of keys on the desk and straightened the picture frame. Billy Joe decided that mankind was doomed.

"The reason I came here..."

"I know why you're here, BJ. George, right?"

Billy Joe tried to conceal his irritation, and managed, "Yeah. What do you think I want to know 'TD' Trevor?"

Trevor blinked. "I don't know where he is, alright? I sent him his last quarterly check in September and it was returned last week saying he no longer lives there. As far as I'm concerned, the money's mine. He didn't forward his mail, it's not my fault."

"Trevor, you're not in trouble. Yet. There's an investigation. We need to find George. He seems to be missing." Bill Joe stood, knowing his bulk could intimidate even Trevor. Billy Joe out-weighed him by over seventy pounds. Trevor had become soft after high school, marrying his high school sweetheart and taking two vacations every year.

"I told you, I don't know where he is. Why don't you ask Pops. He told me he seen him up at the casinos in Kansas City this summer."

"I thought you said you didn't know where he was, Trevor."

"You're not gonna catch me lying, Sheriff. Trust me, if George doesn't want to be found, he won't be found. He's been running from the mob for a decade now. You know that, I am sure." Trevor gave him a sly, superior look. He thought he had the Sheriff in a bad spot.

"A day of reckoning is coming to George one way or the other. I suppose it's coming for us all. We can't escape it. Remember that, Trevor, next time you balance your books funny. The next time you roll back the odometer on your demos or cover up the structural damage on your used cars." He straightened up to his full height and pulled his belt up.

"Pop is out back, chewing the fat with Carmine and Ed Jr. Like I said, he'll know better than me where to find George. Thanks for stoppin' by BJ."

Billy Joe just turned on his heel and slammed the door as he left. The sound of the paneling cracking put a smile on his face as he marched around a bright red Impala.

He could hear the fellas in the back yucking it up. He was pretty sure that Trevor was hiding something and was beginning to think he wasn't going to get much more information. At least he had tried.

"And I told him he could keep his rotten apples. You shoulda seen his face slump. It was precious." Everyone laughed. Ed's face was bright red and Carmine continued to talk, encouraged by their reaction. "I should have slammed the door in his face but that look he gave made me soft in my heart."

"You sure are soft, that's for sure," Pop said and Carmine laughed along at his own expense.

"Oh. Hey Sheriff. What do we owe the pleasure of your visit this slow afternoon?"

"Just dropping by asking some routine questions. I won't bring you in for that bad oil change you gave me last time." Pops had grease and grime under his nails, in his hair and in every fiber of his clothes. His smile was just as greasy as the rest of him. If he was born in the 1800's he would have been a snake oil salesman, Billy Joe was certain.

"Sounds like he needs to trade in that old Dodge for a real car, huh Ed?" Carmine piped in. Ed was the rookie salesman. His father had been the manager under George for over two decades until he had a stroke four years ago. Trevor had supplanted him and now Ed Jr. was following in his father's footsteps. More accurately, Ed Jr. was still living in his father's shadow and was barely struggling to meet quota.

"Just business, fellas. It won't take but a minute. You wanna come outside and visit with me for a bit, Pops?"

"Who, me?" Pops pointed his grimy finger at his sunken chest. He was at least sixty but was built out of bailing wire and bull manure. "I thought she was of legal age, officer, promise." He crossed his heart and his cohorts gave him his comedic due with guffaws and snickers.

"Yeah, that's what they all say, Pops. Now, stop foolin' around. I'm losing light."

Robert Michael

"Well, that's all you're losing, big boy. But I'll humor ya." He started for his little office, wiping his hands on a dirty terry cloth towel. Billy Joe didn't notice a difference in the amount of grease on either the towel or Pop's hands. It appeared to be an equitable exchange.

Billy Joe closed the door as they entered the cramped room. Pops raised his eyebrows and took off his Pennzoil cap and put it on the counter as he sat in a rickety task chair. Billy Joe just stopped and crossed his arms.

"Where's George." Direct. No nonsense. Billy Joe hoped this approach would cut through Pop's natural tendency to goof off.

Pops looked stunned for a second and then let out a nervous titter. He looked down at the streaked linoleum floor and then back up to Billy Joe.

"That's what this is about? And you're serious?"

"He's missing. An investigation into his disappearance is underway by the feds. I've been asked to help locate him." A little white lie to push Pops a little further. A veiled threat.

"Look. If Trevor told you I knew where he was, he's not remembering our conversation correctly. I barely had anything to do with George even when he ran the place. I just do what I do and keep to myself. Harriet won't let me mess around with the stuff George was mixed up in. I'm gonna retire soon and I didn't need none of that monkey business."

"Let me make this clear, Pops. You are not in trouble. I only wanted to talk to you privately to protect you. Give you some privacy so you can be open and honest with me. When was the last time you seen George?"

"I didn't see him, but Gladice did. Harriet's sister was up at the casinos in Kansas City and said he was hanging off of some cougar."

"A cougar?"

"Yeah, you know, a middle-aged, good-looking gal. Gladice didn't call her that, but the way she described her and the way she said she was dressed just forced me to consider her a cougar." He shrugged.

"I see. How exactly did Gladice describe this lady?"

"I dunno. Medium height, dark hair, and she said she wore a short black skirt and a red blouse cut down to here." Pops put a finger in the middle of his chest and raised his eyebrows for emphasis. "Quite the looker from what Gladice said, but she's known to stretch things."

"Women are generally better judges of beauty than us, wouldn't you say?"

"Yeah, well if Harriet was such a good judge, she woulda never married me, that'sfer sure." He chuckled.

"Yeah, but you are God's gift to women, anyway, right?" Pops smiled, two of his teeth stumps visible and his stubble bristling.

"That's right, Sheriff."

"So, Kansas City in July or June?"

"Gladice stays up there all summer with one of her kids. They took her to play the slot machines at one of them Indian Gaming places. Harrah's was too crowded. This was a place on the west side over on the Kansas side I think. I'm not sure. But, it was June. That's all I really know Billy. You gonna bring me in for more questionin'?"

"Nah, you'll give Stella heartburn and I'll never shut her up for a week complaining about you. Unless you, Harriet or Gladice can remember something else, I think I got all I can." He turned to open the door and then looked back.

"Gladice doesn't know many folks from around here, does she?"

Pops shook his head and squirreled up his mouth. "Nah. She barely shows her head anymore. She just has her nephew drive her up to our door and she totters up, plays bridge for two hours, criticizes Harriet's cooking and then leaves. I can't get the smell of her farts out of the house for a week. Why?"

Billy Joe shook his head. "I don't know. Just a hunch. Could it be possible he knew the lady from around here?"

Pops shrugged.

"I suppose, but from what Gladice said, it sounded like an affair or something. Nothing more exciting than a stranger, from what I hear. But don't ask me, I know nuthin' about it."

"Gotcha. Hey, thanks for your cooperation, Pops."

"Not a problem. Any time I can help you out, Billy. You know, I tease you a bunch, but you're respected around here. We all appreciate what you do. Don't you worry about George, though. Nothing he was involved in was any of your concern. Everyone knows that."

Uncomfortable, Billy Joe nodded and left the room. "Thanks," he mumbled and walked back to his squad car. He ignored Ed and Carmine as he passed them in the service bay and walked out into the bright fall Arkansas sun. Something about this whole mess bothered him and he couldn't put his finger on it. He couldn't fight the feeling that more had been going on in his county than he was pretending. He closed the door of his cruiser and sat there for several minutes before he turned the key and headed for the Carother farm, thoughts of George's demise nagging him as he snaked his way through the county roads.

CHAPTER TWENTY-SIX

Brian stood transfixed. The scene before him was surreal. Two of the three bale spears on his father's John Deere 3020 had impaled the recliner and had lifted it about three feet from the floor. The house smelled of diesel and dirt. Two thirds of the front wall had collapsed, the ceiling was sagging, and the tractor had come to a stop about seven feet into the living room.

Victor lay sagging across the steering wheel, one hand still on the shifter. *He must have had it in eighth gear,* Brian thought. The engine clicked as it cooled and the lights on either side of Victor blinked as the electrical system shorted again.

Molly lay on the floor beside him, her face in the tan carpet and the knife beside her. She sobbed, her body rocking, but Brian barely noticed. He watched as the beam above where the front door had been fell over the rear tires of the tractor and came to rest across Victor's back. Victor didn't move, didn't even grunt, as the heavy wood studded with nails fell.

Brian wasn't scared anymore. His blood ran cold as he saw how his future was to unfold. He wanted it just to end. Slowly, he walked over to the fire place, dodging the displaced furniture and the remains of the lamp. He grabbed the poker. Its weight and balance felt good in his hands. He looked back to Victor and watched as his back slowly rose and fell. *Still alive, but not for long.* The time for running was over.

Before he could walk over to finish it all, he heard the wail of an engine and the crunch of tires on gravel. He looked out the only remaining window and saw the Sheriff driving toward the house. He spun the car parallel with the house and got out. He moved faster than Brian would have imagined he could. He knelt behind the hood of the car. He had a gun.

A part of Brian was disappointed. He wanted to end this on his own terms. He wanted revenge, not justice. But, it appeared fate had stepped in and taken his place. With regret, he dropped the poker to his side and walked to the window. With effort, he raised it and crawled through.

"Where are you going?" Molly asked behind him. Her voice sounded small and scared. He didn't care. He ignored her, didn't even turn. The Sheriff pointed the gun at him and Brian could see the fear in his eyes, see the gun shake furiously. Brian had a flash of premonition. He saw how it would all end. They would all die. He panicked.

"Don't shoot! I'm Brian! I didn't do it! My dad's inside and he's the one. He's hurt. Please, Sheriff, we need your help."

"Get down here." The Sheriff stood, his eyes glancing back to the house and the spectacle of the tractor embedded in the front of the house. Brian saw that the porch roof had completely collapsed and lay about the remains of the swing and the porch Brian had painted with three coats of gray paint last summer.

Brian obeyed, his steps slow and his eyes watching the Sheriff closely. He pointed with the gun to show Brian the path he wanted him to take. Brian complied.

"Put down the poker, Brian. It's alright." He lowered the gun and reached for his cuffs. A sense of dread came across Brian and he looked back to the house. Victor was gone. He heard Molly scream.

*   *   *   *

Billy Joe was shaken. All this was almost too much for his heart. The form of George on the ground with his face beaten in was enough to make him want a strong drink. But then, to find a woman he assumed was Patsy Carothers lying face-down with a hole in the back of her skull the size of a Skoal can made his eyes water.

He hadn't cried when Becky had called him from Sturgis to wish him well with his life. In fact, the last time he cried was when he was twelve. He had gotten beaten up at school and when his father asked him how the other boy looked, Billy Joe had broken down. His father claimed that the whooping he received was for crying, not for getting beaten.

But now, he felt like crying. He grabbed Brian's wrists. His revolver was on the hood of the car, the poker between Brian's feet. He did his work quickly; he could feel the danger rising around him. His eyes were brimming with tears and his nose was beginning to run. His face was hot and his hands shook. He wasn't sure his aim would be very good, but he was determined despite his fear.

He heard a girl screaming and assumed it was Molly. Confused, he pushed Brian against the car door.

"Stay here," he muttered. He grabbed his revolver and headed toward the house.

His feet felt like they weighed tons. He shuffled ahead, his gun ahead of him. He looked for an entry. There was no way to squeeze into the opening between the broken siding and the John Deere tractor. The window Brian had come through wouldn't accommodate his bulk, either.

He saw a side landing and a door. He went around to his right, stumbling over broken pieces of the porch. Shingles lay everywhere. He shook his head in disbelief. He wouldn't have ever believed this story if someone had told him.

The grip of his .38 was cold in his hand still. Despite this, his palm was slimy with sweat. He could feel the heat of his own body. He made his way to the door and tried the handle with one hand.

Of course, it was unlocked. No one in the country ever locked their doors, it seemed. Who would want to rob from folks who lived so far out, had so little and carried guns to protect it? Crazy folks: that was who. Crazy folks like the Carothers.

As he had squatted there on the damp grass inspecting Patsy's body, he had pieced together what had transpired to the best of his ability. None of it made sense to him.

In his career the only dead bodies he had encountered were from folks who had died in car accidents. Then there was Corey Casey, a black man who had been crushed beneath three tons of pipes over at Johnson's Oil Supplies. These were accidental deaths, tragic and messy. But the personal brutality of violent malevolence and hate were foreign to the Sheriff.

Violence was etched all over this scene as well. The intent was obviously murder, yet there was Brian and he could still hear Molly. He hoped this was the end of it. He thought for a moment to go back to the cruiser and put everyone on alert and get Dr. Vardamon, the local psychiatrist out here.

He put away this thought. There was no time for procedures and trying to explain what had gone on to Estelle. Better to get his hands dirty, get the work done and then call them in to help clean up. This would help tidy up the State of Arkansas investigation.

The door creaked open and he was surprised at how cold the house felt. It was dark and he had entered in by the kitchen. He noticed an open drawer. The house was swaying. It would probably collapse soon. He gripped the gun tighter.

"Molly? You there? This is Sheriff Shoemaker. You can come out."

He heard footfalls in the hall. Then, framed in the doorway, Victor stood holding Molly out in front of him. Billy Joe did not remember him with a beard. It made Victor appear like that guy from that Stephen King movie, *Dreamcatcher*. His eyes were calm, though. He smiled, his bloody teeth shining in the gloom of the kitchen.

"Howdy, Sheriff. Looks like you showed up just in time."

Stunned, Billy Joe stood there, the sights of the gun trained on Victor's head. The man looked like he was worse for wear. Plaster and blood clung to him everywhere. Billy Joe saw the gun Victor held too late. Victor had hidden it behind a throw pillow with flowers and a green fringe.

The Sheriff wanted to pull the trigger, but didn't want to shoot Molly. He hesitated.

"Stop right—" he started. *THWUMP!!*

He felt a hot bolt enter his chest. His eyes blinked fast. He couldn't feel his hands and he dropped his revolver. He looked down at the front of his uniform at the hole just under the pocket.

He hadn't even heard the shot. The world spun away and he felt himself sinking, felt his considerable weight hit the cold linoleum of the kitchen, his temple smacking the edge of the countertop and his hat toppling away to fall nearby as he fell. He was numb and his consciousness slowly ebbed away. *So this is what it feels like*, he thought.

*   *   *   *

He was dreaming about Luke. He watched as Luke returned from the concession stand with a burger, a quarter pound hot dog and some nachos. It was ridiculous how much food teenage boys could consume. The stadium was loud and the people around them were crammed in tight. He watched as Luke smiled and handed Janice a large cola. She thanked him and kissed him on the cheek. It was sweet. Jacob could feel himself smiling.

Robert Michael

But something wasn't right. He heard screaming and he woke. He could feel himself trapped under some kind of weight. His face was smashed into a rough, moldy carpet. He could barely breathe and all he could see were the fibers of the carpet and the dirt.

Then he remembered. He was at the Carothers. Victor had driven the tractor at fifteen miles an hour into the front of the house, piercing the walls with a farm attachment meant to impale bales of hay. And that was Molly screaming.

"No! Stop it! Brian! Jacob! Help!"

"Jacob? Now who is that?" The voice was unfamiliar, but he knew. It was raspy and condescending. It was prideful and mad.

Then Jacob could hear the crunch of footsteps across the glass and wood on the carpet. Jacob struggled to get up, pushing against the weight at his back. He ducked his head and closed his eyes. He felt the weight give way and was concerned by the sound of the remnants of the wall as it slid from his back. But stealth didn't seem as important as getting free of the rubble.

The first thing he saw was the tractor, green and menacing beside him. Then he saw Brian's back, hunched, the light from the window and the house's new entry shining on his sweat-stained white t-shirt. The dust swirled in the air, the sun cutting through in beams. Brian was holding something at his side but Jacob couldn't make it out. He was heading across the living room toward the hall. That was when he saw the other figure huddle there, his back to Brian.

It happened so quickly, Jacob couldn't react. He was still crouched on the carpet, his hands bloody and his eyes still adjusting to the brightness of the sun and the gloom of the hall ahead. Victor whipped around just as Brian was raising his weapon over his head. Jacob could see now that it was a fireplace tool. He also noted from the glint of light off of the metal that Brian had handcuffs on.

Where did he get those?

Victor shot twice and Brian brought the poker over his head like he was chopping wood. The tool came crashing down on Victor's head.

Blood gushed from the wound like a burst hose. The smaller side pike was buried in Victor's skull. He backed away, wrenching the tool from Brian's hand. Brian held his stomach and collapsed to his knees. Victor shouted.

"You fool! You think this will kill me? Look at me you whelp! You need to man up if you are gonna take this devil!"

He grabbed the poker and pulled it from his head with disdain. Blood was everywhere. Brian was swaying and blood was pouring down his jeans and pooling in the floor of the hallway, thick and dark. Jacob stood and started forward. He meant to tackle Victor. He knew he had the element of surprise. Of course, so had Brian.

Three shots rang out. They were loud in the house, quick and deadly. Victor vaulted forward and his face hit the doorway. He fell backwards and lay motionless.

Jacob, half way across the living room, stared at Molly. She was holding a .38 revolver. She was shaking. Tears streamed down her face, streaking the dirt and grime there. He heard Brian moan.

"Oh, God," he said. "Please take me. Please." His voice was small, a whisper. Jacob leaned forward, his hands on his knees. His heart was still pounding and his head was aching. But it was over.

Molly dropped the gun and rushed over to Brian who had fallen over onto his side. Victor was on the other side of the hall door, blood issuing from several wounds. Jacob gave the brother and sister some room and checked to make sure the deed was done.

Victor had no pulse, and no breath came from his nose. Jacob closed his eyes and said a prayer. It seemed the most logical thing to do. Something had to cleanse this evil. There had to be balance and closure. He tried not to eavesdrop as Molly and Brian huddled together on the floor of their home, their former prison. He couldn't resist.

"Brian. I'm sorry. Please don't die," Molly cried.

Brian coughed. "Oh, Molly. I'm done. It's best this way. I'm just as corrupted as they are. I was coming back to save you, but I guess it didn't work out." He coughed again.

"Don't say that. Come on, I can't go on without you. Who else do I have?"

"You're strong. You'll survive. It'll be better this way, you'll see." He smiled and he pushed Molly's hair back from her forehead.

He coughed again, blood splattering his shirt and droplets flipping onto the carpet in rivulets. "I've been so selfish, Molly. I'm sorry about Vixen. I know how much she meant to you. I just wanted to make it all right." Molly nodded.

"I understand."

"No. I'm beyond all that now. I'm doomed. Mom's dead, dad's dead and I'm to blame for it all."

"No. No you're not! Stop talking like that and just hold me, Brian." Brian looked miserable. He grunted as he sat up. More blood gushed from the wound in his belly. Jacob could see the stain on his back as well, now. He knew this was fatal.

Molly sobbed. They hugged. Jacob rose from Victor's body, feeling like an intruder now. That was when he saw the body lying in the kitchen. It was the Sheriff. He shook his head at the insanity of all this.

The kitchen was darker, but as Jacob stood over the Sheriff, he could see that the man was dead. He had taken a bullet through the heart. There wasn't even that much blood.

It was odd, but Jacob had seen his share of corpses. Sometimes the dead countenance belied the last thoughts. Victor's face was contorted with the rictus of hate and pain. The Sheriff's face seemed serene and accepting. Jacob felt guilty for hating this man. He didn't even know him but had reacted to his bigotry with a prejudice of his own. He wished him peace, wherever he was.

Jacob reached down and closed the Sheriff's eyes. He said another prayer and waited in the kitchen as Brian slowly died and Molly continued to cry. It was almost dark by the time the first car arrived. The lights and sirens were harsh. It was midnight before he was back in Bexton, lying in the bright lights of the emergency room.

CHAPTER TWENTY-SEVEN

T he following day, Jacob lay on his bed, his sheets across his lap watching the Razorbacks play Vanderbilt. Trooper Nunez had been by earlier to ask some questions. Jacob had answered the best he could. He had given directions to the cabin. He remembered several landmarks that were familiar and the officer assured him that they would have an FBI forensics team there tomorrow.

Jacob asked about Molly. Nunez said Molly was fine but being held for questioning by a child psychiatrist. Brian and Billy Joe were at the coroner's along with Victor and Patsy Carothers and another victim named George Foster.

" It's a bloody mess," Nunez declared.

"I think when you look a little further, it's going to get bloodier. But at least it's over."

"Yeah. I've known Officer Shoemaker for almost a decade. He was a good lawman." Nunez smiled, put away his clipboard and started to leave. Just as he reached the doorway he looked back. "Tell me, Mr. Barclay. Why did you get involved in all this, anyway?"

This question had been bothering him since the cabin. He still didn't have an answer.

"I guess it was destiny. God had me in the wrong place at the right time. Besides, other than be a witness, I wasn't able to help at all. Some cop I am, huh?"

"Well, you can be humble, but your information is going to be valuable to our investigation. Oh, and I'll have my office relay the tip to the feds about that coroner over in Kentucky. All this vampire stuff really makes my skin crawl."

"Yeah, me too."

Jacob was relieved when Trooper Nunez left. Jacob felt practically worthless. He had made every mistake in the book. He had left behind his phone, misplaced his rifle, possibly destroyed evidence at the cabin and hadn't even leant a hand to bring Victor to justice. Much of what had happened had taken place out of his control.

The rest could be squarely placed on his shoulders. His mental debriefing was scathing. It was a good thing he was retired, because it was experiences like this that paralyzed and scarred even the best officers.

Jacob was still berating himself mentally when Janice walked in. She bore a bouquet of mums and a bright smile. Jacob didn't know whether to beam with happiness or cower in fright.

"Hey, handsome. See you're up and around. Wanna eat some Chinese take-out?"

"Janice." He pulled the covers up higher, insecure and vulnerable. "What are you doing here?"

She frowned and put the flowers on the dresser by his bed. She picked up his pants from the chair beside his bed, reached in for his phone and held it up, accusingly.

"I came down two days ago when I didn't hear from you. I just had a feeling you were up to your neck in trouble. Your phone is dead, by the way."

"Uh. Yeah, that's what the officer said. But, how did you know I was in the hospital?"

"Are you kidding me? The whole town is talking about you and the Carothers." A blonde nurse came in and checked his chart, ran a thermometer across his forehead and smiled brightly at Janice.

"You want me to tell the young man to come in now?" She asked, addressing Janice.

"I suppose. Although, I don't know if Officer Barclay here is ready for this."

Jacob looked at the two of them, confused. The nurse left, a smile playing at her lips.

"What is she talking about?"

Janice smiled and sat on the bed opposite of him. She had her hair back and he could smell her perfume over the antiseptic hospital odors. She was different somehow.

"Hey, dad."

Phillip entered the room, his sister behind him, shy and quiet.

"Ok. Now I'm really confused. What's going on?" Phillip stood beside him and Clarice grabbed Janice's hand and gave her a wan smile.

"It's great to see you again, dad." Phillip leaned in and hugged him. Phillip smelled clean and masculine. His brown button down shirt was open at the collar and his khaki's looked freshly pressed. *Is this Sunday?* Jacob wondered.

"Believe it, babe. You are Oscar-Mike. We're getting you out of here and back home." She reached behind her and gathered his things. She pulled a pair of pants from his gear and threw them at his face.

"Go ahead, get dressed and let's go. I've got your walking papers."

Jacob smiled and threw back the covers. Clarice groaned.

"Dad! I am just getting over you walking around in your tighty-whities when we were younger."

Jacob slid his jeans on under his hospital smock. He pulled on the clean shirt. The floor was cold on his feet. Clarice handed him some slippers.

"You're not driving, so you won't need your boots. The rest of your clothes smell awful so I just chucked them."

Jacob was too stunned to comment. He felt ambushed, in a good way. Now, if only someone would walk through the door and hand him a three-foot high check with six figures his life would be complete.

"I suppose I have you to thank for all this," he whispered.

"Of course.And Clarice. She arranged all the flights and convinced Phillip to leave the kids behind with Vivian." Janice said.

"Swell. Now, you gonna tell me where we're going?"

"Sure. We're all going to get something to eat. Phillip and Clarice are joining us."

"Dad, we're glad you're well. We've never been on one of your excursions. We can see now why you want to get away. These things always end up pretty exciting for you."

Phillip was doing his best to be humorous. He had his mother's sarcasm.

"You're right. I love adventure, but I don't always plan on things going crazy somewhere along the way."

Jacob grabbed his backpack and began to throw it over his shoulder. Phillip shook his head and took the backpack from him.

"Well, let's get going then," Janice said, grabbing his elbow.

"Not so fast. Let's pray first. I think we're fortunate. I know I am." He looked at Phillip who nodded, satisfied. Jacob smoothed Clarice's blonde hair and brushed it away from her porcelain cheeks. She had her mother's bone structure. He loved his family more than ever. They bowed their heads and before Phillip could begin praying, Jacob stopped him.

"No. I'll do it." He reached around Janice's waist. Janice took Clarice's hand and they formed a close circle. A nurse stopped in, and promptly left the family with some privacy and closed the door.

As they finished, he looked over at Janice. She was crying. He reached up and touched the tear just below her eye.

"Hey. I'm alright. It will be alright." He pulled her in close. Feeling her sniffle against his chest was a sensation he had forgotten. She stepped back, his shirt damp from her tears.

Janice smiled, almost a grimace as she grabbed a tissue from the counter and dabbed at her eye.

"I know, you big jerk," she teased. She gave him a playful punch in the shoulder.

"Where's my truck?" Jacob asked as Phillip and Clarice led them from the room into a brightly lit hall. Through the glass front of the tiny hospital, they could see that fall in Arkansas was in full swing.

"It's in police impound. I have already arranged to have it delivered back to your apartment on Thursday," Clarice said.

"Oh. I see."

Janice walked up beside him and took his arm. Her cheek nuzzled up against his shoulder. He was taken aback by her emotion, but it was welcome. He needed to know that she still cared. He understood now that he cared, too. Somehow, they would make it work.

Janice mumbled into his shirt, "Your vacation isn't officially over." She looked up at him, her eyes red and puffy, her smile genuine. "Anywhere in particular you'd like to go now?"

Jacob continued on, a smile playing at his lips. He shrugged. Phillip glanced back. Jacob beamed with pride. He was glad to have him here.

"Well. We haven't done anything as a family in years. I thought maybe we could all go see the Cardinals play tomorrow. I hear they have a double-header scheduled." Janice looked at him, puzzled.

PROLOGUE

M olly rested her chin in her hands and read the passage again. Her doctor, a wiry, short man, had told her that this passage had brought him great peace when he faced impossible things. Molly just didn't see what it held for her. She put the book down, its gilded face shiny under the bright lights of her room. The inside flap had a hand-written passage:

>*"Almost nothing of this world has come unveiled or pure,*
>*But the words of the Messenger preserve their purity*
>*undefiled, and still wait to be understood fully."*

She agreed, because she didn't understand. Her state of mind was not conducive to absorbing complicated platitudes or great truths. She was drained and felt a hollow shell of herself. She failed to register any emotion. She no longer cried. She had cried more in the last two days than she had since she was a baby. She could no longer bring herself to feel sad.

Brian was gone. That was the only thing she had to feel sad about. She missed seeing Jacob. She wanted to thank him, to see his eyes again. She had almost lost faith in him there at the end. He had seemed so capable and then he had lost the gun and walked around like he was in a dream or something. It had left her feeling disappointed.

As she had recalled the incidents there at her old home, she repainted them to fit her original view of Jacob as a hero. She even dreamed at one time that it was Jacob who had pulled the trigger. She liked this re-inventing part, even though she knew it was a lie.

There were no heroes. Even though she had pulled the trigger, had ended the madness, she didn't consider herself a hero. Brian had died in her arms. That should count for something.

She stared at the little window in her door. She was hungry and she hoped they would bring by a plate soon. The food was plain, but she needed the nourishment. She had already become accustomed to having the food provided for her. After her experience, she never wanted to have to fend for herself ever again.

She felt weak and alone, but chastised herself. Her situation was exciting. She was free and her dreams of that perfect family were just days away. She knew that she would be taken in, knew that her psych profile would warrant that she was normal and deserving of care.

She had made sure to play the role of victim. She had pretended to be disoriented, to feel remorse. She had even cried when she spoke about pulling the trigger and watching her father die. Of course, she was glad he was dead.

She had never regretted doing it. Regrets were for the weak. She only regretted that it had to be her to do it. She ended up being the one that survived, had overcome. She was the only one to not succumb to the madness that engulfed her family.

When Molly thought back on it, she blamed her mother the most. Her mother had been the one to feed the monster that was Victor. It was Patsy that had been lulled into thinking that she had the monster under leash. It was her mother that had lured the men and it was her mother that had hurt her the most. Victor was a monster from the beginning, he couldn't help what he was.

Brian's only sin was that he was too young and too afraid to do anything until it was too late. No, it was her mother and Molly wasn't prepared to forgive her. She didn't hate her—that emotion was saved solely for her father.

The only emotion she could muster for Brian was pity. Holding him in her arms as the life flowed out of him, she realized that she only wanted him to live for her benefit. She didn't hold some sentimental motivation. She didn't want Brian to overcome his breeding, didn't want Brian to become a good man. Molly only wanted Brian to live so he could save her. Once she realized he couldn't do that, she had discarded his memory, had relegated his entire existence to an acute sense of sympathy.

She sat up in her bed, and rubbed her curly brown hair. She was impatient. She felt caged but endured it because she knew it would be better for her to seem compliant.

She wanted to gnash her teeth. She wanted to lash out at everyone. Inside, she would growl at them, bare her teeth and sniff the air menacingly. She saw through their games, understood their intentions. She was above them and so would use them to serve her own means

Molly sat back against the wall and put the flimsy pillow behind her back. The wall was cold on her shoulders. She picked up the Qur'an that her doctor had given her. She was tired of books, tired of all the ideas of other people.

Something about the thickness of the book, something about the leather cover and the copper gilding reminded her of her favorite book in her mother's library. Molly had discovered it when she was eight. It had a silhouette of the moon on the cover and the inside lining had a repeating pattern of a wolf chasing a thin moon and a wolf baying.

She had read the book from cover to cover and had been entranced. When Brian had brought home Vixen and they had huddled in the barn in the scent of the hay, Molly had rubbed her hand across Vixen's back reverently. She had read long passages to the wolf cub, imagining a future where she would run the dark woods near their house and live with Vixen and her kin.

It had been hard on her when Vixen had run away. At first she thought it was her invitation, her initiation to join them, to run with the wolves of the Ozarks. After a month of failure to find either Vixen or her sisters, Molly had just felt betrayed.

Sitting there in the stunningly white room, with the florescent lights and the white gown and white slippers with pink bows, Molly slowly caressed the cover of the Qur'an and remembered the words of the book, *Slaves to the Moon.*

"Learn the hearts of men and twist them to your bidding. Pray to the goddess of the moon, lean on the backs of your fellows."

It wasn't a passage that gave Molly peace, but a passage that gave her direction. She smiled for the first time in days as she thought on her future. She allowed a small whimper and a growl escape her throat. She felt feral, felt alive in so many ways despite her weakness and hunger.

She longed for the hunt, longed for the waning of the moon. She felt her blood coursing through her veins, felt the power in her heart. She knew she had not yet triumphed, knew that her victory was not complete. She spent the next few days waiting: impatient, fidgety, barely sleeping, biding her time, hatching her plans, and carefully considering her past.

ABOUT THE AUTHOR

Robert Michael is a writer and commercial roofing sales director. His love for books, family, and God fill his time and his spirit. He enjoys reading, writing, sports, fishing, and gaming. He lives in Broken Arrow with his wife and four children.

Robert has been writing for over thirty years, honing his craft and biding his time.

Look for more titles from him soon.

Connect with the Robert at:

www.infinitewordpress.com
www.facebook.com/infiniteword
www.robertamichael.blogspot.com
www.twitter.com/InfiniteWord

or download his short stories at Smashwords.com.